STONE CIRCLE

KATE MURDOCH

For my mother Pat

HIGH PRAISE FOR *STONE CIRCLE*

"Kate Murdoch's STONE CIRCLE is a stunning historical fantasy debut set in Renaissance Italy, packed with rich imagery, well-developed characters, and an enthralling plot. The execution of the love triangle is both captivating and refreshing, weaving love, jealousy, and rivalry into a complicated but realistic story of one young seer's journey into alchemy and adulthood. I can't wait to read more by Kate Murdoch."

—Madeline Dyer, author of the Untamed series

"…Kate Murdoch's characters are so greatly human, that it's easy to sympathise with them: to cheer them on during hard times and to admonish them for being foolish. Her characters' interactions with each other and their individualities helped shape the book into something wonderful; at the same time she excels at pacing the story with her characters, all within a framework designed to help readers understand the world of seers and alchemy she has created.

Aside from the tension-filled rivalry between Nichola and Antonius, her story also gave me a glimpse of how the lower class, the simple-minded, and the women lived in the past, which only added to the appeal of the overall plot and strengthened the story's quality. Overall, the *Stone Circle* is an excellent work that I would definitely recommend to historical fiction fanatics everywhere."

—Jessica Barbosa for Readers' Favorite

STONE CIRCLE

KATE MURDOCH

Close your eyes and let the mind expand. Let no fear of death or darkness arrest its course. Allow the mind to merge with Mind. Let it flow out upon the great curve of consciousness. Let it soar on the wings of the great bird of duration, up to the very Circle of Eternity.
—Hermes Trismegistus

PROLOGUE

Antonius trailed his hand in the dark water, feeling its coolness between his fingers. As Nichola's paddle propelled their boat forward, the moon cast shimmering ribbons of light across the surface. Nichola's strong back barely moved from his labour, the paddle dipping in and out of the sea as if it were part of him.

Across from them in his own boat, Savinus paddled alone. His white hair glowed in the muted light.

Gazing into the distance, Antonius did not see the paddle as it swung in an arc towards his head, striking him on the back. The impact winded him and, for a brief instant, the sharp pain emptied his mind, before he tumbled over the side. Dragged down by his clothing, he flailed and gasped. Looking up, he saw Nichola sitting motionless in the boat, studying him with a blank face. The water in Antonius's ears blocked out most noise, but he could hear Savinus yelling at Nichola from the other boat. Sucking in a final breath, he hugged his knees and dropped to the murky depths. There was a splash, as the old man jumped overboard to try to save him.

Antonius plunged deeper. The currents were cold on his body, rushing past his ears as he swam. In the murky depths, tentacles of seaweed swayed beneath him, and small fish darted out of his path. He reached the shore near the cave, and waited in the shallows.

Holding his breath, he tried to think of his family and Giulia, instead of his constricted lungs.

Finally, he raised his head and saw Savinus climb back into his boat. The two men paddled into the distance and it was as if he were watching his life departing. In a sense this was true. After spending the night in the depths of the caves, he would walk away from all that was familiar to begin his new life.

CHAPTER 1

One year before
Pesaro 1585

Tomas Albizi had requested the reading for the next morning, yet Savinus did not hurry as his quill scratched numbers on the parchment. The additions and subtractions appeared haphazard, but were the result of a formula used since boyhood. Allowing his instinct to dictate the calculations was as familiar to him as the mannerisms of his daughter, Giulia. The scrawled numbers suggested symbols. These basic shapes foretold the success or failure of a crop, a love affair, or a battle.

His talents were well known in the town of Pesaro. From the age of ten, he had studied with a seer, Bartholomeus Giovari, who instructed him in both seeing and geomancy. The two men worked together for decades until, one winter, his mentor succumbed to the plague. Savinus found himself in charge of a thriving business, and soon gained the patronage of Conte Leonardo Valperga.

The numbers on the parchment blurred as his eyes watered. His eyesight had been unreliable for some time. This and other maladies were signs of his advancing years, reminding him of the need to find a successor. Giulia had begged him to allow her to take over, and he explained the danger to her reputation. The last time she had spoken about it, he patted her hand.

"You would deny me the pleasures of grandchildren, would you?"

"No, Papa, I just don't understand why you would spend so much time teaching me about geomancy, and all the other skills, only to marry me off to some dull nobleman."

"Giulia, do I really need to be blunt with you? If everyone knew what you were capable of, they would report you to religious authorities. In a man, what we have is a talent. In a woman, it is witchcraft or sorcery. I'm very sorry, my dear, but that's how it is. You can use your abilities secretly—to help your children and your husband. That is all."

As he worked, she sat near the fire at her loom, absorbed in her task. Her long fingers laboured, coaxing the multi-coloured silk threads. Her lips were pursed in concentration, and her auburn hair was loosely pinned. Wide-set green eyes were either tender or flashing with determination. Visiting suitors were taken aback by her outspokenness, and Savinus worried about her marriage prospects. At the same time, he realized her mother had a similar temperament, and it had not deterred him. In the months since Giulia reached maturity, he often missed the wisdom of his wife. Sitting alone at his desk, he would pretend she was nearby, and imagine conversing with her about their daughter.

Carmen, she will not budge on this. I have tried everything. She is spending too much time in her bedchamber, what on earth could she be doing in there? Give me a sign when it's time to find her a husband. I'm worried I will do it too soon, or too late.

Later that day he would visit Conte Leonardo Valperga, who lived in a palazzo on the hill behind the town. His patronage was useful. It allowed him to employ the services of a housekeeper and a skilled tutor for Giulia. Although his ambitions for her were no more than to find her a kind and prosperous husband, he wanted her to have an understanding of the world. Knowledge of Latin verbs and Greek philosophy complemented her esoteric education. He knew wealthy men desired educated wives, skilled in conversation. It was essential for the garden parties and balls they attended. He had asked his patron for help in searching for a suitor, as the Conte knew many eligible young men through his eldest son Gianni. He responded with enthusiasm, and Savinus felt he could relax over the matter.

"Shouldn't you be concentrating on your work?" Giulia was studying him—she knew his thoughts.

"I was distracted, yes."

"Papa, can't my marriage wait for a while? I want to learn more about mathematics and philosophy before I let my mind wither away."

He smiled at her. "Yes, my dear. We haven't yet found a suitable husband anyway. I suppose you know the Conte is looking for someone?"

She nodded and looked down at the floor, turning the comb in her hands. "I don't have a lot of confidence in his choice. Every aristocrat I've met has been completely dull. I prefer shopkeepers, or perhaps a musician."

Savinus concealed his amusement. "Yes, I'm sure they're interesting, but would they be able to keep you at least as well as I have? I think not. Practicality is not one of your strengths, my dear."

He turned away to indicate they should go back to their tasks. As well as the job at hand, the anxiety about his successor plagued him. For weeks he had mulled over the idea of a test. A basic method to assess psychic ability. The question was how it would be performed. He thought there should be a limit on how many youths were tested, as the exercise could become chaotic. As he searched for a solution, he realized the idea would not come unless he distracted himself. His mind needed to find an answer without pressure.

In the end, he placed his work aside. His thoughts were too scattered, and he knew this made for an unsatisfactory reading for Signor Albizi. Sighing, he laid down his quill and addressed Giulia.

"Would you please tell Agnese to go to the market and buy a small amount of pork, some polenta, and whatever vegetable is the freshest? Perhaps a good supper might help my mind with this reading."

Giulia jumped to her feet. "Yes, Papa, I think she's in the courtyard."

Savinus opened his book on hermetic alchemy. It was covered in a layer of dust. He blew it away, revealing gold lettering that decorated the deep blue cover. Opening it at random, his gaze fell on an illustration of a man in a black robe sitting under a tree, his eyes closed. On the opposite page, the same man was surrounded by a swirling wind, streaked with vivid colours. It concealed the lower half of his body. A third image on the next page was an eagle, its coal-black wings extended, its noble beak a flash of gold. Traces of the coloured wind still curled in front of the creature. Savinus had stared at the three illustrations before, without understanding their meaning. He now knew they depicted complete transformation.

CHAPTER 2

Outside the servants' quarters, the sound of axe meeting wood reverberated. The paved area connected with the vast kitchen of the palazzo. Katerina, the elderly cook, stirred a cauldron of lentil and prosciutto soup for the evening meal.

It was late in the afternoon. Before Antonius could retire to his straw mattress, he had many jobs to complete. His work was indicative of his low status in the servant pecking order—emptying chamber pots, chopping wood, assisting in the kitchen, and taking on tasks that others disdained.

Katerina had asked for more wood. Her soup was almost finished, and the fire close to burning out. He pushed back a stray lock of hair from his eyes, and rested an arm on the axe. The old lady seemed to take pleasure in ordering him around. As soon as she observed any hint of relaxation, another order was given. Yet he was fortunate to have the position. His mother's eyes were failing from sewing by candlelight, and his sister was needed at home. It was fascinating to live in close proximity to nobles. He had heard stories about the Conte and his family, but never imagined he would see them. These viewings had been fleeting—snatched glimpses caught at the doorways of their quarters, taking their chamber pots from a page. It was strange to think they eliminated their waste like commoners.

As he had taken the pots, he craned his neck to see behind the liveried servants. He saw the back of a young woman, resplendent in a dress decorated in silver thread. On another occasion, he glimpsed the profile of a middle-aged man with a large nose. The gold embellishments and rich colours of his clothing were too varied for Antonius to take in. More overpowering than the fetid stink of the chamber pots were the heady aromas of cedarwood and bergamot. He was stunned; his senses reeled.

At the age of six he discovered not everyone could hear the thoughts of others. He was fishing on the beach with his friend Timo, who confessed his father was ill and would die. His friend's eyes were swollen, and his round cheeks shone with tear stains.

"That's awful. But you already told me."

"What do you mean? You're the first person outside my family I've told."

"You did tell me—but not with your mouth. You told me in my head a few days ago. When we were at church. Don't you remember?"

"Ant, people don't tell each other things in their heads—you're crazy."

"People tell me things in my head every day, Timo. Has it ever happened to you?"

"No, never. You're teasing me, aren't you?"

"No, Timo, I'm telling the truth."

"Prove it. What am I thinking now?"

"You're scared my powers are dangerous, and you're thinking of telling your Mama."

Timo's eyes widened and he scratched the top of his head with his free hand.

"You are really strange."

"Will you still be my friend?"

Timo threw his line back in the water, where it made a small plop. He looked at Antonius sideways and his bloodshot eyes shone with affection.

"Yes. But I feel a bit worried you'll know all my thoughts."

"I can ignore them if I want to."

"Please do that, at least some of the time."

Antonius and Timo were both the sons of fishermen, as Pesaro was a town that made its living from the sea. Their fathers were close friends who had met through their work, often sharing a drink in the tavern after a good day's haul.

Whilst Timo was content to follow his father's trade once he turned fourteen, Antonius learned he had little aptitude for fishing, becoming restless within minutes. He would fidget and shift in his seat until the men became irritated. His agitation was impossible to contain. This was not a problem, as he had a strong build and would find labour without much difficulty.

Fiora's lips were a thin line when the fishermen commented on her son's lack of prowess. In contrast, his father Girardus shrugged his shoulders, and ruffled his son's hair. He was an unassuming man of slight build, yet the few words he uttered earned respect.

"He will do greater things than I, you'll see." He silenced his wife's protest by holding out his hand.

"Fiora, he's made differently than the rest of us, that's all."

Girardus showed his acceptance of his teenage son's divergence from the familial path by taking him to the tavern. Tankards of dark ale were placed before them, and his father spoke of his youth in Genoa. To Antonius's embarrassment, he described how he courted Fiora when she was a pretty young girl.

They sat in silence, gazing at the amber liquid in their glasses, lit from behind by dim candlelight. Antonius considered telling his father about hearing everyone's thoughts, but dismissed the idea. He knew him to be a simple man whose comprehension was limited to that which he could touch and see.

"You're a good boy, Antonius. If anything ever happens to me on the boat I know I can trust you to look after the family. Your brother will always have the mind of a young child, I'm sure you realize."

His younger brother had been born simple. Despite this, he breezed through life unaware of his difference. Every day he laughed with abandon and hugged everyone. Often he met with cruelty—taunts in the street and trickery from other children. They would pretend he could play with them and hold the ball out of reach. Undeterred, he would chase them, his arms flailing like windmills and his face confused. Adults were discomfited by his overt friendliness. Antonius learned to shield him from malice.

He was aware each time his father stepped onto the boat it could be the last. Immense storms occurred at sea, crushing the flimsy fishing boats like giant hands gripping parchment. Girardus had lost several of his friends, and knew one day it might be his turn.

In the end, it was contaminated water that claimed him. He visited friends who lived in the poorest part of town, and they offered him the tainted cup. It only took a few sips. The following week he coughed and complained of headaches. Days later, he developed a high fever and took to his bed. His nose leaked blood, and his insides emptied themselves until there was nothing left. Within three weeks he was dead.

For Antonius, the worst thing was the harrowing noise made by his mother. It was an unrelenting guttural moan—sometimes loud and accompanied by sobs, and other times low and inconsolable. The louder, higher one was better, as the softer one made him worry she might give up. He fought the temptation to lie down and pull a blanket over his head, realizing his responsibility to hold the family together. In a haze of grief, he walked to the market to buy food, kept Piero out of trouble, and made sure his mother ate. It took almost a month for her to emerge from her despair. Antonius sat down on her bed one autumn morning, and explained the reality of their situation. They were now almost penniless. He was helping out at the docks by repairing boats and doing other odd jobs, but the work was sporadic.

∞

The spectre of poverty jolted Fiora out of her depression. To ask the neighbours for help was unthinkable. Looking out the small window, she noticed the fig tree had lost most of its leaves. She could feel the chill permeating the air—it was becoming colder every day and would soon be winter. She knocked on doors and offered her services as a seamstress. Within weeks, money trickled back into their household.

Her income meant a steady supply of food for a diet of thin gruel, polenta, and potatoes. There was not enough for more varied fare, such as the occasional cut of meat, or more vegetables. When Girardus was alive, they ate substantial meals, and sometimes had new clothes. One evening, as they sat around the table consuming the gruel, Fiora looked at the drawn faces of her sons and daughter and decided it was time for Antonius to find more stable work. As she cleared away their dishes, she informed him of her idea. He met her gaze and nodded, eyes shining.

"It's time to take my father's place. I'm seventeen. We must try and live as we did before. I'm sorry to say this, Mama, but I can't eat this gruel every night for much longer."

His sister laughed. "I agree. Mama, I'm getting so thin that no man will ever want me as a wife. I think it's an excellent idea."

Fiora slid the dishes into the brass washing bucket and wiped her hands on her apron. She looked at the three faces before her, two smiling at their joint decision, and the third with beatific ignorance, his gruel making an oily trail from the corners of his mouth. He opened his arms wide and said, "I like clowns!"

Fiora patted his shoulder, ignoring the interjection. "Good, then it's settled. My friend Paloma knows Katerina. You know, the old cook from the palazzo. She told me they're always looking for extra help. She's at the market in the mornings. I can go and introduce myself."

∞

Lying on his mattress, Antonius watched the crescent moon glowing outside the window. He could hear the creaking cart of the night watchman making his circuit along the town walls. The moonlight bathed the room in deep blue, outlining the sleeping forms of his sister, mother, and brother. None were silent in slumber, and he listened to the varied rhythms of their breaths. He was always the last one to fall asleep since his father died. It was a habit. Girardus had always returned home late at night, and his son had waited for him. As soon as he heard his father's exhausted footsteps on the flagstones, he succumbed to sleep. His body had not adjusted to the truth of his absence. He lay awake, often until just before dawn, and the lack of sleep was starting to affect his waking hours.

In spite of his proclamation, he was fearful about working in the palazzo. It would mean separation from his family. The child in him was unprepared. His mother's tenderness, and the physical proximity of his siblings were all that kept him from being mired in grief.

The next morning, he sat hunched at the table as his sister Theresa placed buttered bread in front of him. He watched his mother's stout form as she walked down the path leading from their cottage, carrying a large straw basket for her purchases at the market. Piero stuffed bread into his mouth until there was no room left and breathed heavily through his nostrils, eyes wide with alarm. Exasperated, his brother reached forward and pulled some bread free.

"Piero, not so much!"

Piero grinned at his brother, and the masticated bread fell to the table. Antonius looked away in disgust and met his sister's eyes. She was slicing potatoes and leeks for supper. She was a hard worker; Fiora often extolled her virtues, saying she would make a good wife when the time came.

"How about a game of cards?" he suggested. She shook her head and flicked her long black braid out of the way as she wielded the knife.

"No, maybe later. I have to fetch some water and clean the flagstones. Then Mama needs me to wash the clothes ready for mass tomorrow."

He shrugged. "All right, I might go for a walk then."

He strolled without purpose through the narrow streets, enjoying the sensation of not being needed. The worst had passed, and his mother seemed herself once more, capable and resilient. Although the market was several blocks away, he could hear the shouts of the vendors as they peddled their wares. A swift breeze blew the aromas of dirt-covered vegetables, freshly slaughtered animals, and the briny sea. He took a deep breath, the strong smells clearing his mind and filling him with energy. Every few minutes he passed familiar faces and greeted them, doffing his cap at the men and nodding to the women. Many of the latter were friends of his mother.

Granite cut by masons from the surrounding hills formed the low structures of the village houses, their roofs laid with a rounded terracotta tile. The windows were small mottled squares, inserted into the houses like pairs of eyes. Some villagers added personality to their dwellings by painting their doors blue or red.

As he approached the Piazza del Popolo, the odours of fish and ripe fruit intensified, as well as the sounds of street performers and animated conversations. In the distance, he could see his mother gesticulating as she spoke to Katerina. He walked around the outskirts of the market, not wanting her to see him and be drawn into the conversation. Small children pushed past him, giggling and jostling each other.

At that moment, he saw the person who most intrigued him in the town, Savinus di Benevento. It was not difficult to spot him in a crowd, due to his erect bearing and sanguine expression. His knowledge of matters both academic and magical was legendary. This wisdom did not cause arrogance, as he was capable of relating to both peasants and noblemen. When people described him, they spoke as much of his personal warmth as his erudition. It disarmed his critics, allowing him to explore the mysteries of his profession with a depth his predecessors would have only imagined. There were some who viewed him as an eccentric old seer, out of touch with the realities of everyday life. Antonius could see the truth of who he was and it left him in awe.

He watched Savinus browse a stall filled with bright silk scarves. They hung in festive rows from the awning and danced in the breeze. The old man appeared lost in thought as he felt one between his fingers, a deep purple hue. Antonius wondered if he were looking for a present for his daughter. By all accounts she was attractive. His mother had clucked that it would be difficult to find her a husband due to her headstrong nature. He looked beyond the market walls to the port, his eye captured by the white-sailed boats at anchor. When he glanced back, the old man had disappeared, as had the purple scarf.

The wide form of his mother hurtled towards him, her expression triumphant.

"There you are! It's Monday, my love! Monday!"

"Monday what?"

"You are to be a helper to Katerina! Her previous helper went on a pilgrimage. He was a young man of great faith. She later heard he joined a monastery in Paglieta. So, Antonius, it is due to God you are fortunate enough to gain this position. Then Timo's Mama came over and vouched for you. What do you say?"

"Uh…thank you?"

A slight frown creased her brow. "Is that all? I have sung your praises to the sky, said you can work like ten oxen, and have the forbearance of Saint Francis. Can you do a little better please?"

"Mama, you are an angel. I hope I can make you proud of me."

This seemed to placate her—she took his elbow and guided him in the direction of home, her pace slowing to a comfortable stroll.

"Mama, I saw Signor di Benevento before. Have you ever seen his daughter?"

"Only once, at a party for women to celebrate the birth of a child. It was some time ago now. She was very lovely. Why do you ask?"

"It's just strange I have never glimpsed her. I'm curious, that's all."

"Women of her class are rarely seen in public. She must keep her honour intact if she is to find a husband. Your curiosity is exactly what her father wants from eligible men."

Antonius walked at a slow pace, his mother's grip reassuring in the crook of his arm. He felt a pang of anxiety at the thought of leaving her.

Fiora looked at him sideways, concern clouding her features. "I must say something else to you. There will be many pretty servant girls at the palazzo. The Conte does not tolerate ugliness in his home. Not even the animals are allowed to be plain. The thing is, you must not bed these girls. You are the only man with all your wits left in our family. Our good name rests with you, so you must act with dignity at all times. If you need to do those things, then find them outside of the palazzo. Understand?"

Antonius blushed. "Mama, I have only heard about it from the other boys. The girls I've met aren't really interested in me."

She nodded, her thick fingers squeezing his forearm. "Forgive me if I've embarrassed you. I understand you're still innocent. But you will know soon enough, and then…"

"Don't worry, Mama, I won't embarrass you. I'll just work hard, isn't that right?"

Her eyes crinkled in a smile.

CHAPTER 3

In the dim afternoon light, Giulia peered at her weaving and sighed. A drizzling rain had begun outside, and she was distracted by the sound of children bouncing a ball beneath the window. She laid down her comb and stood near the fire to warm her hands. Her father's irritated thoughts filtered into her mind. He had not been able to devise a test for potential seers. She considered whether or not to share her idea with him. It was possible he would find it ignominious to be outsmarted by his daughter.

Gazing out the window, her voice was casual. "You know, Papa, Agnese told me she saw a funny game at the market the other day. The man had three silver cups and beneath them he hid different objects very quickly. The person playing the game must tell him which item is under which cup. If they're right, they win two florins."

Savinus raised his eyes to her and sat forward in his chair. If he understood her ruse, he did not show it. His dark blue eyes sparkled and his lips formed a slow smile.

"Giulia, that's it! I've been thinking of complicated tests, when this simple game would do just as well. I can do exactly that, but without showing them what the objects are. They will simply have to tell me the names of the items beneath the cups. Three items would be ideal. I'll need to test them more than the man at the market, to eradicate chance."

"Well done, Papa. I think that's a brilliant idea. I can make some signs for Agnese to pin up in the piazza, if you can tell me what to write. When do you think you would like to do it?"

"Next week. I need an apprentice as soon as possible. I want to do some more research into the First Matter. A fresh mind would invigorate my studies, perhaps give a new angle to things." He stroked the wiry grey hairs of his beard. Giulia knew this gesture well; it was a sign her father was excited.

"I can have the posters ready by tomorrow if I start now. Agnese can take them to the piazza in the afternoon. Then perhaps you can conduct the test next Friday?"

"Yes, that sounds good. I'll test no more than six boys. Otherwise it will be too chaotic. We will assemble them on the Wednesday and I can choose the candidates. The poster must state the time and place of both the original selection and the final test. I'll write it down for you now. Thank you, my dear." He took some blank parchment and picked up his quill, dipping it in the ink well.

As she stood by the fire, she listened to the noise of his quill scratching across the parchment, combined with the sound of the crackling flames. He finished within minutes and crossed the room to hand it to her.

An anxious expression flitted over his face.

"It's all right, Papa. I'll start now."

He shuffled from one foot to the other.

"Why don't you go for a walk and when you get back I might be finished?" She spoke in a soothing voice, patting his forearm.

He nodded. "Yes, I'll do that."

There was a break in the rain, and the darkness had lifted. She watched her father shrug his cloak over his shoulders, before he kissed her cheek and left.

Giulia was relieved. As much as she enjoyed her father's company, she found it difficult to concentrate when he was impatient for a job to be done. She pulled some parchment out of a drawer.

∞

Savinus walked with his hands clasped behind his back, enjoying the feel of the salt-tinged air on his cheeks. It held a chill he knew would be icy in a matter of weeks. He dreaded the autumn and winter days, as the cold penetrated his bones. Preparations for the saint's festival of San Terenzio were taking place. In the doorways of many houses, women sat sewing costumes and making masks. Bright ribbons, coloured paper and fabrics, and mirrored sequins spilled out of baskets. The half-finished masks were whisked away by children who held them to their faces and chased each other up and down the streets. Although he almost tripped over them on several occasions, he found their excitement contagious. They sang the song marking the celebration, and he found he could not stop humming it as he rounded the corner near his home. He realized he had been gone for over an hour, having walked the entire perimeter of the town.

Giulia was standing at the window, her posture taut with impatience. He raised an eyebrow.

"I thought you would still be hard at work."

She turned and smiled. "Agnese has already taken them to the piazza. I worked quickly. What took you so long, Papa?"

"I had forgotten about San Terenzio. It's only a week away now. There's much to look at." He stood over the desk to look for evidence of her labour.

"So. You are industrious today. Did you not keep one for me to admire?"

"Perhaps you should go for another stroll tomorrow and you will see them around the piazza."

"Yes, of course. I'm rather hungry now. Would you please go and ask Agnese to bring me some almond pastries and wine?"

∞

Giulia nodded and left the room to find Agnese, scuffing her heels on the tiles. Her father had not thanked her for her efforts. This was not unusual. Yet he was prepared to give her an education, a privilege not afforded to her friends. They were instructed only in sewing, weaving, singing, and managing servants—the skills necessary for marriage. She viewed the world through the mottled glass of their windows, and the black gauze of the veiled hat she was required to wear outdoors. Part of her looked forward to marriage— she had heard married women could be seen in public more often.

Her thoughts returned to the test and she wondered whom her father would choose, and how their powers might compare with hers.

CHAPTER 4

Katerina rebuked Antonius five times that afternoon for dreaming on the job. She had been pushed to the breaking point by the carelessness of her new charge. So far, he had left an empty cauldron on the fire, missed a log chopping wood, which broke the axe head and dripped a trail of water on the tiles, causing her to fall on her impressive behind.

She cornered him in the kitchen, wiping flour off her red cheeks with a chubby finger.

"Are you going to tell me why you are so absentminded today, or should I just relieve you of your position?"

He blushed and stared at his shoes. "There is a competition. I saw a sign at the piazza when I went to get vegetables this morning. It's for boys who think they might be able to help Signor di Benevento."

Katerina frowned. "So this job is not good enough for you? You have higher ambitions?"

"No! Not at all. I just thought perhaps, if I were selected, I could do both."

"Well, I suppose we would have to consider that. Perhaps you could work here in the mornings and for the Signor in the afternoons for less pay. I am not sure what the Conte would say about it, although the two men are good friends. Anyway, you are in grave danger of injuring both of us if you don't concentrate on your work today. Can you try to be in the present for now?"

"Yes. I'm sorry. Do you need me to sweep the courtyard?"

"I do, young man." She handed him the broom. "Off you go. Hopefully you can't hurt anyone with that."

He swept the courtyard until it was spotless. The selection for the competition was the next day and he could not stop imagining the outcome. He felt his destiny was involved with the old man in the same way he had known it would not involve catching fish.

The poster had been attached to a stuccoed wall near the sea, just before the market came into view. It was on thick parchment, the neat script decorated with curlicues and gold dust. Whoever made it had gone to great lengths to make it eye-catching. "Do you wish to become a Seer's Apprentice? We are holding a competition to find the most talented young seer in the district to assist Savinus di Benevento in his work." At the edges, gold stars glimmered amidst blue swirls of paint. He had memorized the date and time, and walked on, his chest pounding.

That night he could not sleep. He felt every lump in the straw mattress, and pushed his pillow into his ears to muffle the sound of Luca's snores. Luca was an affable, corpulent man who tended the Conte's large stable of horses. He had a thick crop of red hair, sprouting at various angles from his head. His round cheeks were flushed from the copious quantities of ale he consumed. The enthusiasm of his grin compensated for his jagged teeth. Antonius had been exhausted since his arrival at the palazzo and had slept well every night. He had not realized his roommate sounded like a crazed bugle when in slumber. Dawn arrived, the rooster gave an ear-splitting crow, and he had not slept for a second.

With weary determination, he started work, trying to avoid mistakes. He knew further negligence would not be tolerated. Katerina had agreed to let him go to the piazza at the striking of the church bells for the selection. He stole furtive glances outside to ascertain the position of the sun. To his annoyance, its climb was sluggish. He tried to distract himself by humming the San Terenzio

Saint's day song.

Katerina grimaced. "Would you please stop that? I've been hearing it from every child on every street for the past week—if I hear it one more time I think I will go completely mad." He gave a meek nod, wielding his knife as he peeled a potato and tapping his foot on the tiles.

When the bells rang out, he had to restrain himself from breaking into a run. He thanked Katerina for allowing him to go, as he realized she would have to work twice as hard to make up for his absence. Then he walked to the door and closed it behind him. It was only then he allowed himself to sprint down the long, cypress-lined driveway and into the street.

It was a warm day, which he took as a good omen. He had lost his only coat and had been suffering the chill with good humour. Every morning he hunched over and blew on his hands before lifting the axe to chop the wood. His mother always worried about exposure to the cold; he knew if she were to see him working without a coat, she would go without food for a week in order to buy him one. It had been liberating to not be fussed over for the first time in his life.

The road leading away from the palazzo was deserted. On either side were wheat fields, where peasant workers were sowing seed. Men walked ahead with the ploughs and women behind, seeds falling from their hands into deep ridges. Overhead, crows circled, hoping to plunder the fallen seeds. The sun warmed his cheeks as he strode ahead. He felt twinges of anticipation in his stomach and tried not to think about the possibility of not being selected.

As he entered the town, familiar sounds intensified. The voices of the children, squeaking wheels of the handcarts, barking stray dogs, and shrill voices of mothers as they chided their offspring. He was accustomed to these noises and missed them. Approaching the piazza, he saw a group of about fifteen boys standing near the fountain. They jostled each other good-naturedly and exchanged insults. He made his way over and tried to join the periphery of the group without being noticed. A couple of them nodded in his direction and continued their banter. After a few minutes they fell silent, and he realized Savinus di Benevento stood before them. He wore a blue cloak with a gilt collar, his posture erect and his expression bemused. Intense blue eyes were deep-set in a face that revealed his age through the wrinkles surrounding them. He fingered his short grey beard as he surveyed the boys, who looked at their feet and shuffled.

"Good afternoon, young men. Thank you for coming today. I need to choose six of you to do a small test to see what abilities you possess. My question to you is this—which of you believe you have the ability to see things that are not visible and hear things in your mind, not with your ears? Please raise your hand."

A few of the boys giggled. Antonius raised his hand, along with nine other boys.

"Those of you who have not raised your hand, please go home. The rest of you, I would like you to please stand in a line in front of me. Very good, that is marvellous."

He walked along the line, looking each boy in the eye and pushing his chin up with his hand if he looked down. With each, he spent a minute of appraisal. Some boys received only a stare, and some were touched on the shoulder. Antonius stood at the end of the line and waited his turn. There was an awkward silence as each candidate tried to guess the seer's thoughts. Antonius did not need to guess. He knew the old man was unimpressed by each boy, except for the first in the line, a boy who stood out due to his regal bearing and fine clothes. It took a few minutes for him to realize it was the son of the Conte, Nichola. Antonius had seen the boy in a hallway at the palazzo, as he was carrying a chamber pot. After wondering why a nobleman's son would be interested in a seer's competition, his turn arrived.

Savinus stood before him and held his gaze. Antonius felt stripped bare. It seemed the seer had the ability to see the trajectory of his life and his entire personality, with one look. Rather than passively allowing the examination to take place, he decided to give the old man something back. He sent him a thought.

Well then, what do you think of me?

If the seer was surprised by the question, he did not betray it in his expression. There was a long pause before he responded, his resonant voice loud in Antonius's mind.

Excellent. I am pleased to meet a younger version of myself. I do believe I may have found an apprentice, but I still need you to do the test to make sure. What is your name?

I am called Antonius, sir.

Good. Have you always been able to do this?

I have never met anyone who was able to converse this way with me.

I see. Do you often hear the thoughts of others?

Yes, but I try to turn them off, because I don't want to know peoples' secrets. With friends and family, I allow them to come. With others, I think it's bad manners to read them without permission.

Savinus suppressed a smile and turned away, addressing them as a group.

"Thank you again, boys. Those whom I touched on the shoulder need to return here for the final test. It will be on Friday, mid-morning. You may go now."

The final six left the piazza. They chatted to one another in high-pitched voices, some strolling arm in arm. The Conte's son walked well ahead, at no point had he deigned to speak. At the north entrance to the piazza they dispersed. Antonius followed his employer's son and soon realized they were both headed in the direction of the palazzo. Outside the town walls, they walked on the dirt road and up the hill, lined with wheat fields. Antonius quickened his pace to catch up with him. As he came closer, the gold thread in his fur-trimmed cloak, and the fine blue wool of his breeches dazzled his eyes. He looked sideways at the refined features: an aquiline nose, light olive complexion, and full, well-shaped lips. Summoning courage, he spoke.

"Hello there. I work at your father's house, mainly in the kitchen. I just did Signor di Benevento's selection with you. It looks like we could have a good chance, do you think?" He cringed, hearing the obsequious tone in his voice. With a sigh, the boy nodded in his direction. Then he strode faster, leaving Antonius in his wake.

Antonius slowed down. He dragged his feet, kicking a stone out of the way. The sun was hidden behind a thick bank of clouds and a frigid wind pressed at his back. A lump formed in his throat and he swallowed. He watched the boy's back recede in the distance, the dust clouds at his heels. For a moment he felt pity—Nichola could not speak to whomever he wished. Then he turned his mind to the rest of the day and the work he needed to accomplish.

At the palazzo, he was able to work twice as hard and with greater speed. He swept the courtyard, shelled a basket of peas, chopped a large pile of firewood, and emptied ten chamber pots. This was accomplished in under an hour. Katerina regarded him with a quizzical expression. For some reason he did not understand, he preferred to keep the good news to himself. It was like a precious jewel he could take out from its box to admire. He did not feel like sharing it with this woman who was still a stranger. After finishing his tasks in a whirlwind of energy, he realized there was time for a walk before supper. He asked Katerina for permission and she acquiesced with a gruff nod. She had been anticipating his company while she made a chickpea and pheasant stew for the main house, and a lentil and cabbage one for the servants.

When he opened the oak door, an icy wind billowed into the kitchen, lifting her apron. She eyed his thin shirt and shivered, despite her many layers of flesh.

"Antonius! Where is your coat? You will catch your death out there."

"I've lost it. I don't have another."

She sighed. "Wait a moment."

Lifting the lid of an earthenware jar, she drew out a handful of florins and placed them in his hand, closing his frigid fingers over the top.

"Go to the garment salesman on Via Torassi. He has a good selection of second-hand coats. That should be enough to cover it. If not, tell him I will give him the remainder tomorrow."

He raised his eyes to her with a shy smile. "Thank you. You're very kind. I am a little cold actually."

She snorted. "Cold? Your lips are turning blue and you have icicles hanging from your nose. Hurry now, I think he closes his shop at four o'clock."

He walked down the hill, rubbing his hands together for warmth. The prospect of a coat made him feel the chill he had tried to ignore. His boots made crunching sounds on the tiny stones beneath, and crows circled overhead in the slate-coloured sky. The ploughed fields were empty of workers. Despite the cold penetrating his bones, he was suffused with anticipation, a new coat, a test of his abilities, and San Terenzio to be celebrated on the Sunday. For the first time since his father's death, he felt content.

Wherever he looked, people were absorbed in preparations for the Saint's day and the festival that followed. It was the most important day of the year in Pesaro. Those with less money went without food in order to be able to afford elaborate costumes.

Outside the tavern some workers from the wheat fields had congregated. Their faces were grimy and slick with perspiration as they clinked their glasses together and guffawed. From the tone of their voices, he understood they were talking about an attractive woman.

At the piazza, the stallholders were packing up for the day. They lowered their awnings and stacked their wares onto carts drawn by donkeys, conversing with each other about their takings. Many were irritable about reduced sales due to the cold weather. He nodded to the ones he knew as he passed.

To the left of the piazza he saw Via Torassi. Arriving at the door to the shop, he knocked and, hearing a low voice asking him to enter, opened the door. He could just make out the wooden countertop, and the indistinct shape of a man behind it. Various garments were stacked on tabletops to either side of him, arranged according to their categories. Through the dim afternoon light, he could see dust motes swirling in the air. They found their way into his nose and he sneezed.

A diminutive elderly man stood behind the counter. He wore a wool cap and had a thin sallow face. He peered at the youth before him.

"Good afternoon, young man. How can I help you?"

His eyes watered as he recovered from his sneeze and caught his breath.

"Hello, I'm in need of a warm coat. Do you have any in good order that might fit me?"

"Yes, someone brought one in yesterday that might fit you. Just a moment, and I'll find it."

With painstaking concentration, he looked through each stack of clothing, careful not to disturb the folds. Antonius was beginning to get impatient when the man exclaimed.

"Aha! I knew it was here somewhere. Come closer and try it on."

Antonius looked at the woollen coat. It was only slightly threadbare and a deep indigo. He pulled it on and fastened the gilt buttons. It was of fine quality, and he wondered if Katerina might baulk at the price.

"How much is it then?" he asked.

"Well, normally, I would ask ten florins for such a handsome coat, but I can see you are not a wealthy man. How does seven sound?"

Antonius withdrew the coins from his pocket, turned away from the man and counted them. There were five florins. He remembered Katerina had said she could return with more money and faced the garment seller.

"I will buy it, but I'm short of two florins. I work at the palazzo. Is it all right if Katerina, the cook, returns with the rest of the money tomorrow?" He placed the coins in the man's outstretched palm.

The man nodded. "Yes. I know and trust Katerina."

Thanking the seller, he left the shop. As he pulled the soft wool closer around his frame, he felt a flash of joy. He had not realized how much being cold had oppressed him.

At the deserted piazza, he saw a familiar silhouette at the south end, waving in his direction. It was his mother. She was heading towards him at such a rapid pace he thought she might start to run. She bellowed in a voice shrill with panic.

"Son, son! You must come home at once and help. Piero has gone mad! Quickly!"

CHAPTER 5

Antonius grasped his mother's shoulder. "What happened?"

"Just come, we'll talk later."

He followed her through the streets until they arrived home. Despite his anxiety, he was pleased to see the familiar blue door and smoking chimney. From inside, he could hear a cacophony—his sister crying in distress, Piero shouting gibberish, and plates smashing. He threw open the door and took in the scene before him. Theresa was trying to restrain Piero as he flung every object he could find on the floor, a stream of obscenities and nonsense erupting from his mouth. His face turned almost purple with fury and his eyes bulged. Saliva frothed from the corners of his mouth and his hair was caked in mud. Antonius walked towards him, calling his name in a soft, decisive tone. When he was close enough, he grabbed his upper arms and forced him to look into his eyes.

"Piero, listen to me, it's Antonius. Calm down. Listen and calm down. It's all right. You're safe now. No one can hurt you."

Within seconds his words took effect. The younger boy's body relaxed and he regarded his brother with confusion. His eyes filled with tears and he sobbed. Antonius hugged him and patted him on the back. After a few minutes, he led him to the bedroom and laid him on his straw mat where he fell asleep.

Antonius came back into the main room and sat down on a chair. Exhaustion weighed him down. It had been possible for him to ascertain what happened from looking into Piero's eyes and hearing his thoughts. Some older boys had decided to have some fun with him. They threw him in a wheelbarrow and took him to the wheat fields. Then they used him as a human plough.

"Mama, do you know what happened to him?"

"No. I suspect some children did something to him, but I'm not sure what."

When Antonius explained what had befallen Piero, his sister and mother gasped with shock. They had long been aware of Antonius's ability to read minds.

"Why would they do such a thing to a poor simple creature?" Theresa asked, her voice incredulous.

"I will find them and give them the hiding of their lives," added Fiora.

They all sat in silence, too outraged to speak.

Fiora sighed and pushed out from the table. "We must eat now." She looked at her son with affection. "Can you stay for supper? I've made linguine."

He shook his head. "I'm so sorry, Mama, but I must go back to the palazzo. I was only meant to be gone a little while, to buy this coat and Katerina will be worried. I'll try and come back later tomorrow."

"Yes, of course, I understand. You go now."

He gave his mother a tight hug, stretching his arms around her wide girth, and kissed Theresa's cheek before leaving.

As they watched, he walked at a normal pace down the path. Then, as soon as their backs were turned, he broke into a run. He had been gone for a long time, and he thought Katerina might be angry as well as worried.

∞

Savinus returned to his desk by the window, unable to stop thinking about the boy. It was not often he met someone with such strong powers—they almost eclipsed his own. The boy might be more adept than he, by the time he reached the same age. He was surprised by the way Antonius carried his powers like a second skin, unaware of how unique they were. The thought of sharing his knowledge with such a worthy recipient energised him. The Conte's son, Nichola, also had some ability, but to a lesser degree. For over an hour he sat in his chair, tapping his fingers on the smooth oak surface of the desk. The test would be just a formality. Antonius was the obvious choice. However, it would be problematic for his relationship with the Conte if he passed over his son. He hoped Nichola would demonstrate more talent than he had observed. Then he would be able to take them both. An arrangement where the more talented youth was the primary apprentice, and the patrician's son the secondary, would be the solution.

∞

To escape her father's agitation, Giulia helped Agnese in the kitchen for the rest of the afternoon. The repetitiveness of the work was soothing, and she listened to the chatter about her three grandchildren. Agnese moved her wiry frame as if she were twenty years younger. Her silver-grey hair was pulled into a large bun, and her crisp white apron was tied around her waist Her arms were sinewy and her hands strong. As she spoke of her youngest grandchild, a boy called Giorgio, her features took on a youthful glow. He had started to walk with the aid of a walker and was, in her opinion, very handsome. She was proud her job provided the family with extra food and even some luxuries, such as meat on the table once a month. If she was taken aback by Giulia's lack of aptitude in the kitchen, she did not show it. She was gentle in her instructions for kneading the dough to make ravioli, and running the meat through the mincer.

"You're such a beauty, Miss, I'm sure you will find a husband soon." Her deep brown eyes twinkled. Giulia had heard similar platitudes before.

"Is beauty really all anyone cares about?"

Agnese looked confused. "A woman's physical charms are what make us different to men. It is how we attract our husbands. You are so fortunate—I'm sure you will marry someone rich with those gorgeous eyes, and your hair, it's like amber-coloured silk."

Giulia realized Agnese had never questioned her place as a woman. She supposed her education was as much a curse as a blessing—it had given her an idea of what it might feel like to be a man. This contrasted with the claustrophobic realm of women. On more than one occasion she wished she had been born male. Men were able to travel, to do as they pleased, and to control their lives. Most married women she had met, particularly from her own class, were cloistered at home. Their minds were kept dull by domesticity. Their fathers, husbands, and brothers made decisions for them. Those who were allowed more freedom were from the lower classes. Indeed, Agnese walked to and from the piazza every day as a requirement of her job. If she had not been their servant, she would have done the same to obtain food for her family.

By the time she returned to the main part of the villa, her father had calmed down. Yet he still brimmed with energy that belied his years. She surmised he must have met someone with considerable ability, and wondered if he would confide in her.

"So, how did it go today, Papa?"

He rose from his desk and sat down next to her by the loom. His white hair was dishevelled and his eyes glimmered with an intensity she had not seen for a long time.

"I've found him."

She felt a shiver of excitement prickle her forearms.

"You have? Who is he? What's he like?"

"He is a servant in the Conte's household and his name is Antonius. His ability is breathtaking. I'm sure I was not as gifted at his age. With my help, he will be extraordinary. I am to test him, the Conte's son Nichola, and four others. Nichola has some powers, but I think they are quite weak. The other boys, well, I doubt very much they will impress me on Friday. So, my dear, very soon I will have some assistance."

"That's wonderful, Papa. I'm so pleased for you. May I come and watch on Friday?"

He shook his head. "No, I think that would be unwise. The boys might feel distracted to have a young lady present, even if you are veiled."

Giulia pouted, and her green eyes narrowed. "I could stand some distance away, they wouldn't know I was there. And even if they do, my presence could be an even greater test of their abilities."

"Believe me, they would know you were there. And don't try to come in secret either, I will be watching out for you. As for testing them further, that's an interesting idea, but I would prefer they concentrate on seeing."

She picked up her comb and turned to her weaving, her shoulders slumped. "Yes, Papa, I'll stay here, just like I always do."

The tapestry depicted a peacock, his plumage displayed in vivid purples, emerald, and teal. She had spent five months on it and there was still much to be completed. The repetition of pulling the silk strands down with the comb was comforting. It was also a useful distraction from her disappointment.

∞

"What's this I hear about you participating in a competition for seers?" asked Nichola's father, a note of amusement in his voice.

Nichola sat up straighter and his chin jutted out in defence. "It's true, Papa. On Friday, your Signor di Benevento will test me along with some peasants from the town. I think he will see my abilities outshine the others."

The Conte adjusted his thin frame in the silk-covered armchair, watching him. He placed his book on a side table and clasped his hands in his lap. It was just after breakfast, and they were in the sitting room where they often spent time together in the mornings. They were left undisturbed by the servants for at least an hour. At times they discussed the affairs of the town and surrounding regions, or family issues. Father and son had been reading until the Conte broke the silence. His two sisters and mother were occupied with their embroidery in the library. They were oblivious to the fact that the women gossiped under their breath as they sewed, using their quiet time to catch up on the secrets of the town.

"It's a good thing you are confident. However, do you think you might have discussed your plans with me first? As a noble, you're not really meant to work. Much less for someone who is an employee of this household."

Nichola shifted in his seat. He had not told his father of his plans because he knew they would be frowned upon.

"Yes, it is a bit different, I know. But, Papa, if I can develop my abilities for seeing things, imagine how it could help our family. I would be able to cast my eye over all of Ginevra's suitors and see immediately which ones were of good character. I could tell you which of our lands were the most fertile for planting and the optimum times to plant. The possibilities are endless! And you could get all of this for free—I know how much gold is spent on Signor di Benevento."

"Is that so? And how do you know this?" His father raised a neat eyebrow.

Nichola looked at the floor with flushed cheeks. "I had a look at your account books."

The Conte shook his head and sighed. "Nichola, I'm disappointed you have been prying into things that do not concern you. On the other hand, I'm impressed by your initiative. I think you don't realize Signor di Benevento is an acclaimed seer, whose abilities are unmatched in the region. Indeed, as far as Florence. I'm unaware of anyone who is his rival, except for one man from Genoa who is a friend of his. I think it's unlikely you will be able to assist me to a similar extent. However, I don't object to you obtaining an education from him. It can be an interest of yours, like my fondness for the hunt. I do insist you not receive payment—it would be demeaning for our family. When does this test take place?"

"Tomorrow morning, Papa. At the piazza."

The Conte took a sip of his mulled wine. He held the cut crystal glass in one slim hand, and opened his book with the other.

"Very well. I do hope he selects you, otherwise you will look like a fool."

CHAPTER 6

Savinus woke at dawn the next day and rang the bell for Agnese to bring him breakfast in the sitting room. He glanced into Giulia's chamber as he passed. She was fast asleep on her stomach. Looking forward to a solitary breakfast, he sat down at the round table in the corner of the room, surrounded by four rosewood-backed chairs. He did not have to wait long. Sleepy-eyed but cheerful, Agnese emerged from the kitchen carrying a tray of steaming oats and a cup of milk. She greeted him without making eye contact and placed his cup and bowl on the table.

Despite the early hour, the noise outside was constant and increasing in volume. There was the groan of rolling cartwheels taking produce to the market, followed by the curses of the donkey seller, as he coerced the reluctant creatures with the aid of a large stick. To Savinus's chagrin, each morning also heralded the arrival of the apple juice vendor, who advertised by singing folk songs at the top of his tone-deaf voice. He often wished his powers were such that he could make the dreadful man disappear.

The previous afternoon, he had submitted his geomantic findings to Tomas Albizi, regarding his crops for the next six months. As the farmer was only semi-literate, he had devised a number of symbols for the various states of the wheat and the types of weather influencing it, to which his client could refer at the beginning of each month. In turn, Signor Albizi found methods to counteract the ravages of the weather which he implemented before disaster struck. Locusts were the only problem he was unable to combat. If they were a part of the predictions, then all he could do was sit and wait in despair.

As there were no more urgent readings, he realized the need for a distraction. Examining his bookshelf, he pulled out the most complex tome, *Hermetic Alchemy*. It was as thick as his arm and gave off a strong odour of mould and dust. He tried to empty his mind, to allow the cryptic words to penetrate his subconscious. This had always been his method for understanding the great alchemical texts. At around nine o'clock, Giulia emerged. She picked up the bell and gave it a vigorous shake before letting her slight frame drop into a dining chair.

"I'm famished. Where on earth is Agnese?" she asked, after no more than three seconds had elapsed.

"Not far away, I'm sure. How did you sleep?"

"Well, thank you, Papa. Goodness, I just realized today is the day! How exciting, when did you rise?"

"With the rooster."

She smiled. "Of course you did. Well, I won't be able to rest until I hear the news. Ah, Agnese, what a relief to see you! Can you please make me some polenta with strawberries on the side? Lovely."

Agnese nodded with good humour and turned on her heel towards the kitchen. She was accustomed to the rise and fall of her mistress's moods.

Mid-morning, Savinus readied to leave, letting Agnese help him into his cloak and hand him his hat. She fetched the box of objects and brass cups, which he would use to conduct the test, and asked if she could help carry it to the piazza. He declined. They both wished him luck, Giulia with less enthusiasm, as she was sad to be left at home.

He took his time walking to the piazza, in part because of his arthritic knee, and also because the box was heavier than he had realized.

The sun had just emerged from dense clouds low on the horizon. He paused several times to set down the box and rub his knee. It was whilst he was doing this that he glimpsed a neighbour. Conscious he would be drawn into an excruciating conversation, he grabbed the box and propelled himself forward, eyes on the ground.

"Signor di Benevento, how wonderful to see you! I was chatting to your lovely daughter the other day and she told me of a test you are doing with the young boys. Signor? Hello? It's me, Signora Umbrico!"

"Good morning, Signora. How charming to see you. As you may notice I am rather encumbered here with this box, and on my way to do the test. I hope you are well. Good day." He tipped his hat and continued on his way, swearing under his breath and limping from the strain on his knee.

On reaching the piazza, he saw the six boys assembled near the fountain. Three of them were attempting to balance on the narrow edge, hands outstretched and laughing. Two others stood and watched the spectacle, and the Conte's son looked embarrassed. He stood apart from the others, as if trying to disown them. His clothing appeared as out of place as his sullen expression.

Savinus observed them for a few moments more before making his approach.

"Good morning. Are you ready to begin?"

They stopped what they were doing and stood to attention in a neat row. All except Nichola greeted him by touching their caps and saying, "Good morning." The Conte's son nodded in his direction.

"Now, you'll have to excuse me while I borrow a table from one of the market people. Just a moment."

He returned several minutes later with a small pine table and a lace tablecloth. He placed the table before them and covered it with the cloth. He took six blindfolds out of his pocket and handed one to each boy.

"Put them on please. I will tell you when to remove them."

They did as they were told and stood in silence, awaiting further instruction. Savinus opened the box and withdrew each object, careful not to make any noises that might reveal something about them. He placed the objects under the three brass cups, which he lined up in a row, on the table.

"You may remove the blindfolds." He pointed to the boy on the far left. "What is your name?"

"Giovanni, Signor."

"You will be first. The test is quite simple—you must tell me what you think is under each cup. You may begin."

Giovanni fixed his gaze on the three cups before him, as did the other five boys. There was a prolonged silence as he studied each one. A few passersby stopped to watch the spectacle and as they did so, his shoulders drooped. He shook his head.

"I'm sorry to waste your time Signor, I do not know what's under the cups. I can read the tarot cards quite well and I thought that would be enough. I will go."

Before anyone could reply, he walked away without glancing back. Savinus looked at the remaining five and pointed to the next boy in line. His name was Mario and he was able to identify just one item—a baby's bonnet. Savinus blindfolded the remaining four in order to change the bonnet for another item in the box. The next two boys were twins, Paolo and Domenico. They had the same mannerism of scratching their red hair as they stared at the cups, faces sprinkled with freckle constellations. They were unable to identify any of the items and hung their heads as they departed.

∞

Nichola's turn arrived. He stood in a languid pose; his right leg crossed over the other, and studied Antonius from the corner of his eye. He thought the long-limbed servant from his father's house was unlikely to possess any skills. If the other boy had been from a similar class, he would have treated him with scorn. Even an insult gave peasants inappropriate status. So, he ignored him.

"Well, Nichola, we have not had a chance to be acquainted

formally, but your father has told me about your talents for archery and hunting. Let's find out if seeing is also one of your strengths. Please, you may begin."

Nichola cleared his throat and regarded the cups with an unflinching gaze. A thin film of perspiration appeared on his forehead, and various images took shape in his mind. The difficult part was designating the objects to the cups. He was aware some of the things he saw were just his imagination. His skills were hazy. Sometimes he had what he later realized were prophetic dreams. He was unable to differentiate between the prophecy and the parts that were merely his subconscious regurgitating the events of the day. It frustrated him that at this crucial moment, he faced a similar problem. In the end, he just guessed. Savinus nodded and shook his hand.

"Well done, you have identified two out of three. We're almost there. Be patient while I test Antonius here. Mario, I'm afraid you have been outclassed. You may go home."

∞

Antonius was undeterred by Nichola's success, as he had seen the objects beneath the cups from the moment Savinus placed them there. His blindfold had not even been removed. It was irritating to have to stand and wait, when he knew the answers. He decided he would not pretend he needed to study the cups. Raising his eyes to Savinus, his voice was assured. He pointed to each cup as he spoke.

"A key, a pipe, and a brass spoon."

Savinus beamed. "Excellent. Now I would like both of you to guess the objects four more times, just to make sure. Blindfolds on please."

Both boys performed well in the next four rounds, yet Nichola made several errors. Antonius was correct in every instance, without hesitation.

Savinus picked up the items and wrapped them in a cloth. "You have talent. I would like you both to assist me and also to learn. However, I must clarify that you, Antonius, will be my primary apprentice, and you, Nichola, the secondary. There are certain practices and research I am only willing to share with one person. I need that person to be as close to my own abilities as possible. Do you have any objection to this, Nichola?"

Nichola glowered. "No, Signor, I am honoured to be chosen in any capacity."

"Good. Now I'd like to take you to my home so you can see where I work. Actually, I do spend a great deal of time working in the front room with my daughter, but I have a room where I keep my tools for seeing. If Giulia is in a bad mood I go there!" he chuckled.

"I imagine now I have some helpers we will spend time there though. So, are you ready?"

The boys nodded in unison. Savinus smiled and led them in the direction of his villa. Antonius straightened his back as he followed, suppressing a smile. He had never been in the company of nobles on the same footing. He tipped his hat to some friends and acquaintances as they passed. Nichola watched him with narrowed eyes, and shook his head.

Arriving at the door of the villa, they were greeted by Agnese. Her eyes glinting, she ushered them inside, waving them towards the sitting room.

"Can I bring you some refreshments?"

"Just a jug of water and sweetbreads please, Agnese. We will be in my workroom."

∞

Giulia waited to be called from her bedchamber. She was restless from having to wait at home.

"Giulia! Come and meet my apprentices. You may leave off the veil."

She emerged and regarded the newcomers, smoothing down her dress and beaming. Both seemed confident, although the boy with the sand-coloured hair was more low-key. His assurance was a steely undercurrent beneath a gentle exterior. The noble boy was haughty. It was obvious he disliked the other boy and thought him inferior.

She found it difficult not to stare at his refined features and sensual lips. If it had been appropriate, she would have felt compelled to speak with him.

"Giulia, this is Antonius and this is Nichola. Antonius will be my primary apprentice and Nichola the secondary."

Nichola looked at Savinus. "May I?"

The old man nodded. Nichola made a display of his fine manners by approaching Giulia, bowing, and kissing her hand.

"It is indeed a pleasure to meet you."

"And you, sir."

It was impossible to remain unmoved by the gesture from a man whose face was as finely chiselled as a statue. When his pale blue eyes met hers, she felt as if he were looking into her soul. Lowering her gaze, she stepped back.

Not to be outdone, Antonius approached her and bowed, before rising and meeting her eyes. The honesty she saw in his expression moved her. He spoke in a low voice.

"I am honoured to meet you."

"And I you. I'm pleased to welcome you both to our home and I hope you'll feel comfortable here."

Savinus was eager to show the boys where they would be working. He gave his daughter a small nod and she understood.

"Well, I have much weaving to do today. I will let you gentlemen become acquainted."

∞

Savinus led his protégées to the workroom at the back of the house. As they stood on the threshold of the large room, he allowed the boys to absorb their surroundings. To the casual observer, the room looked ransacked. Books were scattered across the desks, opened at various pages, and piled in haphazard formations on the ground. A floor-to-ceiling bookcase housed hundreds of other tomes, and beakers and vials connected with tubes of differing lengths were arranged on the remaining surfaces. Some of the vials contained amber, blue, and red-coloured liquids. Another larger one contained mercury. A luminous crystal ball sat on a smaller table, beneath a dust-streaked window. In front of it, yellowed parchment, a quill, and the presence of a green, velvet-upholstered chair, indicated this was the eminent man's desk.

Savinus walked over to it, and was about to sit down, when he realized the lack of seating for his pupils. He bellowed to Agnese.

"Agnese! Bring in two of the rosewood chairs please! And hurry—these boys look tired!"

His resonant voice carried through the rooms and Agnese returned looking harried, a chair slung over each broad shoulder. She was panting from the exertion. Behind her was Giulia, bearing a tray with the water and biscuits.

"Here they are, Signor."

Savinus was taken aback to see his daughter acting as a servant.

"Thank you. Antonius, Nichola, do take a seat. Thank you, Giulia."

As the two women exited, Savinus watched the boys, enjoying their awe and fascination.

Nichola's upbringing allowed him to conceal his reactions, taking in the contents of the room with many small glances, feigning nonchalance. Antonius had never needed to hide his reactions and sat slack-jawed, his eyes darting around with unbridled curiosity. He returned Savinus's gaze with a broad smile.

"This room is like a cave of treasures. I would like to read every book and smell every liquid."

Nichola rolled his eyes. "It's bad manners to stare at another man's possessions. Signor will think you are coming back later to fill your pockets."

Savinus laughed. "I think no such thing. Antonius has not seen a room such as this before, and I daresay, neither have you. He is entitled to show his reactions in a different manner. I have chosen each of you because you demonstrated some skill in seeing. However, you have much to learn. I started in these practices when I was a few years younger than you, because my parents approached the seer in my village. They were concerned that I seemed to know everything that was about to happen, before it occurred. As they were deeply religious, they thought I might be possessed by the devil. They wanted the seer, Bartholomeus Giovari, to tell them if their son was like him, or evil."

"Thankfully, they were told I was talented and I was spared an exorcism. We have moved to more progressive times. Those who have this talent are now more respected than feared. Nichola, what you learn here can be used within your family. I am sure they will appreciate not having to call on me for their less important divinations. Antonius, you will one day take over from me. You must be diligent and committed in a more serious manner than Nichola. We must study some subjects alone so you are ready to take over from me when the time comes. Nichola, I understand this may cause some resentment. Please, tell me now if you feel this arrangement will not suit you."

Nichola shook his head. "No Signor, I accept that my role will be different. It's not a concern to me."

"Very good. Now I must explain my workroom to you. One of the most important things I will teach you is the skill of geomancy. I use various symbols, with which I make additions, subtractions and an overall calculation. It's time consuming, but I have found it to be an extremely accurate method. I do this work at my desk. For matters of the heart, it's different. Then I use my skills of seeing. I might ask for a personal object to assist me. But I digress. Over here, you can see my apparatus for experiments into the First Matter—also known as hermetic alchemy. Nichola, you may as well know now, this will be out of bounds for you. Only seers with higher powers are fit to investigate this subject. Here are my many books on all that is unseen in the universe. You are welcome to look at them when I am not teaching you. Any questions?"

∞

Antonius was transfixed by a shower of dust motes swirling in circular waves through the light cast by the window. Although he had been listening, his attention had drifted just before the question.

Nichola poked him with a tapered index finder, held delicately, as if he feared he might catch the other boy's poverty.

"Yes, Signor. Are you sure this dolt will be your primary apprentice?"

A brief look of consternation passed over Savinus's face before he replied.

"To see beneath the surface of existence, one must be able to access a state between alertness and slumber. It is apparent Antonius is well attuned with this state. Isn't that so, young man?"

Antonius reddened and cleared his throat. Straightening his posture, he answered in what he hoped was a confident voice.

"Ah, yes, Signor. My mother calls me a dreamer and I'm pleased to hear this is something useful in my new work."

"Very good. I have something more to say to you both. It is clear you are not getting along very well. Nichola, I understand you have never had to associate with someone of the peasant class before. You think Antonius is beneath you. In my workroom, and in any place where the three of us are working together, he is your equal. You are to treat him as you would someone from your own class. Otherwise it will be impossible for me to impart any of the ancient wisdom to you. It's not necessary that you be great friends. Only that you can work in harmony. Although, as I have pointed out, at times he will be learning at a higher level. Antonius, you must gain confidence in yourself as someone who will one day be in my position. Is that clear?" -

The boys nodded in unison. Antonius shifted in his seat, glancing over at Nichola. He could see how difficult it was for someone in his position to be secondary to a servant from his own household. He resolved to be kind to him. Following this thought was the realisation he must assert himself to create a good impression. He knew this opportunity to develop his talent was the best chance he would ever have. By contrast, his rival's life was one of endless possibilities. Gazing once more into the dust motes, he decided he would tread the middle road between ambition and benevolence. He would not wither into passivity, but nor would he be cruel.

Once again, he was wrenched from his thoughts.

"Antonius, please help yourself to a biscuit and some water. I have been talking too much."

"Thank you, Signor."

The conversation drifted from alchemy to the festival due to start the next day. Although all three were excited to see the town erupt into celebration, they saw the preparation that made it possible as "women's business." To indulge in hedonistic preparation for San Terenzio was to be ignorant of worldly affairs, the domain of men.

Nichola contributed to the conversation in the well-mannered way that was expected of him. His face was flushed, and he kicked the table leg in an agitated rhythm. When the time came to leave, he shook hands with the seer and gave Antonius a curt nod. His rival nodded back, bemused. Savinus informed the boys which three mornings they were required. Antonius was told to come on an additional morning to learn about Hermeticism. As they walked down the path, Nichola made sure he was well ahead. By the time they reached the street, he was yards in front.

Antonius was thrilled to be the primary apprentice, but also uncomfortable. He had heard of people from his class becoming wealthy in larger cities. Only on rare occasions had this happened in Pesaro. The workers did not often try to rise above their station. When they did, ridicule followed, and sometimes hostility. Most found it reassuring when people just did what was expected of them. As his elevation was based on talent rather than ambition, he hoped he would be spared judgement.

Arriving back at the kitchen, he concealed his excitement as he sat down at the table. Katerina turned to him as she wiped flour-covered hands on her apron.

"So, how did it go? What is he like, this magic Signor?" she asked.

Antonius shrugged. "He seems very kind. Smart too. I'm to be his primary apprentice and the master's son the secondary."

Katerina drew a sharp breath. "Are you sure? The Conte will surely be insulted. His family are always in charge, not secondary.

Do you know why you've been singled out?"

"I'm more adept than he. The Signor needs an apprentice with similar powers. He's allowing Nichola to be secondary apprentice, out of respect for the Conte."

Katerina thought for a moment. "This is a big day. Do you realize, by your association with the Signor, you now have a higher status? However, you still need a job, so you will have to speak to the Conte regarding your new role. Go and find his valet, Ignatio, and ask for an audience. Go now and you might be able to see him before he readies for his supper. Quickly."

Antonius darted though the servants' quarters and reached the courtyard dividing them from the main villa. Entering through the large oak doors he half-ran along the wide carpeted hallway, at the end of which lay the Conte's rooms. He had seen Ignatio standing outside the rooms many times before. He managed to look alert and dignified at all times. Antonius had been impressed with his resolute manner; given the hours of boredom he endured waiting for his master's requests.

Ignatio stood erect in his gilt-edged blue uniform, staring at a fixed point on the wall in front of him. For a moment, Antonius struggled to form the words he had practiced.

"Excuse me sir? I'm Antonius, the boy from the kitchen?"

At first he thought the human statue had not heard him. Then Ignatio turned in his direction and an indifferent gaze fell on a spot just above his head.

"What is it you want?"

"I have a job helping Savinus di Benevento and I need to discuss the arrangement with the master. Can you please ask him if I may speak with him?"

With a nod the man responded. "Wait here and I will find out."

Ignatio ran a hand through russet-coloured hair, cleared his throat, and gave a soft knock on the door behind him. A distant voice gave permission and he disappeared inside. Antonius felt a shiver of excitement at the realisation he would see the Conte's private rooms, the splendour of which he had spent hours imagining. Low voices could be heard as he waited. A few minutes later he heard the click of the door opening and Ignatio beckoned him forward. He intoned in a low voice.

"Speak only when spoken to, other than when you greet him, and look at his collar, not his eyes. Bow as you approach him and say, 'Good evening, Your Eminence.' Good luck."

Ignatius pushed open one of the double doors and gave him a small shove forward. At first, Antonius could not see very far ahead and gazed down at the ornate Persian carpet beneath his feet. His mouth was dry and a dull ache throbbed in his stomach. After a moment, he was able to see the room more clearly. It was large and decorated with voluminous grey silk drapes at the windows, and small groups of chairs clustered together, upholstered in deep red brocade. Brass wall sconces held candles, bathing the room in a muted gold light. A Carrera marble fireplace contained a roaring blaze. A tall man stood in front of the fire warming his hands. His breeches were dark green and woven with gold thread. His tunic was in a lighter green silk and belted at the waist. Turning towards Antonius he smoothed his neat grey beard. The boy studied the carpet, feeling the Conte's stare.

Remembering his instructions, he bowed low at the waist and spoke in a clear voice.

"Good evening, Your Eminence."

"Good evening, what is your name?"

"I'm Antonius Sardi. I work in the kitchen with Signora Giallo. I also do other jobs as required."

"And what is your reason for wishing to see me?"

"I've obtained a position four mornings a week as apprentice to Signor di Benevento. I would like to know if Your Eminence might allow me this time away from my job. My work here is very important to me, as it supports my family. My father died one year ago."

The Conte was silent for what seemed a long time, but was only several moments.

"I see. And how do you propose to make up the time you are

absent from the palazzo? I do not have an extra boy to do your work. Will the Signor be paying you a wage?"

"I will work Sundays, Your Eminence. Also two nights per week, I could help with serving the dinner banquet. This would add up to the four mornings I am gone. The Signor can only afford to pay me five florins per week. This is just an idea, Your Eminence, and I would like to know what you would suggest."

The Conte examined him, a long finger stroking his beard. Antonius reddened as his eyes travelled from his head to his battered shoes.

"I think your idea is appropriate. I'm satisfied with it. You've shown initiative in working out how to repay the lost hours. Signor di Benevento is an excellent seer and you will learn many things. I hear you will be accompanied by my son?"

"Yes, Your Eminence—"

"Please, you may refer to me as Don Leonardo."

"Yes, Don Leonardo."

"He thinks very highly of himself. Don't be offended by him."

"I won't, Don Leonardo."

"Very good. You may go."

"I'm much obliged. Thank you very much."

"It's nothing. Please tell Katerina I would like some spatchcock for tomorrow night's banquet. Good night."

"Good night, Don Leonardo."

He bowed once more and exited at a pace he hoped was neither too fast, nor too slow.

CHAPTER 7

Eager to learn the mysteries of seeing, the boys arrived at the same time on the first morning. They had not realized they were earlier than Savinus had requested. Agnese opened the door a crack and looked at the mismatched pair.

"It's just after dawn. Was Signor wanting you so early?"

Nichola never suffered from uncertainty. He responded in an authoritative tone.

"He has a lot to cover as it's our first day. It is the right time."

Not believing him, she hesitated for a moment before standing aside. "Well, you will have to wait in the sitting room. Signor is not yet ready."

They sat in armchairs opposite each other. Antonius shifted in his seat and looked around the room to distract himself from the waves of antipathy coming from Nichola. He watched the fire crackle in the hearth and glanced at the watercolour portrait of Giulia as a child hanging on a nearby wall. Her cheeks were plump, but her eyes held the same inquisitive, determined stare. The early morning sun flooded through the windows, forming a shaft of light on the wood floor.

Agnese returned and placed a jug of water and some glasses on the side table, before exiting without a word. A clearing of the throat preceded Savinus's emergence from his bedchamber. He stood before them, his thinning white hair askew, his eyes shining.

"A bit eager to start are we, boys? Good, good, nothing wrong with that. Although I think our Agnese was a bit put out, to open our door so early. Never mind. I've been thinking about what we should begin with today and here it is. Firstly, we can do an introductory lesson in geomancy. Then, when your minds wander, we can head down to the marshes for some exploration. Let's go to the workroom."

They followed him into the back room where he had placed two chairs at a long desk set against the wall.

The next hour evaporated in an introduction to geomancy. They covered a multitude of symbols and mathematical calculations, combined with the trajectories of the sun and the moon that foretold anything from a crop failure to a pregnancy. Their teacher explained that, when combined with the skill of seeing, geomancy was more accurate than any other form of divination. There were sixteen symbols. Savinus told his pupils to copy them onto parchment at random, using their intuition. Following this, they were to choose from the symbols and write them down in a shield chart, a special table, on another sheet of parchment. The symbols were compared with astrological charts to discover meaning.

As soon as he saw their attention wavering, Savinus announced it was time for the next part of their lesson.

"I've recently added a new aspect to my services. I was collecting herbs and other plants for my investigations into the First Matter. At the time, I had a terrible cold and I noticed a certain combination, when inhaled, made me well again. Giulia also tried it when she had a completely different ailment and it cured her too. This was around one year ago and I've been selling the liquid, I call it my health potion, to others in Pesaro. The results have been very encouraging. Even if one is not sick, it seems to give added vigour and energy. So, we'll go by horseback to the countryside outside the town, to the salt marshes. I keep three boats there for my explorations. There is a small island nearby, with a large cave. We call it the blue cave, as the walls are streaked with blue agate. A special plant grows there, both inside and outside the cave. I don't know its name, just that it's somewhat like a dandelion except purple in colour. We'll collect it. Then it's combined with certain herbs and crushed with a mortar. I mix it with salt water and distill it. After that, the potion is ready to be used. Shall we go?"

The boys nodded, excited at the prospect of an excursion. At that moment, Giulia poked her head around the door. After a small curtsey, she smoothed the skirt of her red embroidered day dress and tried to make her smiling face more serious. She knew of her father's plans for plant gathering.

"Good morning Papa, Antonius, Nichola. I hope I'm not intruding, but I thought you might need some assistance at the blue cave?" She looked at Savinus who was already shaking his head in exasperation.

"Giulia, can we speak privately please?"

"Of course, Papa."

He took her elbow and guided her to the hallway. "Dear girl, it's my first day with the boys. I really wanted them to focus on the job and you are fetching enough that if you come, they will be distracted. Can't you just be patient and wait for a day, when they have learned some of what I hope to impart?"

Giulia regarded him with a calm expression.

"You are such a wonderful teacher Papa, and I understand what you're saying. But these boys have never collected the healing plant before and your eyes are not so good. You need at least one person there who knows what to look for. Also, I'm quite sure noblemen don't know how to manoeuvre boats, so Nichola will need me to row—" She raised a hand to his objection. "We both know you're having trouble paddling with your bad knee. Antonius can row you."

Savinus looked defeated and bemused at the same time.

"Good. It's settled then. I'm so glad I can accompany you all."

"Yes, dear. There is some reason in what you are saying."

On returning to the workroom, Savinus explained that Giulia would be joining them. There was some organisation required before they were able to set off. Savinus borrowed extra horses from a neighbour and Agnese prepared water bottles. Giulia changed into an old dress, more appropriate for boating and plant gathering.

It was mid-morning by the time they left. Savinus led the way on an attractive brown mare. Nichola was next in line, followed by Antonius, and Giulia at the rear. At the insistence of her father, she wore her veiled hat, which made navigating the cobbled streets a challenge. Once they left the town walls, she was allowed to place it in the bag tethered to her horse. Their procession drew the stares of the townspeople, curious to see who had been chosen to help the seer. There was much whispered discussion about the son of the Conte. Fewer people knew the identity of the peasant boy.

They travelled past the wheat fields, into the countryside bordered by the shimmering sea. The sun was soon high in the sky, and they stopped to swig from the glass water bottles. They passed apple orchards and olive groves as they made their way closer to the coast. Giulia covered her mouth with one hand as the horse's hooves kicked up yellow dust from the road. It was not yet spring, and the heat took them by surprise. As the sun beat down, she became mesmerised by Nichola's blue cape fluttering in the breeze. She paused to take her straw hat from the bag and put it on her perspiring scalp.

"Almost there now," Savinus called out.

She noticed with amusement that Antonius seemed unruffled by the heat, in direct contrast with his rival, who breathed heavily and mopped his red face with an embroidered handkerchief. She supposed nobles were unused to physical discomfort.

To their right, she could see the beginning of the salt marshes, olive green spikes of the reeds rising like sentinels from the still water. Her father kept the boats hidden in their depths, tethered to two heavy wooden stakes. She felt anticipation and fear at the thought of strangers being introduced to their secret place. It had always been a source of closeness between them. The necessity of sharing both the cave and her father with the boys gave her a jolt of insecurity.

As they approached the marshes, a large black crow flew towards them and hovered in front of their party. Giulia knew the meaning of its appearance. It warned of someone unworthy to visit the sacred space. She glanced at her father; his expression was troubled as he watched the bird recede into the distance.

At a signal from Savinus, they dismounted and waited while he stepped through the reeds to find the hidden boats. He waved his hand and called out; he had not needed to go very far. They were long vessels that sat low on the water, hewn from whole logs.

"Boys, I need some help dragging these out. Come here with those strong young bodies of yours."

They rolled up their breeches and waded into the murky water, Nichola wrinkling his nose at the dank smell. His steps were tentative. The others had already brought up one boat by the time he touched the other. He undid the tether holding it to the stake and hauled it to the shore. Short of breath, he stood with his hands on his hips, looking pleased with himself.

Antonius smiled in his direction. "Well done Nichola, they're very heavy."

He shrugged. "I've lifted much heavier things."

As Giulia had predicted, she took the boat with Nichola and her father with Antonius. Nichola frowned and stepped forward to take the paddle.

"Please, you sit in the back," Giulia said. "I'm quite capable of taking us."

Nichola gaped, his brows knitting.

She tossed him an amused glance. "Forgive me, but I've paddled through these marshes and to the cave countless times. Even if you can use the oar, which I doubt, you wouldn't know which direction to go."

He stepped into the boat and sat glaring with his arms folded as she steered them away from shore.

Long-necked herons populated the marshes. They floated with grace on the surface of the water and flew over their heads, stretching out their wings. Due to his many excursions, Savinus had cleared a path through the reeds, which became sparse once they reached deeper water. Having emerged from the reeds, all that could be seen was an infinite stretch of calm azure sea, flecked by the gold of the sun. Soon the tiny island came into view. It appeared barren, with a towering granite hill jutting out of the centre. A black cavity could be seen in the hill—the cave.

As they approached, Savinus indicated where they should go ashore. There was a sliver of sand. It was only possible to land one boat at a time. Giulia and Nichola waited for the others to go ashore and then followed. Savinus led them to the copse of olive trees on the island, the only shade. From his pocket he pulled four small burlap sacks. He handed them out and spoke to Giulia.

"My dear, I need you to go and collect a sample of the plant, so the others know what to look for. Take the boys with you and show them how to twist at the stem, so as not to lose any of it. Thank you."

Giulia led them to the base of the cave. The purple-flowered plant grew there in great profusion. She crouched down and demonstrated the correct way to gather the plant, twisting at the stem. It was then placed inside the sack.

"Your turn now," she smiled with encouragement. "Just be careful not to pick all of them or they won't be able to keep growing for next time."

She darted away, lifting her skirts to better navigate the slight hill curving up the side of the cave. The two boys watched her for a moment, her steps agile as she landed on stones to reach the top and disappeared around the corner. Nichola turned to his rival with a glacial expression. Antonius shrugged and bent over to collect the healing plant. Soon his sack was almost full. Every few minutes, Nichola would push in front of him to collect his intended plant.

Savinus sat on a rock, the sun warming the top of his head. He closed his eyes and saw vivid orange. On previous excursions to the island, he had spent hours straining his eyes and bending to find the requisite amount of healing plant. With his new assistants, it would be finished in half the time and all he had to do was supervise. He kept a close eye on Nichola, who was intent on sabotaging

Antonius's efforts.

Giulia sidled up to him and laid her hand on his shoulder. She frowned.

"Papa, that boy is trouble. He keeps jumping in front of Antonius every time he finds a plant."

Savinus sighed. "Yes my dear, I'm quite aware of it but we must choose our battles."

"Why do you think he acts like that?"

"He's spoilt. No one has ever denied him anything. I believe this would make most people rude."

"Perhaps. Would you really lose the Conte's patronage if you sent him back?"

"Without a doubt."

"Oh. Well, we've got enough of the plant now. Do you want to see the bags?"

"No, I trust you. Tell them to come to the mouth of the cave. I'd like to talk to them."

"Yes, Papa."

They clustered together in front of the gaping black mouth of the cave before entering. The air was rancid and dank. The darkness was broken only by the sharp glints of light that marked a universe across the interior walls. Antonius breathed in the musty air, and felt the compressed space of the cave around him. In that moment, it reminded him of the church in Pesaro. He could feel them everywhere, pressing down on him; the countless people who had stood there before him, filled with fascination and dread. He touched the jagged wall and waited.

CHAPTER 8

In the dim light of the cave, Savinus cleared his throat to speak. "It's not just the healing plant we collect here. There are about a dozen herbs I gather for various remedies. Some of these I use for my investigations into the First Matter. Each month, on the new moon, and sometimes on the half moon, I conduct a ceremony here at the cave. I call on my protectors to guide me in my work. I burn certain herbs on a fire and perform incantations. Following the ceremony, my powers are enhanced. Seers are never alone in their abilities. They are dependent on their protectors, and the source of their powers, God himself. We should never be arrogant and must operate with complete humility. Those who have these abilities are our allies and should be supported. I like to think of it as a brotherhood." With this last comment, he cast a pointed glance at Nichola, who shifted on his feet.

"Here in this cave lie the ashes of my original teacher as well as those of other seers. They are my protectors. Sometimes, when I perform rituals here, I can see them standing behind me. When I die, my ashes will be scattered here too. Next week is the new moon. We will return here to perform the ritual together. I need the two of you to cooperate and work together until then. For the rituals to be successful and strengthen our powers, there needs to be cohesion between us. Do you understand?”

“Yes, sir.” The boys responded in unison.

Savinus was satisfied. “Good. We will go back into town now. Place the sacks at the front of my boat and I’ll make sure they stay dry. Are you ready?” Without waiting for their response, he headed to the shore, stepping with care to avoid aggravating his knee.

Nichola seized the opportunity to talk to Giulia. “I have heard your ability is almost as good as your father’s. It seems a shame that, just because you are a woman, you can’t help him.”

She glared at him. “What do you think I’ve been doing today? Looking at the scenery?”

The words came out before she could stop them and she blushed.

“I’m sorry. I would prefer you do not talk about it with anyone, but I help my father all the time. I simply can’t do it openly. And as for my ability, I would never say it is at his level. Around these parts, he is the most talented seer we’ve had for generations. The only one who’s superior is his friend, Lorenzo di Montefiore. He visits quite often; you might be fortunate enough to meet him.”

Once in the boats, they freed them from their moorings, and glided away from the island. Antonius watched Giulia and Nichola conversing, and clenched his jaw. Looking away, he tightened his grip on the paddle. The wood cleaved the surface, and he could see the pebbles lining the sand beneath. The heat was intense as it reflected from the water, and he felt a trickle of perspiration travelling down his back. Another flock of herons took to the air, the beating of their wings so deafening, he flinched as if they were beside him. He took a swig from the water bottle and tried to think of something clever to say to the Signor, who was seated behind him.

“Are we to make healing liquid when we return, Signor? What would you like to show us next?”

He could hear the smile in the reply. “The next thing on our agenda will be filling our stomachs, young man. One cannot learn without sustenance. We shall stop at a roadside stall—there is a good one near the piazza with excellent polenta and vegetable soup. How does that sound to you?”

"It sounds wonderful. Thank you."

When they reached the shore, two of the horses stood in the water and the others had wandered as far as their restraints allowed to chew grass. Antonius felt the low rumble of his stomach as he climbed out of the boat. He held out his hand to help Savinus, but the old man waved it away.

"I may look frail, but I'm as fit as a twenty-year-old. You'd be better off getting my horse ready."

Antonius led the handsome brown mare to him. "Here you are, Signor."

"Thank you."

Once on the open road, lethargy settled on all of them and they fell silent. Some farmers passed on their way to the wheat fields and tipped their caps. Overhead, a flock of crows swooped low, before careening towards the bluish-green hills surrounding Pesaro. Soon they reached the town walls. Savinus led the way to the roadside stall, tucked behind a row of houses near the piazza. A few diners sat at small round tables out front and a corpulent man with flushed cheeks stood behind a counter, stirring a large copper pot. Behind him was a makeshift oven, with a wood fire burning underneath. His wife was at his side, serving the customers. Savinus dismounted, tied the horse to a post, and approached him, signalling to the others to follow.

"Good day, Jonas. What do you have today—the polenta I hope?"

"Yes, Signor. I have that and a beef stew. What can I get you?"

Savinus placed his order and indicated there were four of them.

"Take a seat over here under the awning, otherwise it might be too warm for the lady."

As they sat around the table, everyone except Savinus felt awkward. They were strangers and did not yet know what to say to one another. Antonius hoped the food would arrive without delay so they could discuss its merits or flaws. Giulia was wearing her black veiled hat, and he tried to glimpse the outline of her face beneath the gauze.

Within a few minutes, the wife of the stall owner returned with four steaming plates of stew and a bowl of polenta to share.

"Enjoy. I ground the cornmeal myself," she said smiling, her cheeks rounded and pink, and returned to the counter to serve another customer.

They descended on their plates, realising their ferocious appetites. For a few minutes, there was only the sound of the conversation of the other diners and their own chewing. Giulia was the first to speak.

"Well, I would say the healing plant expedition was a success. Do you think you would be able to find it on your own then?"

Nichola made a scornful noise. "It wasn't exactly difficult, just at the base of the cave. If you had told me the colour, I could probably have found it without you."

She raised an eyebrow. "Well, quite the confident one we have here. What if I told you there is an almost identical plant but with a different scent. Do you think you could find it?"

He shifted on the stool and looked at his knees before raising his eyes to her.

"Perhaps we should return and you can demonstrate the different smells."

"Yes, perhaps we should."

An awkward silence followed. Savinus cleared his throat and looked absorbed in his stew. Nichola tapped his leather-shod foot on the ground.

"Signor, I have to leave an hour early today. The Conte has some guests coming for a hunt and I need to help saddle up the horses." Antonius spoke in a soft voice; worried his request might not be received well.

Savinus looked up from his examination of his food. "Yes, of course young man, that's perfectly all right." He switched his attention to the other plates. "Are we all finished? Good. Let's get back then, we have a lot to do."

∞

Agnese was waiting with a tray of warm milk and sweetbreads.

She led them into the workroom and placed it on the desk.

"I trust the expedition went well, sir?"

"Thank you, Agnese. Yes, we have a couple of quick learners on our hands."

Savinus waited until she had exited before speaking again. Her shoulders were slumped as she closed the door, leaving a gap. One eye peered through. Savinus cleared his throat and turned to the door. It clicked shut.

"We only have a short time before Antonius leaves. I want to talk to you about the herbs you must take to enhance your seeing. I collect them every few months from the forest behind the town. I brew them up and drink them, or sprinkle them on my evening meal. They serve a dual purpose: firstly, they cleanse the system of impurities to facilitate seeing, and secondly, they cause the mind to more easily access the state in which we see things. I have prepared a jar for each of you to take with you. Now we will make the healing liquid together. Put on these aprons please."

He held out two blue cotton aprons and waited until they had tied them securely. Leading them over to the bench with the alembics, he picked up the sacks they had carried back and handed one to Nichola.

"Divide the contents of this sack between the two of you and I'll show you how to ready the flowers for distillation."

As they did so, he emptied the flowers from the other sack onto the bench, not wanting to waste any time. He had a client the following day who was in need of the liquid and was in short supply.

They stood at the bench and awaited their instructions.

"Yes, well, first you must strip all the leaves from the stem. Then remove the flower from the top. You grind both the flower and the stem in a mortar and pestle. We distill the essence of the paste over a fire I will make in the courtyard. You must work together— Antonius, you strip the stems and remove the flower, and Nichola you do the grinding. Swap tasks every ten minutes or so if you are getting bored. We'll do the distilling when you return on Wednesday. Although I must do some on my own when you have left, as I need it urgently. You may get started now." He waved them off with one hand and picked up a flower with the other.

Antonius and Nichola worked in silence, careful to keep their distance and avoid conversation. They inhaled the scent of the flowers, bitter like almonds. The bench was long and narrow, with plenty of room for the three of them. Savinus hummed the San Terenzio song in a low voice. Soon a rhythm emerged in their work and they laboured as if in a trance, conscious only of the movement of their hands as they stripped the flowers and wielded the pestle. From outside the church bells rang, announcing afternoon mass. This merged with the melodic warble of the sparrows in the tree outside the window. Nichola heard the bells and watched Antonius, his tongue poking out as he peeled off the leaves. He was sure he had not heard them, and knew he would be late for his work at the palazzo. He smirked and ground the pestle in a circular motion.

So absorbed were they in their task that an hour passed in what seemed like an instant. Antonius jumped and looked around him, readjusting to his surrounds.

"Sir, please, were they the afternoon mass bells I heard?" he asked.

"Yes, they were."

Eyes wide, he yanked his coat from the back of a chair and said some hurried farewells before darting from the room.

Luca was waiting for him at the stables when he arrived. He was standing with his back to him, adjusting the straps on a saddle. He could tell by the stiffness in his back he was angry.

Antonius approached him with wary steps—he had heard stories about Luca throwing punches at the tavern and he had never been taught how to fight.

"I'm sorry Luca, I lost track of time," he said.

Luca turned to him; his face flushed a deep pink.

"The master will be here soon with his hunting party. How are we to tell him the horses aren't ready? Just because you have a job doing hocus pocus doesn't mean you're too good to do your real job. Quick, get that saddle over there and put it on the grey mare."

"Please Luca, don't tell the master it's my fault."

Luca shrugged and pushed him in the small of his back towards the saddle. He picked it up and found it heavier than anticipated. It was the second time he had helped in the stable and he had forgotten how to fasten the saddle to the horse. He watched Luca from the corner of his eye and remembered the order in which to fasten the buckles. Then he hoisted the saddle onto the mare that snorted and shifted with her back legs, creating a small cloud of dust. Giving her a gentle pat on the neck, he finished the task and looked to Luca for instructions.

"It's your lucky day—it seems our master is running late. The black saddle there is for his stallion, I'll do that. You do the brown horse in the corner. The saddle is at his feet. We're almost finished."

Grateful to have avoided further anger, Antonius saddled up the horse. His caramel coat gleamed with health. He wondered what it would be like to ride such beautiful animals, and imagined they would be more even-tempered and obedient than the horses of commoners. Without warning, the Conte entered the stables. The atmosphere changed and both Antonius and Luca stood straight with their hands clasped in front. Their heads were bowed and they greeted him in low voices. At his side were three noblemen, dressed for the hunt in long leather boots and gilt-embellished grey coats. On their heads were small suede brimless hats, favoured because they did not fall off during the hunt. Their chests were crossed with the leather strap of their quivers, full of arrows. They ignored the servants and examined the horses, admiring their shining flanks and good breeding. The Conte gave credit to Luca, who spent hours each day on their grooming.

The four men took swigs from silver bottles of brandy they extracted from their coat pockets, before being assisted by Luca and Antonius onto their chosen mounts. As they rode away, Luca played a fanfare on a small bugle. When they could no longer be seen, his body slackened with relief. He wiped perspiration from his forehead with a handkerchief and winked at Antonius.

"His friends, eh? Have you ever seen such a bunch of girls in your life?"

Antonius smirked. "How about their balloon pants, they were so puffy I thought they might just take flight!"

"I'll say, and what about those coloured feathers sprouting from their hats? They might be mistaken for prey by some other hunters."

They laughed together before Antonius returned to the kitchen. He was sure Katerina would have a long list of tasks ready for him.

CHAPTER 9

The library shelves were a vertiginous height, crammed with the thick leather spines of his father's books. A long ladder stretched almost to the ceiling. Nichola had only seen his father climb the ladder once. He had been looking for a particular reference about birds and had leant too far in one direction, causing the ladder to come away at the top and sway slowly. Nichola and his mother stood aghast during the several seconds that passed before it came to rest against the shelf. His mother had watched with her hand over her mouth as he made the perilous climb down, the thick tome in the crook of his arm. He walked over to them with great composure. It was only when he placed the book on a table that his son observed his trembling hands.

On this afternoon, he sat with his father and his older brother Gianni in burgundy leather chairs facing the fire. They cradled cups of spiced mead. Gianni spoke very little as he had spent the previous day and night immersed in the San Terenzio celebrations. Grey-faced he nursed his mead as if it might save his life.

The Conte and Nichola kept the conversation to a minimum when they realized he winced every time they spoke. Nichola was frustrated. He wanted to talk with his father about the problem of being secondary apprentice. It was outrageous Signor di Benevento expected him to assist. Members of his family had not assisted anybody for countless generations. Without exception, they led.

"How was the lovely Violetta?" asked the Conte in a teasing voice.

Gianni took a sip of his mead and squinted at him. "She's well, thank you, Papa. I saw her only briefly, at her balcony. She dropped her handkerchief and turned inside. Her father forbade her to take part in the celebrations. She even wore a veil, as he was concerned about drunken revellers seeing her face."

The Conte nodded. "Ah, I see. Signor Bonacci is very preoccupied with virtue. He does not even permit his wife to go unaccompanied to the markets."

Gianni had been in love with Violetta for two long years. During that time, they had conversed only twice. The first time was at the wedding of a mutual friend of their parents. They had found a quiet doorway, away from the revelry of the banquet table, and talked about plants. Gianni was an avid gardener and had his own vegetable plot and flower garden near the servants' quarters. He described to Violetta the downy petals of the irises and the green tips of the snowdrops. Taking her hand in his, he confessed he loved nothing more than plunging his fingers deep into the moist earth and pulling out muddy fistfuls, before planting daffodil bulbs, or snow peas. Touched by his passion, she said she loved to arrange flowers in vases, often spending hours on one arrangement. Their enthusiasm spent, they felt awkward and looked at the parquet floor.

Their second opportunity to speak had come about by chance. Violetta had accompanied her mother and the cook to the market. On their way, her mother ran into a friend and they became absorbed in conversation. She saw Gianni talking to a shopkeeper nearby. Lifting the veil of her hat, she signalled to him with her eyes that she would meet him in the opposite street. Once there, they walked until they found a deserted alleyway. After a furtive glance around, they ran into the nearest doorway, away from prying eyes. Without hesitation, Gianni lifted her veil and grasping her waist, found her lips. They remained like that for some time before pulling away.

Awkward once more, and cognisant of their limited time, they had a brief discussion about how all their mothers talked about was food and servants. They found time to kiss again before leaping away from the doorway and walking as far from one another as possible as they returned to the market.

Nichola knew from his brother's mannerisms that although his body was there with them, his mind was with Violetta. He stroked one tapered hand with the other and his eyes became unfocused. It irritated Nichola. Since they were small boys it was apparent that aside from blood, they had little in common. Gianni had a gentle disposition and a love of beauty in all its forms. He believed the highest ideal was to help others. From an early age, he rescued foxes from traps, ducks with broken wings, and on several occasions, street urchins. His parents explained they could not keep stray children and either arranged adoptions with local families or sent them to the orphanage. To his brother's annoyance, this nobility of spirit did not make Gianni a bore. He was gifted with immense personal charm and made friends with members both of their class and many of the servants. His only flaw was naivety—he was unable to see the shortcomings of others. Unkindness from Nichola was met with bewilderment. He loved his brother and defended him when he was accused of being haughty or callous.

By the age of seven, Nichola knew his role in the family. Gianni was the good son and he the amoral one. He played his part with skill, regularly playing tricks on his brother and offending the servants. After a misadventure, his father would call him into the library for a discussion about kindness. He explained that very few people enjoyed the privileges of their family and he should show his gratitude through benevolence towards the peasants. Nichola had heard the speech so often he knew it by heart. It did not penetrate his resolve to be as different from his brother as possible. The disapproval of his father was counterbalanced by the love of his mother. She was able to show him affection and ignore his shortcomings. This prevented him from becoming a complete reprobate.

From the hallway, his mother's voice called out. Gianni was

needed to intervene in a dispute between the sisters. He hauled himself out of the chair with some difficulty and left the room. Nichola seized the opportunity to speak with his father.

"Papa, did you realize I'm a secondary apprentice to Signor di Benevento? A servant boy of the lowest level is the primary apprentice. His name is Antonius and he has a half-wit brother. Do you think it's appropriate for me to be beneath this boy?"

His father appeared not to have heard him. He read his book and did not raise his eyes. When he spoke, his voice was exasperated.

"The Signor is a great seer. He needs his primary apprentice to have skill which is close to or matches his own. The boy has strong ability and is to be commended for securing the job. You have minimal abilities and are fortunate to have been given the secondary role. Do you know why you have it?"

"Because I was the second best out of all the boys whom he tested."

"That is correct. However, did you realize the Signor only required one apprentice? He has appointed you only out of respect for our family and his friendship with me. Stop complaining and show some appreciation. I don't wish to hear any more about it."

The Conte dismissed Nichola by turning his attention back to his book. Stung by the rebuttal, Nichola stared out of the tall windows, where a team of gardeners trimmed the hedges. For a few minutes, he tried to distract himself by reading his book, a dull description of the history of Roman architecture. Then he rose from the chair and left the room. The plush Persian runners were soft underfoot as he made his way towards the sitting room. He knew his mother and two sisters were there working on their embroideries. The agitated voices of his sisters reached his ears, and the placating tone of his mother. For as long as he could remember, his mother had been supportive, even when he was wrong. It was not necessary to explain his predicament, only to show distress. He entered the room with his shoulders slumped, eyes downcast, and waited for her reaction.

"Dear boy, whatever is the matter? I've just stopped their bickering, and now you're here looking gloomy." She placed her embroidery on the side table and held out her arms. His sisters, Ginevra and Francesca, rolled their eyes in disgust as he went his mother and buried his head in her considerable bosom. He was too old to do this, but knew he had some time left before she would forbid it.

"I am an underling to a peasant, Mama. That boy from the kitchen is the primary apprentice to Signor di Benevento."

"Dear me, how undignified!"

"Can you speak to Papa?" he asked.

Contessa Ilaria Valperga was still an attractive woman, despite approaching middle age. Her gowns had elaborate drapery to conceal her girth and she wore her dark hair fastened with tortoiseshell combs. A regime of splashing rosewater on her face each morning meant her complexion required only a dab of rouge to appear youthful. Her great passion was her three Bichon Tenerife dogs, which she kept close at all times. When she had her weekly milk baths, they were permitted to accompany her.

She ran her fingers through his hair and contemplated his question. "I think not, my darling. You see, it's not a normal job. The Signor must appoint as his primary apprentice someone of great talent. And I'm afraid talent does not care if you are the son of a conte or the son of a street sweeper. It's important you accept your position with good grace and show your fine manners. In this way, our honour will be enhanced in spite of your lowly role."

He drew back with a scowl and flopped onto a chair beside her, crossing his arms and turning away from her.

"Now my love, don't be a crosspatch. Mama must tell you the truth sometimes."

Ginevra raised her embroidery circle to her face and stifled a giggle.

"And what are you laughing about, you dimwit?" he growled.

"I think perhaps that's the first time Mama has told you the truth in ten years. Everyone knows you only got the job because of Papa. You should realize how lucky you are."

Nichola clenched his fists. "How dare you speak to me like that!

I've a good mind to go to that suitor of yours—what was his name? Vittorio? I'll tell him you eat fifty cream cakes a night, you fat sow!"

Ginevra was unperturbed. "Vittorio thinks I am pillowy and beautiful. He told me so. We are peaceful here, won't you please go?"

His mother gave him a weary smile. "Dear boy, perhaps you should go for a ride on your horse to clear your head. It's not good to argue with your sister. And stop worrying about your secondary role. It will be good for you"

"Arguing clears my head, and I'm not worried, because I will show that kitchen hand his place."

CHAPTER 10

In the kitchen, Antonius peeled potatoes at a dangerous speed, pausing to gesticulate with the knife as he told Katerina about his day. She deboned a spatchcock and listened with wide eyes. After wiping her bloodied hands on her apron, she spooned a honey and herb mixture onto the bird.

"Does he sell this potion to everyone? Or just rich folk like the Conte?"

"I'm not sure. I imagine if you have the money he would sell it to you. I can ask him if you like?"

"Yes, if you would. And tell me about the daughter—I hear she's a beauty."

Antonius blushed. "She's the loveliest girl I've ever seen, but she's not allowed to show her face very often. She's fearless and has almost as much knowledge of alchemy and seeing as the Signor."

Katerina smiled. "Ah, I see. You're already falling for her but are worried you won't be viewed as the right suitor?"

"How did you guess? Perhaps you should be the Signor's apprentice!"

"No, my dear, I've just had many years observing the love-struck."

"I think the Signor would prefer to see her with someone like

Nichola. Not a penniless nobody like me."

"What rubbish! The fact that you are learning from him proves you're not a nobody. And if you're to take over from him one day you won't be penniless. Have confidence and the young lady will be drawn to you."

His smile was uncertain. "I'd like to go to the festival tonight if you don't mind. It's the masked celebrations and the parade. You never know, she might be there."

"Well, you'd better get a move on with those potatoes, and I need you to pick some carrots from the vegetable patch, and do the sweeping. Then I suppose you can go. Don't be too late or you'll be asleep on your feet tomorrow."

"Yes, I shouldn't be too much after midnight. Thank you."

She glanced at the small wooden shrine of the Virgin Mary, placed near the fireplace, and crossed herself. Its candles flickered next to the porcelain statue.

Antonius smiled. "What has this to do with Our Lady?"

"Our Lady influences everything. I am asking her to have you back by midnight."

Luca was also planning on going to town. The two of them slipped out of the gates just after sunset, as the sky turned from russet to indigo. The luminous moon cast a soft light. They had fashioned masks from papier maché, which they swung at their sides. After talking about work, they settled into a comfortable silence. Both were excited to be attending the masked night—the highlight of the weeklong celebrations. The anonymity of the masks was known to encourage trysts and covert behaviour of all kinds. The previous year, Luca had started a dalliance with a barmaid, which had lasted for several months. He had high hopes of repeating his success. For his part, Antonius anticipated some innocent fun and perhaps a sighting of Giulia.

As they walked down the hill, the sounds of the festival increased in volume. Shrieks of delight, singing, drunken shouts, and the cacophony of badly played instruments met their ears. Their noses were filled with the smells of street food. The sudden boom and whine of firecrackers caused them to jump. Once through the town gates, they saw the parade was still in progress. Altar boys held aloft a large papier-maché statue of San Terenzio, complete with silver tears on his cheeks and a painted red mouth. His blond hair was fashioned from yellow-painted horsehair.

The statue wobbled precariously as they wound their way past the onlookers. Following the altar boys was a couple dressed as Mary and Joseph, who held a sinister papier-maché baby Jesus. Many others snaked behind: tattered orphans, jugglers, flute players, the pious bearing wooden crosses and muttering prayers under their breath, and party-goers in spangled costumes. Anyone was permitted to join the parade, the only exceptions being prostitutes, known criminals, and Jews.

Luca and Antonius followed behind the procession, hanging back a few feet, as they did not wish to draw attention to themselves. Closer to the piazza, the voice of Lisabetta Romano held the attention of the crowd as she sang with celestial beauty. Even the most intoxicated revellers fell silent.

Stalls selling beef ragú, cakes, and soup to accompany enormous carafes of ale and wine surrounded them. Before Antonius realized he had gone, Luca returned with enough ale for four men. They found a table and chairs nearby and took in the atmosphere. Children were climbing all over the fountain, and in some cases swimming, to the horror of their mothers. The spectre of illness was always present. Others had donned masks and were taking advantage of their anonymity to steal jugs of ale. After a while Antonius and Luca became restless and decided to go for a walk. They joined a tide of people at random that led them to one of the alleyways surrounding the piazza. As they walked, Antonius felt the warmth of the alcohol spreading through his body.

The ebullience of the crowd was contagious. The men put on their masks, allowing them to ogle the young women more freely. In a doorway, a young fiddler playing a raucous tune had attracted a small crowd. Children danced with their parents and couples were grateful for the opportunity to hold one another close. Luca broke into a jerky dance, his arms and legs moving in a spasmodic rhythm. Antonius snorted with laughter and imitated him. At that moment, he saw the delicate frame of a girl standing to the side. She wore a gold mask decorated with peacock feathers and a simple white muslin dress. Her mask concealed most of her face, other than her lips and chin. Sensing her eyes on him, he was certain it was Giulia. Excusing himself from Luca, who was deep in conversation with an attractive brunette, he made his way towards her.

"Is it you?"

"It is. I'm meant to be having supper at my friend's house. We made the masks a week ago."

"It's beautiful. You have many talents. Where is your friend?"

"Over there." She pointed behind him. A slim blonde wearing a similar mask in blue was dancing by herself with her eyes closed, immersed in the frenetic pace of the music.

He smiled. "Don't you like to dance?"

"I like to watch others. You're a little drunk, I see."

"Perhaps. Is that a crime?"

"Not at all. I'll dance with you if you like."

He nodded and placed a tentative hand around her waist, drawing her to him whilst being careful to keep a small distance between them. She smelled of rosewater and vanilla.

"You've been cooking today?"

"I helped Agnese make some biscotti."

"You smell delicious."

The blush returned, this time starting from her cleavage and climbing up to her face. Her hand was so pale it had a bluish tint. It felt cool on his forearm. By contrast, her chest radiated heat. He was not prepared for the sensation of having her at close proximity and he had difficulty meeting her eyes. When he did she was regarding him with an open curiosity. Her eyes were a deep green. He tried to think of something to say whilst ignoring the desire to kiss her.

They turned to see a clown cartwheeling down the street. In his mouth was a fiery torch, flames snaking out towards a frizzy red wig. As he landed on his feet, clad in oversized leather shoes, an errant flame leapt out and the wig was set alight. Within seconds his head was engulfed, a flaming medusa. For several moments the crowd stood motionless, paralysed in horror. Then a plump woman flew out of one of the houses, carrying a blanket that she tossed over his head. He sank to the ground where he lay very still. Someone yelled out for the physician and one of the children was sent to find him. Several women attended the burned clown with wet cloths and soothing words. Antonius heard someone whisper that he had been practicing his cartwheeling torch routine for weeks. At almost the same time as the physician, his wife arrived. Her face was streaked with tears and her body convulsed with sobs.

"Vittorio! My darling! You are a cobbler, not a clown! Leave the clowning to the clowns. Oh, dear God, look at you!"

On his left cheek, a jagged purple burn was already visible. He gave a loud moan and clenched his fists. Beside him, a blue curve of smoke snaked from the extinguished torch.At the edge of the crowd, unseen by Giulia and Antonius, stood Nichola. He had walked to the festival with his friends, Matteo and Giorgio. Within minutes, the throng separated them and he wandered on his own. He spotted a couple dancing—something about them looked familiar. As the girl turned, he noticed her gold locket; the one Giulia always wore, and realized it was she and Antonius. He watched the interaction between them, heat burning his cheeks. Lifting his tankard to his lips, he drained the liquid in one long gulp. Staggering away, he smashed his fist into a wall, and yelped with pain.

The shock of the incident left Antonius and Giulia stunned. They made excuses and parted, dispersing into the crowd and searching for their friends. They did not have to search for long.

The beer and wine flowed, and couples paired off in quick succession. Luca dragged Antonius over to a table outside the tavern, where several of his friends were carousing. He accepted another pitcher of beer and was soon swept up in their exuberance. Giulia sat on a bench with Luisa and watched the intoxicated crowd, twisting in every direction like one disordered entity. Cries of delight intermingled with those of pain, as feet were trodden and ribs were elbowed. She held her small sequined purse closer to her chest, aware that many of the children took the opportunity to delve into pockets.

The moon cast a silver glow over the festivities as Lisabetta Romano took to the small podium once more and the pure, bell-like sound filled the cool air. For the length of the aria the crowd was subdued. Its beauty was as ethereal as that of the choirboys in the cathedral and reminded the pious of their sins.

Antonius kept glancing around, hoping for another glimpse of Giulia. He had felt a spiderweb bond between them. At the same time, he mocked himself. He knew she was a woman unlike those in his family. As a member of the middle class, she was refined and educated. He imagined her wringing out steaming washing in the courtyard of his home like his mother, or descaling fish with slimy pink hands. He almost laughed—she could not, would not do these things. To have any hope of winning her he knew he must elevate himself to at least her status. The apprenticeship was a start. It was an opportunity to one day fill the shoes of his teacher.

He had seen Nichola watching them and glowering—had felt the heat of his jealousy. Never had he experienced such hatred and knew it was his talent that had provoked it. He did not have anything else. His chest felt tight. He could not understand how someone with everything would begrudge his modest success. There was a temptation to walk away from the situation. The thought of Nichola trying to impede him filled him with dread. Then he remembered his father coming home each day reeking of fish guts, falling exhausted onto his straw pallet, the battle to have food on the table. The second-hand shoes donated by neighbours, sewed up by his mother with fishing line. There was no option but to fight for his position. Anything else would be a betrayal of his parents' struggle.

At half past midnight, the pace of the festivities slowed and many of the revellers straggled home. Antonius and Luca climbed the hill with drooping shoulders, chatting about the people they'd seen and the amount of ale consumed. They were satisfied they had extracted as much pleasure from the evening as possible. Antonius did not mention the encounter with Giulia. It was too important to him. He was aware Luca might share the story with another friend. In Pesaro, even a conversation with a man was enough to stain the reputation of an unmarried girl.

Nichola preceded them by half an hour. He lay in his four-poster bed, surrounded by swathes of deep red velvet. The silk comforter was filled with down and he was feverish with heat. In his mind, he replayed the coy glances. He clenched and unclenched his fists as he stared at the gold stars on the fabric above him. They were painted in curving swirls on indigo silk. The scent of the hyacinths the maid had placed on his bedside filled his nostrils. His vision blurred with tears.

CHAPTER 11

It was just after dawn when Savinus filled the retort with liquid. He had made a fire underneath with rushes, and the acrid smoke caused his eyes to water. The boys were due to arrive later that morning and he wanted to get ahead with the distillation of the healing liquid. Multiple orders had been placed both from the people of Pesaro and some nearby towns. His old friend, Lorenzo di Montefiore, was on his way from Genoa and his work would fall behind.

The celebrations were over, and a lull fell like a blanket over the town. Everyone was exhausted. Those who had participated were drained from the drink and stimulation, and many had taken to their beds.

Some people, like himself, who had stayed indoors and tried to wish the clamour away, were tired from the constant noise and heightened atmosphere. Even though he had made a decision to avoid the party, there was a part of him that wished to be twenty years younger so he could have joined in. Without him noticing, Agnese had placed a cup of mead on the ground behind him and he picked it up, gratefully inhaling the spiced smell and feeling the warmth of the china cup on his palms. He estimated that by the time the boys arrived, most of the order would be completed. Then they would be free to learn from Signor di Montefiore.

The finches in the olive trees edging the courtyard trilled as the saffron disc of sun ascended. Water in the stone fountain burbled and splashed as it fell. The pain in his knee abated and he wondered if it was due to his inhalation of the liquid. Inside the house, he could hear Giulia's excited tones mingling with another female voice. He sipped some mead and crouched at the woodpile to gather twigs. As the steam rose, beads of perspiration broke out on his face.

When the sun was much higher, he guessed it was approaching mid-morning. He called out to Agnese for some water to extinguish the fire. He would need to do one more distillation the next day but was almost finished. Fifteen glass bottles with cork stoppers were lined up against the courtyard wall. After pulling on heatproof gloves, he picked one up, uncorked it, and placed it near the scalding retort. With great care, he unscrewed the receiving flask filled with liquid and, placing a funnel on top of the bottle, poured the distillate into it. Ten bottles were filled and he placed them with satisfaction into a crate he had left near the door. Removing the gloves, he stepped inside and greeted Agnese before making his way to the sitting room. Giulia was seated on one of three armchairs covered with deep blue brocade. Opposite her sat Luisa Pepolo, her long-time friend and the daughter of a prominent businessman. They were giggling and tried to suppress their laughter as Savinus entered.

"Good morning Luisa, I hear congratulations are in order for your nuptials. What month have you chosen?"

Luisa's brown eyes sparkled. She looked at her hand, adorned with a large ruby. "It will be January the eighteenth, Signor, and Mama is already putting together a guest list. Of course, you will be invited. I do hope Giulia won't be too far behind me with her own good news."

A cloud of anxiety passed over Giulia's face before it reassumed its expression of calm.

"One needs a suitor to progress to marriage."

"It's entirely my fault." Savinus replied with a guilty smile, "I did mention it to the Conte but have forgotten to remind him of it.

Forgive me, my dear."

"Don't be silly, Papa. It's not solely your responsibility. I could meet my future husband through my friends, or purely by chance."

Savinus laughed. "Chance? What a terrible idea. The temperaments and backgrounds of both the bride and groom must be thoroughly considered before they even cross paths. It's the only way to a strong marriage. Your mother and I, God rest her soul, met this way and we had five good years together before the consumption took her. I'm sure Luisa and, what is your betrothed's name?"

"Federico."

"I'm sure the two of you did not form a relationship based on chance. I know your father well and he is not a gambling man."

"You're right, Signor. Papa has been friends with Federico's father for a number of years. They hunt together every Saturday."

"Indeed. Well, I've said my piece. I'll leave you two to gossip. If you need me I'll be in the workroom. Good day, Luisa."

"And you, Signor."

Savinus walked towards the workroom with a slight limp, the pain in his knee returned with the thought of trying to find a husband for Giulia.

∞

Giulia lowered her voice. "I had a flirtation, at the festival."

Luisa leaned forward, her face lighting up. "And why didn't you tell me straight away?"

"I don't think Papa would think him appropriate for marriage. He's attractive and very good at what he does. He is kind and has had a difficult time, as he lost his father. I can't tell you who he is. I feel like I want to keep it to myself for the moment. There is also another boy I am interested in who is not as kind. It's just that when he looks at me I feel a bit queer in my stomach. Has that ever happened to you?"

"No, never. Is it because you would like to kiss him?"

Giulia laughed. "Yes! I think that's it. He is more the sort of person Papa would like me to marry."

"Do you mean because he's rich?"

She nodded. "I'm not sure I care so much about that, although I wouldn't want to be poor, and I certainly wouldn't like to do my own washing."

"Yes, I think I would draw the line there as well. So you can't tell me who they are?"

"No. Let's talk about the wedding, shall we?"

Each time they had spoken in recent months, little else had been discussed. Luisa had told her about the Spanish lace on her gown, the wild boar that would be hunted by her father for the wedding feast, her fear of consummating the marriage, and her mother's wedding jitters causing her to shatter five water goblets a day.

She had met her betrothed whilst riding her stallion in the woods near the town. He was riding fast and came towards her in a blur, clods of earth flying in his wake. As he drew the reins in a dramatic stop, she saw a muscled youth with fine hands. His velvet cap was tilted forward on his head and thick brown hair curled from beneath. He flashed a crooked smile and asked the name of her mount. Luisa had said she knew from his hands and the well-tended horse that he was from a good family. His clothing was of a fine cut and his manners impressive. As they spoke, she realized he was the son of her father's friend whom she had not seen for several years. Within weeks, they were betrothed.

Luisa studied her and smiled. "What's wrong? You seem subdued."

"Well, I know fathers make the decision based on similarities between the two families. This worries me. What if my father chooses someone dull, basing his decision on his relationship with the father, instead of his regard for the boy?"

Her friend shook her head. "Your father is a good man, and intelligent. I think you can trust his choice."

She glanced around before whispering, "I hope you're right. My mother is no longer here to intervene if he makes an error."

CHAPTER 12

As instructed, Nichola and Antonius did not arrive until mid-morning. Shortly after, there was a knock at the door and Agnese presented a tall, rangy man who swept into the workshop in a flowing black cape. His body seemed possessed of a peculiar crackling energy and his every movement was charged. His angular features were hawk-like and his lips full. It was an intimidating face set off by large black eyes. He stood in silence, examining the boys with an intensity that made them flinch. Savinus shook his hand as he made introductions.

"Boys, this is my dear friend and colleague in the Hermetic Arts, Lorenzo di Montefiore. He is the only man I have ever met who was privileged enough to read a scroll originating from the great library of Alexandria. It was written by Hermes Trismegistus, and detailed many secrets of our craft. Signor di Montefiore has been a practitioner of the highest order for the last fifteen years. He has much to share with you."

The giant of a man pushed a lock of lank black hair out of his eyes and ran his fingers over his chin, contemplating what to say. He accepted the stool Savinus pushed in his direction.

"Good morning, boys. It is difficult to know where to start, but I may as well tell you something of Hermeticism. There are two parts to the Hermetic tradition—that of philosophy and that of practical magic, potions, and alchemy. Our philosophy is based around communion with the sun, moon, and stars. We aim to purify our bodies so our consciousness can rise to a higher level of knowledge. For many years, Signor di Benevento and I have been trying to find something called the First Matter. It is the inherent power that resides in all things. If we can establish what it is, then our ability to help others will be greatly increased."

The two apprentices sat motionless, mouths agape, unable to look away from his soot-black eyes. His powerful gaze made them imagine he could see into their depths. Lorenzo opened his mouth to speak once more and as he did so, looked intently in Nichola's direction. Flushed, Nichola averted his eyes.

Lorenzo turned to Savinus, "Could I have a word with you outside?" he asked.

Savinus was taken aback but nodded. "Of course." The two men walked out to the courtyard.

"I was going to share some of my findings with all of you today. I have found the First Matter, it is simpler than we imagined. The trouble is, that young man is an unsuitable recipient for the knowledge. He cannot be trusted to use this information, or the skills, for the benefit of others. There is a great impulsiveness and I can also see a lot of self-interest. Not to mention righteousness. Whatever possessed you to take him as an apprentice?"

Savinus sighed. "He is the son of my most important benefactor. I had no choice in the matter. You do mean the aristocratic-looking one?"

"Indeed. Can you perhaps find an errand for him to run? I have something I would like to show you."

He glanced at the crate of healing liquid. "Yes, I think I have something he could do. Lorenzo, I think I now understand the First Matter too. It is all in the purification of stillness—am I right?"

"You are. But there are other things that must be done for the transformation to be achieved. Speak to the boy now, send him away."

They returned to the workroom where Nichola and Antonius waited.

"Nichola, we have almost finished the orders of healing liquid. However, I'm out of jars to put it in, except for this one." He reached for a jar from the shelf. "Could you please go to the market and find the glass seller? His name is Franco. Ask him for twenty of these. If you can't carry them, then ask him to deliver them tomorrow. Here are ten florins, that should cover it."

Nichola gritted his teeth. "Yes, Signor, I will go there now."

"No need to hurry. We'll fill you in on our discussion when you return."

∞

Nichola slunk away, shoulders hunched. Once he was outside the front door, he cursed under his breath. He ambled down the street, tempted to fling the jar at a wall. Halfway to the market he came to a stop. A smile spread on his lips and he turned around and walked in the opposite direction.

He knew there was a small window between two of the bookcases. It faced onto a seldom-used alley. He could listen to their conversation from there.

Reaching the villa, he glanced around to see if anyone was looking, and ducked into the alley. Peering through the grimy window, he could see the back of Antonius and Savinus as they listened to Signor di Montefiore. He could hear the low hum of his voice but was unable to make out distinct words. Growing bored, he kicked some pebbles at his feet. When he raised his eyes, he had to blink several times, as he thought his eyes were deceiving him.

The Signor had disintegrated into millions of points of coloured light. They danced in swirls that leapt in all directions before forming into the shape of a hawk. The bird extended wings that were stippled brown and white, the low hum of the man's voice emanated from the winged creature. He remained a hawk for several minutes before dematerializing once more and resuming his human shape. Light-headed and queasy, Nichola reached out to the wall to steady himself. He felt the urge to run to the palazzo and hide in his bedchamber. Then he looked at his left hand, the knuckles white from clutching the glass jar too tightly. Taking a few deep breaths, he walked out of the alley and turned towards the market. His heart thudded in his chest. Looking down at his free hand, he saw it shook with violent tremors.

The glass seller had a wooden crate for the jars. Wincing as he lifted, Nichola carried it with an awkward gait, stopping several times to rest. Embarrassment burned his cheeks on seeing a friend of his mother. The news would soon spread amongst her circle, Contessa Ilaria Valperga's son doing the work of a labourer. He had never even had to carry a cup of water, much less something as cumbersome as the crate. His forearms were soon thrumming with pain and his fear gave way to anger. Approaching the front door, he banged his palm against it and half dropped the crate on the step. The jars tinkled against one another. Agnese opened the door with a frown.

"Goodness, what's all this noise? You're lucky you didn't break those. You'd better come in then and bring them with you."

He glared at her. "I'm not accustomed to doing the work of a servant. They're too heavy. Tell the other boy to fetch them."

"Signor assigned you to the task and he'll expect you to bring them inside."

"Certainly not. I simply won't do it. I'll tell the Signor that you're being impertinent. Good day."

He gave her a contemptuous look and turned towards the workroom, shaking his head. His day was not progressing well. Carrying a crate and a peasant addressing him with impertinence. Striding into the room, he bristled with outrage.

"Signor, your servant spoke to me inappropriately. She had the gall to suggest I carry a crate inside when I had barely managed to carry it from the market. It's not right and I won't stand for it. Can you please speak to her?"

Savinus had been deep in conversation with Lorenzo and Antonius. He looked up distractedly.

"Nichola, I'm sure Agnese didn't mean to offend you. She's from the countryside near Perugia and is not familiar with the protocol of speaking to nobles. I'm sure Antonius would be happy to assist you with the crate."

Antonius nodded. "I'll get it. You can stay here, Nichola."

With one sentence, Antonius had made him look churlish. His cheeks burned once more as he watched his rival leave the room. Giulia appeared at the door, radiant in cornflower blue chiffon. She looked down when she felt his eyes on her.

∞

"Good day, Agnese told me we had a visitor."

Savinus beckoned her inside. "Hello, dear, do you remember Signor di Montefiore?"

"Yes, how do you do, Signor?"

He approached her and touched his lips to her outstretched hand.

"I'm so pleased to see you again, Signorina. Your Papa told me you have grown up and he didn't lie. Soon you'll be out in the world."

"Perhaps. But first I'd like you to teach me everything you know."

Savinus laughed. "She doesn't mince words, did I not tell you, Lorenzo?"

He beamed. "Of course, you may sit in with the boys and I'll share some of what I have learned." He indicated a chair. "Please, sit down."

Antonius returned carrying the crate as if it were an extension of his arm. He placed it near the workbench and found his seat, ignoring Nichola's hostile stare.

Lorenzo sat down on a wooden bench and crossed his legs. He gazed for a moment out of the window, lost in his thoughts.

"As I mentioned before, to achieve the results we want in alchemy we must first purify ourselves. Those who are consumed by negative thoughts about others cannot possibly reach the level of purity required." He gave Nichola a pointed stare. "I generally begin by going to the woods. The time of the full moon is the most auspicious. I burn twenty different herbs and recite an incantation in Sanskrit. I dance whichever way my body tells me to. Then I find a grassy place, usually near a tree, and allow my mind to be free of thoughts for several hours. I spend the rest of the night there. In the morning, I'm able to perform whichever form of alchemy I wish. There are many forms, from the most basic of turning a base metal to gold, to the most difficult—that of turning oneself into whatever one wishes to be. I'm also able to converse with my guides. I have eight, and they advise me on which of my skills would be best suited to a given situation. Any questions?"

Giulia held up her hand. "Signor, where did you learn these things?"

"From a variety of sources. The most important, of course, is the same one used by your father. Hermes Trismegistus. The founder of Hermeticism. The language of his writings is coded and difficult to decipher. This was intentional so the knowledge was not easily intercepted. The logic being that if someone is willing to spend years trying to understand his writings, then they are a true seeker and would not use the knowledge to harm others."

Nichola interjected. "I don't agree with that logic. If someone wants power to do something negative they will try just as hard as someone who wants to do something positive."

Lorenzo smoothed the crevice between his eyebrows with a long finger. Dust motes swirled in the shaft of sunlight from the window, forming a golden halo around his head.

"You are entitled to your opinion, but history has proven otherwise. There has never been a successful attempt by those who seek dark rather than light. Granted, many have tried. I like to imagine the spirit of Hermes Trismegistus himself, skillfully manipulating events from the next realm. I know there are a multitude of spirits whose sole job is to prevent the knowledge from being understood by the wrong people."

Antonius raised his hand. "How long has it taken you from your first exposure to the writings, to being able to use the knowledge on a regular basis?"

He smiled. "Every day I'm still learning. I never feel I'm finished and an expert on the subject. I will continue to learn for the rest of my life. But to answer your question, it took about eight years from when I first set eyes on the scrolls to really being able to perform superior alchemy for my clients. I suppose for a young fellow like you that seems like an eternity."

Antonius smiled back. "Yes, it is rather a long time. But I imagine the results are worth it."

"Indeed they are. There is a rumour amongst Hermetic circles that Signor Trismegistus lived until he was one hundred and thirty years old. Apparently, the body purification achieves more than just magic. Yet, I'm not sure of this. Perhaps I can be a living experiment of this theory!" He chuckled to himself.

He turned to glance at Savinus. "Well, it has been a long time since Signor di Benevento and I have had a chance to speak together. You may go."

With this he stood and waited for them to leave. Savinus rose and stood alongside him. He gave an apologetic smile in their direction.

"Yes, I'm afraid we do have rather a lot to catch up on." He picked up a sheaf of papers and thrust them at Antonius.

"I know you wanted to do some work. Here is the case of Signora Girondio and her daughter Maria. She wants us to do some geomancy to find out Maria's marriage prospects. All the information about birth dates and the background of the family are there. It's a good opportunity for the two of you to practice your new skills. Go and sit in the other room and see what you can come up with. Giulia, you may sit with them in case they need help."

The three young people left the room. Lorenzo leaned towards Savinus and spoke in a low voice. "You realize your young aristocrat saw my metamorphosis. I could feel his eyes, but did not halt the process."

Savinus nodded. "Yes, I felt it too. Why did you allow him to see it?"

"I'm afraid it was my darker nature—I wanted to scare him,

shake him up. I was annoyed by his complacency."

Savinus shook his head. "You are subversive, and you have succeeded. The boy is indeed shaken."

Lorenzo hesitated before speaking again. "I think you should know, Tomas di Ignacio has been stirring things up again in Genoa. They view some of our work as sorcery. I have been searched several times, and they warned they would come again, next time unannounced. You must be careful whom you work for, and more stringent in concealing your interest in Hermeticism."

Savinus frowned. "Thank you for telling me. This is troubling. I hope with God's grace, the Church will not be interested in a town as small as Pesaro."

∞

In the sitting room, they perched on the edge of three armchairs, the two young men on either side of Giulia, glowering at each other from across the table.

"Don't you two need to sit next to one another to do the work?" Giulia asked, bemused. "I'll swap with you, Nichola."

Nichola wrinkled his nose. "I think our friend here has been cleaning out the pigsty this morning. I would rather not. If you could hand me those papers, I'll figure it out with Giulia."

Antonius sniggered. "You may as well do it then, Giulia. This dandy has about as much skill with geomancy as a pet dog."

"If I were at your level I would be wringing your neck for that insolence. As it happens, I am well-bred and I will merely say that you are a heathen and beneath my contempt. This is hopeless. Why don't you head back to the servants' quarters and get your orders for the rest of the day. I cannot abide you."

"The feeling is mutual. An even better idea would be for you to head back to the palazzo and have a nice game of cards while talking about clothing fashions with your sisters. This job is out of your depth."

Giulia stood up. "I've had just about enough from you two! Please stop arguing. If you fail to work together on this job, I think my father will dismiss one of you. He is tired of all the hostility. Now which one of you is going to swap seats with me?"

Their eyes were downcast; they both looked like six-year-olds chastised by their mothers.

Antonius rose and nodded. As he sat down in her place, Nichola leaned further back in his seat as if attempting to avoid a nasty waft of air. Somehow they managed to speak about the details of the job. Antonius handed him a sheet of parchment and a quill for making calculations and they concentrated on the geomancy. It was a combination of mathematical thinking with psychic insight. At one point, Nichola raised his head to ask Giulia a question.

"Which figures do I assign to the house chart and which to the shield chart? I'm a little confused?" He gave her a smile so filled with sheepish charm that she blushed.

"Let me see." She approached and stood over him. He looked sideways at her pillowy white cleavage straining at the top of her dress. Her breasts were small and rounded. Antonius also found it difficult to ignore the view, but tore his eyes away and glared in Nichola's direction.

Giulia continued her explanation. As she spoke, Nichola fixed her with a look that was warm and knowing. It was the confident stare of a man accustomed to women wanting to share his bed. In actual fact, they had shared a mound of hay, as he was too frightened of his mother's disapproval to bring his conquests to his bedchamber. To date, he had bedded every pretty servant girl at the palazzo, and one of noble birth whom he met at a garden party. Giulia had never been stared at in such a forward manner, and her mouth went dry. His long sun-streaked brown hair and azure eyes were as difficult to ignore as his arrogance.

Antonius watched as they edged closer, their heads dipped together. He rustled the parchment and shifted in his seat.

"Can you please concentrate? We'll never get this finished and the Signor will be angry. He may not be able to keep two apprentices if only one shows the desire to work."

The barbed comment worked. Nichola pulled away from Giulia,

but not before whispering in her ear to meet him in the gardens of the palazzo the following afternoon at four o'clock. With flushed cheeks, she muttered an apology and darted to her bedchamber.

For a few moments the boys sat in silence, bereft of the sensory pleasures of Giulia. Her rosewater scent and gentle femininity had been a buffer for their hostility. Antonius handed Nichola the page of calculations, averting his eyes.

"Can you please do this chart here and I'll do the other? I've almost finished it; there are only about six to go."

Nichola nodded and picked up a quill, dipping it carefully in the ink well.

CHAPTER 13

Katerina had given Antonius permission to spend the night with his family. It was late afternoon and the town was bathed in golden light. As he walked, he was unable to stop thinking about his apprenticeship, and Signor di Montefiore's transformation. It was an incredible stroke of luck he had been given the opportunity to work for Savinus. It would be too much to expect to have a relationship with his daughter. It was understandable she would want to be with someone like Nichola.

As he approached his house, the aromas of ragú and polenta wafted into his nostrils. The door burst open and his mother stood beaming, splashes of sauce on her apron and her chubby arms outstretched. Her cheeks were flushed from the cooking fire and when he did not immediately rush into her arms, she took a few rapid steps and enfolded him into her bosom.

"*Caro! Mi sei mancato.* I have missed you so much. Are they working you so hard at the palazzo that you are not allowed to see your mama? Shame on them. Come in, I've made your favourite."

Close on her heels was Piero, who sidled up to him, clutching at his hand. Antonius did not realize that during his absence, Piero had been beaten twice and abused every other day. His right hand had developed a tremor from anxiety. He did not speak but took hold of his brother and would not let go, cradling his head in his unaffected hand. Antonius was moved and stroked his brother's back.

He then detached himself and found a seat at the dining table. It was an ancient, gnarled object whose provenance no one seemed to remember. On the legs were horizontal cuts he had made with a knife when his mother was not looking. The surface was marked with the circular burns from cooking vessels still hot from the fire, combined with ink spills from letter writing. Unlike the children of their neighbours, both Theresa and Antonius had learned to read and write from their father, who in turn had learned from an itinerant priest who had taken refuge in his childhood home. He had not attempted to teach Piero.

The floor was hard-packed earth. In the warmer months, it became dusty and needed to be swept. The walls were whitewashed and the ceilings low with rough wooden beams. On the wall was an ornate wooden cross, embellished with gilt. It was their most precious possession. They had few furnishings other than the dining table and chairs. A small living area adjoined the kitchen with two rush-backed wooden chairs. For extra seating, there were canvas cushions filled with straw, kept in the corner of the room.

In the middle of the table sat two enormous pots of ragú and polenta emitting curling trails of steam. Theresa gently urged her mother into a chair and took charge of serving the family. She took a cloth from the side of the fireplace that she tucked into Piero's collar before ladling the food into four bowls and handing them out. Once seated, she lowered her head and mouthed a blessing. They all crossed themselves in response. She then made a sweeping gesture with her hand they understood. It was time to eat.

The food was delicious. He wondered how many times they would have been eating cabbage for supper in order to save enough for the meat. The countless sewing jobs his mother would have needed to complete. These thoughts brought tears to his eyes that he blinked away. For several minutes they sat in silence, savouring the complex flavours unique to Fiora's cooking. Theresa was the first to speak.

"Giorgio Butera is engaged to Francesca from two doors up. They say the marriage will take place in two weeks. All the nonnas from our street have been saying they will have a family by the end of the year, as Francesca is looking more rounded every day."

They all snickered except Fiora, who clicked her tongue.

"Gossip, gossip, gossip. Why do you get involved in this, Theresa? How would you feel if you were poor Francesca? Have you nothing better to do than listen to the silly nonnas? It's the occupation of the idle. Perhaps you need to take on more of my sewing?"

She shook her head. "Mama, you said my stitches were clumsy and too large. That my work was not good enough for your clients who demand perfection. Is that not right?"

"Like anything, it takes practice. If you could be a little more patient, I could teach you the small stitches."

She sighed. "But you're unfair! I'm far too busy caring for our house and clothes, and buying and preparing food to find the time to practice sewing!"

Antonius held up his hand. "Please, you two. I don't come home very often. Can you save your bickering for another time?"

They looked shamefaced and fell silent. Piero grinned, his lips smeared with the glistening red sauce.

"I kicking the ball to the boys in the street. I kick hard!"

"Good boy, Piero, you are such a good kicker. I will come and watch later."

Piero puffed out his chest and flung out his arms, knocking his bowl to the floor with a clatter.

"I the best in the street. I kick so hard I knock over Signora's dog."

"Piero!" exclaimed Fiora, "You have spilt your supper everywhere. Now it is only good enough for a dog." Sighing, she pushed herself to her feet and cleaned up the mess with a cloth.

Theresa rose to help, but not before asking Antonius in a low voice, "What is he like, the son of the Conte? I have heard he's very handsome and charming."

Antonius grimaced. "He may be that to young women of high birth. To me, he's very unpleasant. He hates the fact that a peasant has the role of primary apprentice. Sit down, I'll help Mama."

Fiora waved him away. "No, please, I've almost finished. Rest in your chair."

She heaved herself upright and dropped the soiled cloth in a bucket of water before sinking back down into her seat. "What's this I hear about the Conte's son?" She had not missed a word of their conversation. "I've heard less of his charm, my daughter, and more of his arrogance. Katerina has known him since he was a small boy. His mother has always had troubles with him. His brother, on the other hand, is apparently a kind soul. Spends all his time in the garden tending plants as if they were babies. What a shame he didn't try for the position instead. Be careful, they do not like to think we are getting above ourselves. It offends them."

"Yes, Mama. I'll do my work and try to ignore him as much as possible."

She fingered the whorls in the table with hands that were red from constant immersion in water. A purple crescent-shaped burn glistened near her thumb. Her blue eyes had turned dark with concern.

"No, son. You don't understand. You must be polite to this boy, friendly even. If he dislikes you, then he might make things difficult for you. Don't forget how fortunate you are to have this opportunity. The down side is having to pretend to like someone you detest."

He opened his mouth to protest but she silenced him with a raised hand. "I will not talk about it anymore. I've said what I needed to say."

Theresa cleared away the dishes and an awkward quiet filled the room. Piero, as was his habit, lightened the mood by breaking into an off-key song. Antonius seized the remaining dishes, lest they be swept onto the floor by his expressive arms.

When he had finished, they applauded and laughed. He bowed deeply and pulled a face. Antonius turned to his mother.

"The dog he hit—I do hope it wasn't Signora Albinoni's?"

Signora Albinoni was a hunch-backed widow whose only distinguishing feature was an unwavering devotion to her spaniel, Gigi. If any harm had come to the dog, Piero would have been the object of her wrath.

Fiora suppressed a grin. "I'm afraid so. Gigi was fine, just a little dazed. I had to keep Piero indoors for several days afterwards or she would have given him an almighty spanking."

"Oh dear—I suppose it could have been worse."

Theresa rose and took away the dishes. Antonius mused that she was fast approaching the age of betrothal and he regarded her as dispassionately as he could. She was pretty in an unremarkable way, with the dark straight hair of her mother and permanently flushed cheeks from washing and hanging out clothes in the blazing sun. Her figure was robust and pleasingly fleshy. He surmised she would attract at the very least a peddler and at best a farmer. As the male head of their family, he felt responsible for her welfare.

"And have we had many suitors visiting recently?" he asked.

Theresa's cheeks turned a deeper shade of red and she ignored the question, dropping the dishes into a metal bucket with a clatter.

Fiora chimed in. "Yes, we've had several—a pig farmer's son from Montemarciano came just last week—a cheerful lad with the most incredible head of carrot red hair. He'd been selling his father's beans to a stallholder in the market and happened to see our girl as she bought a loaf of bread. Absolutely smitten he was. He said their well was two fields away and he needed a wife who was capable of lugging large quantities of water to their house without spilling a drop. He saw Theresa's strong arms and thought she was perfect. He also said she looked quite fetching. A couple of weeks before that, Federico the cobbler dropped in to declare he'd heard of her housekeeping skills and good character. He asked if he might come and see her so they could get to know each other. I was rather flattered by that one, as he has never shown interest in any other village girls before. He's rather a loner and I believe he does quite well for himself—"

"Mama! Slow down. I need to know what Theresa thinks of

these people, not just you. Sister, tell me, did you like any of these suitors?"

She sat down with a sigh. "I don't like being peddled like a leg of ham. Mama is in a hurry to marry me off and I would like to find the right man. The first one who came was the one I liked best but Mama won't let me see him again."

"Who was that?"

Fiora slapped the table with the flat of her hand.

"No *cara*, he was an acrobat in the travelling circus! What would you do for your life then—sit in a cart mending costumes and travelling from pillar to post? Ridiculous! Have your babies on the side of the road because you're homeless? Pah!" She made a small exhalation of disgust and folded her arms.

Antonius was bemused. "Mama is right, dearest. You can't marry an acrobat; it's not a good life. Which one did you prefer out of the farmer or the cobbler?"

She hunched her shoulders and looked at the table. "I suppose the cobbler and then I could be close to Mama. But I need to see him some more. I'm worried that he's a loner because there is something wrong with him."

Fiora shook her head. "I've heard he is only shy and has a kind character. It's very brave that he called if you consider that. Good girl, I will send word he may come and visit next week."

"Very good" said Antonius. "I'm pleased we're making some progress. Do you mind if I retire to my bed now? The day is catching up with me."

"No dear, get some rest. Theresa, did you prepare his bed?"

"Yes, Mama."

"Good night then," she leaned over to plant a kiss on both his cheeks. Theresa did the same and Piero grasped him in another tight hug.

"Night, night, night, night," he sang whilst patting him on the back.

"Good night Piero, you're very sweet to me." He peeled his brother's arms away and turned to the bedroom. He washed his face with the bowl of water next to his bed and fell onto the soft straw mattress.

CHAPTER 14

The juice from one of Gianni's strawberries ran down Nichola's chin in sticky rivulets. He pulled out a handkerchief to wipe his mouth clean. Leaning over, he picked another and devoured it in two bites. The plant had been heavy with fruit and he had consumed most of its bounty. It sat to the side of the vegetable garden, and Gianni had announced to the family the day before that it had borne fruit for the first time. He had been flushed with pride. Nichola let the stem drop to the ground. He glanced towards the road. It was a quarter after four o'clock and he did not like to be kept waiting. He ground one of the stems into the dirt with the front of his boot. Then he heard the sound of hesitant footsteps on the gravel and she was there, dressed in a demure yellow muslin dress. Her eyes darted left and right and she almost jumped when she saw him. Her face was drained of colour. She whispered, her voice urgent.

"Is there anywhere we can speak privately? I'm sure every servant in your house can see me from here."

He shook his head and watched her with languid eyes.

"This is the back entrance. No one can see you here. We can talk in the stables if you like. It's this way."

"I mean it—just talking," she said. "Don't you dare touch me."

He glanced at her sideways, amused. He opened his mouth to

speak and then closed it. They followed a winding path through tall rectangular hedges, then across a green field. The stables were housed in a large brick building flanked by a well and sheaves of hay stacked high against an adjoining wall. He motioned her inside and raked some hay into a long pile for them to sit on.

∞

Giulia lowered herself onto the hay and it prickled the backs of her thighs. For a few moments, there was only silence. She took a few deep breaths, filling her nostrils with the sweet scent of hay and the less pleasant odour of horse dung and dust. She tried not to think about the stories she had heard of peasant girls deflowered in stables. Snorts and whinnies echoed through the cavernous space. Silent as sentinels, bats hung high in the rafters. Then her fear left her.

She crossed her legs and stared at him. "What is it like to be told only good things about yourself?"

He cleared his throat and raised an eyebrow. "What on earth do you mean?"

"Well, you are the son of a noble. Therefore, no one ever tells you the truth about yourself. And that's why you are quite difficult to like."

He drew himself up. "Well, you're quite the charmer, aren't you?"

"See? You're shocked to hear anything less than stellar praise from someone. That is because from the moment you were born you were told you were perfect. Your servants are even paid to tell you that you're perfect. Don't you see?"

He shrugged. "And what in the world is wrong with that?"

"Well, no one is perfect, and it's not healthy to never be told the truth. To hear both the good and the bad news about how you come across."

"Actually, you're wrong. My father doesn't like me. My mother does, but she worries about me. It's my brother who is perfect. He's as faultless as the Archangel Gabriel. I am the wicked son. I do as I like. For example, if a beautiful redheaded girl is seated next to me, I find it near impossible not to do this—"

He took her wrist and before she was able to object, pulled her to him, pressing his lips hard against hers. His other hand clasped her back, massaging her shoulders. The kiss deepened, and she became lost in it before rearing back and pushing his chest. He fell backwards and landed clumsily on the dirt floor. She stood over him; her mouth opened, but she could not speak. Then she sputtered, eyes blazing.

"I am the daughter of your employer. Do you not have any respect for anyone? I am a lady, not one of your peasant wenches. I enjoyed the kiss. But please refrain."

He sat up and dusted off his breeches. "I do respect you, Giulia. Otherwise I would have kissed you weeks ago. I've been very self-controlled."

She gave a small snort of disgust, but the edges of her lips turned up. He watched her.

"Why did you come here then? I thought you might like to kiss me." He looked at his shoes with feigned humility.

"Perhaps," she said. "But not in such a rush. I wanted to talk a little, get to know you."

∞

Nichola made patterns in the dust with his shoe. It was always the same with girls, they wanted to converse. His mother had instructed him in the art of conversation and he was able to give them what they wanted, infused with enough charm to obtain his desires. As he opened his mouth to speak, she interjected.

"Why are you so nasty to Antonius? You should be charitable to people of his class."

"Have you not noticed he is unpleasant to me? He is so full of himself because he is better at geomancy and has more insights than I. All I've done is attempt to defend myself. I'm sure you would do the same. Let's not talk about it—it makes me depressed. Let's talk about you and what it was like growing up as the daughter of a seer."

He turned to her and let his eyes traverse the long line of her powder-white arms, her fingers resting on her knees, and imagined the sinuous legs intertwined beneath the muslin skirt of her dress. His gaze was heated and she reddened.

"It was like being the daughter of an academic, except he was capable of reading my mind. It was difficult to hide anything from him. It still is."

He smiled and poked her thigh with one finger. "That must have been difficult; you could never hide your vegetables in your napkin, or, oh dear, sneak out to meet an extremely good-looking noble? What a pity."

She laughed but averted her eyes. "He thinks I've gone to visit my friend, Luisa. I'm hoping he's distracted by Lorenzo di Montefiore visiting at the moment and he won't have an insight as to where I really am."

"You're being very naughty. I like that. It shows you have character. I'm often naughty, my mother would say too often. But without it, I'm terribly bored. In fact, I've already been good for much too long. Come here—"

∞

He took her arm and pulled her onto his lap. With his free hand, he pressed his palm against hers and she was forced to meet his eyes. Her resistance crumbled in the face of his gaze, his cerulean eyes inquisitive. When she remembered the kiss afterwards, she could not recall a moment where it had begun, as when she met his eyes, all reason left her. She opened her mouth to his and was consumed. His hand cupped her breast whilst the other stroked her thigh, inching closer to her waist. For a long time she savoured the woody scent of his skin, and the salt taste of his mouth. Then, from nowhere, an image of her father flashed into her mind and she jumped from his lap as if scorched by a fire. Her eyes were downcast and she covered her mouth with her hand.

"It looks as if I've behaved like one of your wenches after all. I enjoyed it, but now I must go." She turned and ran, a small cloud of dust rising in her wake. Nichola was left speechless and aroused. He remained where he was, his forehead damp and his breath ragged. All he could think about was when he might see her again.

CHAPTER 15

"You like to collect stones. They are lined up neatly on your windowsill. Every night you touch each one before going to sleep. You are convinced they ward off bad luck." Antonius told him without hesitation.

Savinus sat to one side in the workroom making notes on a large piece of parchment as he watched Antonius and the village boy, Massimo. Next to him sat Nichola, his mouth a hard line of consternation. The old man did not need to ask if the insight was correct, taking in Massimo's slack jaw and stunned expression. The boy's long limbs contrasted with his round freckled face as he sat hunched on a stool, savouring the attention. Antonius raised his eyes to the seer, a question in his eyes. *Shall I do more?* Savinus shook his head and motioned for him to rise, muttering, "Good, good" under his breath. It was Nichola's turn.

∞

Nichola crossed the room and sat on the straw seat, still warm from his enemy. His heart thrummed in his ears and blood flushed his cheeks. The certainty of failure left his mouth dry. Catching the boy's eye he let his mind go blank to allow space for images. Nothing came. After several long minutes, he saw the boy drawing patterns in the dirt with a stick. He was unconvinced, but decided to

110

take a risk.

"You like to draw in the dirt with a stick."

Massimo's gaze was impassive. Nichola fell silent, knowing he was expected to come up with more. Clearing his mind again, he waited. Then, an image of wet clothing hanging from a tree and over chairs. A large woman stirring washing in an iron tub, the grey water circling and frothing.

"Your mother is a washerwoman. She takes in washing from the neighbours?"

"Well, Massimo?" asked Savinus.

The boy hesitated. "My mother isn't a washerwoman, but I have five brothers and sisters, and she must wash many clothes every day. The other thing, about the stick, that's not true."

Savinus made a gesture with his upturned palm; he wanted Nichola to vacate the chair. "That will be all, Nichola. And thank you, Massimo. Please tell your friend Franco to come to us the same time next week."

Nichola rose and felt pressure building in his head. A headache of frustration was almost upon him. Every week it was the same. Savinus had started the exercise a few weeks earlier so they could practice their skills. Antonius demonstrated great accuracy and had been wrong only once. Nichola was correct for around one in three of his insights. Once he had not come up with anything. He found the difference in their abilities humiliating.

During the second week of torment, he approached Savinus when Antonius went to purchase more herbs. "Sir, it's evident that he's more talented than I. It makes me very uncomfortable to be subjected to this practice every week. It is demoralising to be shown up in such a way. Can we perhaps reduce the frequency to every few weeks?"

The pause before his answer was prolonged and he wondered if his question had been heard. Savinus sat at his desk, his snowy head bent over an enormous dust-covered tome. He turned and looked at Nichola, pressing his thumb on the deep furrow between his brows.

"Tell me, are you at all interested in learning to see, to feel, to understand what it is that I do?"

Nichola gave a vigorous nod. "Yes, sir, I do wish to learn. It's just that I feel my capabilities are limited. I'm frustrated."

"If you were bereft of capabilities I wouldn't have you here. You must let go of your pride and absorb what you can. It's important that you cease comparing yourself to Antonius. It's true he has more sight than you. This is not important. Just do your best and don't be so petulant."

He turned back to his reading and waved his hand. Nichola remained behind him. He was dismissed but had no idea what he was expected to do next. He cleared his throat."Uh, what would you have me do now Signor, until Antonius returns?"

Savinus remained bent over the desk and replied in a low voice. "Go to the bookshelf. There are many books about geomancy to choose from. You need to read about the formation of the diagrams as yours are very shaky."

∞

Antonius returned around midday and Savinus suggested an excursion to the blue cave. Orders had been placed for the health potion and they needed to collect more plants. The new moon also necessitated a ritual.

They set off after consuming a rabbit stew prepared by Agnese. As was her habit, Giulia accompanied them, abandoning her veiled hat on the outskirts of town.

Antonius observed a crackling energy between her and Nichola, an undercurrent beneath their banter. He used the whip on his horse more than necessary, giving the animal a brutal kick with his heels when it slowed. Savinus asked him questions about the stallholder at the market, his health, and the amount charged for the herbs. He answered with few words.

There was no question whom she would accompany to pick the herbs. Her face glowed when Nichola addressed her. Yet she spoke to him in a brusque tone, only meeting his eyes when it could not be avoided. When they dismounted at the salt marshes she was betrayed by both the slight incline of her head towards his, and her joyous laughter after a joke.

Antonius shaded his eyes from the brilliant light reflecting from the water in a dance of silver and gold. He looked at his feet and kicked a hillock of mud. Turning from Nichola and Giulia, his eyes met those of Savinus. The old man shrugged.

Her head may be turned now, but as I have explained to you before, the nature of our existence is that of continual change. Do not show your disappointment—she must not know your feelings, not yet.

For a moment Antonius thought he spoke out loud. Then he glanced at the others and saw their heads were still close together, their voices low and intimate. It was not often his mentor chose to communicate this way, and it was a privilege. He blushed.

Sometimes I forget nothing escapes you, sir. It's true, I'm fond of your daughter and what I'm seeing causes me pain. I will try to follow your advice, but may I ask, why must she be ignorant of my feelings?

Savinus's hand closed around a reed, pulling it out and twisting it around his gnarled fingers. He gave a tired smile.

I know my daughter. Like many of her sex, she is attracted to that which is not too attainable. She will respect you more if you keep silent. It will serve you well when she realizes the limits of his personality. I am unable to see exactly what will transpire. Now, do not answer me, they are growing restless and we must go in the boats now.

His deep voice resonated across the water.

"Nichola, the first boat is tied up there, next to your left foot. Please untie it and help Giulia inside. We will see you at the island. Antonius, you take the next one and I'll row alone. I like the quiet and the exercise. My arms, at least, have not failed me."

Nichola did as he was told. The rope was tied in several knots and it was soon apparent he could not untie a single one. He looked to Antonius who had them loose within a minute. He basked in Giulia's admiring look but avoided her eyes, nodding to Nichola, who gave grudging thanks.

Savinus had already pushed off, gliding towards the island, his back straight and his face serene. Three regal herons floated in his wake.

Antonius waited for the others to embark and then stepped into his vessel, his feet refreshed by the small pool of water on the boat floor. For a few minutes he forgot the tightness in his chest. He enjoyed the purity of motion, the searing white light, and the sound of his paddle cutting the water. Once again, he rebuked himself, for it was enough to have a job that should have been out of reach for a fisherman's son. To desire his mentor's daughter was to desire his own downfall. He had heard about highborn women at the tavern. They expected manners and refinement, qualities he was only beginning to learn. By the time he reached the island, he had almost talked himself out of Giulia. Then he felt his chest contract on seeing her, and knew otherwise.

Savinus took him aside on reaching the island and instructed him to gather a different plant, *Caltha polypetala*. Its flower had deep orange petals and was found at the base of rocks. He muttered something about a full moon ceremony and Antonius felt his skin prickle with excitement. Since Lorenzo di Montefiore had visited, he knew his initiation would soon occur. The signor had spoken of Hermetic rituals taking place at the time of the full moon. To witness his ability to transform himself had filled him with awe. He was electrified by the idea that through initiation he might be able to do the same.

The honour of this task distracted him from his sadness. He filled two baskets with the strange-smelling blooms. His fingertips were stained orange.

On returning to the mouth of the cave, Savinus waved them inside, where a fire was crackling on the stony ground. From a leather satchel, he took a jar of dried herbs and scattered them on the flames. They made a popping sound as they were consumed, whilst the bitter scent of cloves and something sweeter filled the cave. The boys stood to one side, transfixed by the flickering flames and the dark patterns thrown onto the walls of the cave like reflections of falling water.

"We ask that the spirits support us in this new moon ritual. That we may be able to see the unseen and be cognisant of their guidance. Antonius and Nichola are here with us for the first time. May they tap into their powers by connection from within and without."

He turned to them and motioned for them to circle the fire. Giulia had removed her shoes and made a slow circle, chanting under her breath.

Savinus continued. "Please repeat after me—
> Nine powers of nine flowers,
> Nine powers in me combined,
> Nine buds of plant and tree.
> Long and white are my fingers,
> As the ninth wave of the sea.
> By all the powers of land and sea,
> By all the might of moon and sun,
> As we do will, so mote it be,
> Chant the spell and be it done."

After each line, the boys repeated his words. At first their voices were uncertain, and then grew louder as they felt more confident. Giulia chanted with them, and skipped around the fire, lifting her skirts so as not to trip over the rocky cave floor. The echo of their chant reverberated through the cave, sounding more like a crowd than a group of four. Antonius felt a prickling sensation in his limbs. Then, as he became more absorbed in the sound of the words and the motion of his body, he felt as if unseen people were touching him with gentle fingertips. He glanced behind, seeing only the dark glimmer of flame shadows dancing up and down the crevassed walls. At the point where he was verging on delirium, Savinus clapped his hands together and motioned for them to still their movements. Giulia smiled at them, her teeth a startling white in the gloom.

"Be still now and listen. I ask that our protectors, here with us now, help Antonius and Nichola in their journey of seeing. As the new moon is born, I request that their insights emerge. I also ask for help in my own exploration into the First Matter."

He chanted in a low voice, in a language they had not heard before. The flames snaked higher, as if incited by the words. The pure sound echoed in a mesmerizing pattern, and time appeared to still.

∞

The tavern was crawling with inebriated fruit pickers from the Veneto. No one was sure why they had arrived en masse the previous day. They spent every minute at the tavern in a drunken state and were unable to answer questions coherently.

Nichola had been sitting near the door with Matteo and Giorgio where the noise of their carousing was diminished. The sound of raucous laughter merged with that of breaking glass. Each man competed to raise his voice the loudest and tell the best tale of conquest. It seemed every woman of ill repute in the town had descended on the tavern, lured by talk of the free-spending fruit pickers. Their bosoms strained at their low-cut, flimsy dresses in jarring shades of orange and pink. Their lips were painted purplish red, accentuating their yellow teeth. The three young men did not make eye contact as they spoke. Their eyes remained on the powdered cleavages and expansive thighs of the women, ill-concealed by the thin fabric of their dresses. When they did speak, they giggled.

"I want to put my head there and just lick," snorted Giorgio, beads of perspiration forming on his upper lip.

"I would just grab that blonde's behind and haul her into a corner," added Nichola.

Matteo was no less aroused but sat in silence, trying to look at his glass of ale instead of the lascivious women. Every so often, he rose from his stool and stepped outside to cross himself and recite a fervent catechism. He was a lanky youth with a pale grey complexion. His face and hands were clammy. To make matters worse, his already thin black hair was falling out and there were only several clumps left, giving him the appearance of an emaciated infant. In childhood he had survived smallpox and this had given him great faith. Every morning he would meet with his uncle, Cardinal Costa, in the small chapel that annexed their villa. They performed a mass together and took the sacraments.

That night, Nichola had told him a story, which distressed him even more than the women. He told of a visiting seer with the ability to morph into the form of a hawk. Matteo had muttered one hundred "Hail Mary's" under his breath, and fear had gripped his stomach until he struggled to breathe.

His uncle had warned him about the dangers of magicians and seers. "Black magic" was to be as strenuously avoided as contact with the plague. It weakened one's faith and caused moral decay. Holding onto the door for support, he stumbled inside to rejoin his friends. To his horror, one of the women, a redhead, had approached Nichola. She was stroking his shoulder with a calloused hand. Up close, her face was pitted with scars and coarsened from drink.

"What have we here? A fancy boy, is it? Don't worry, I won't eat you. Want a cuddle?"

Nichola inched backwards, his nose wrinkled in distaste. "I'm not feeling very cuddly tonight. Giorgio here is a very affectionate man. You might have more luck with him. I, uh, might just get some more ale. Gentlemen? More ale?"

Giorgio nodded dumbly, transfixed by the mountain of cleavage. Matteo crossed himself once more and mumbled excuses, before stumbling in the direction of the door and out into the night.

CHAPTER 16

At the breakfast table, sitting next to Giulia's plate of strawberries, lay a scented letter. It was pale blue in colour and bore the seal of the house of Valperga. She recognised the scent as being Nichola's cologne. She consumed the strawberries with such alacrity that Savinus was worried.

"It is terrible for the digestion to eat like that. Whatever is wrong with you?"

"Nothing Papa. I promised Agnese that I'd fetch some fish from the market. The fishmonger leaves soon and I must hurry."

Savinus let out a sigh. "Giulia. I can read your thoughts. How many times must I catch you out before you understand it's pointless to lie to me? You will have to go to church on Sunday and make a confession. You're a silly girl. Go and read your love letter."

Her eyes were downcast. "Sorry, Papa."

Clutching the letter, she dashed to her bedchamber to savour its contents. It was written in an elegant looping script and announced the birthday banquet of Nichola's brother, Gianni. There would be dancing, entertainers, and fine food. On the reverse side he had written a message:

"I hope you can join me—wear your best dress, although your beauty hardly needs assistance! I think of you night and day. What happened between us feels like the most exquisite of dreams. *Con affetto*, Nichola Valperga."

Without hesitation Giulia opened her oak armoire and pulled out armloads of dresses. She called out to Agnese for assistance before remembering she had gone to the market. Cursing, she clutched each one to her chest whilst standing in front of her full-length mirror. Turning left and right, she tried different poses before settling on a mauve chiffon with delicate silver beading on the bodice. She thought of Nichola—his high cheekbones, long fingers, and soft, full lips. Under his gaze she felt beautiful, treasured, like an exotic bird. She sat on the bed, remembering his kiss.

The banquet was only one week away. Never before had she received an invitation to an event of this grandeur. For a moment, her ecstatic mood gave way to despondency as she wished for guidance. Other girls were assisted with preparing for balls by mothers who fussed and helped with grooming. Her mother, Carmen, had died giving birth to her. Giulia kept her miniature portrait in a gold locket, which she never removed other than to bathe. There was one other portrait in a gilt frame hanging over the fireplace. It depicted her mother in a white silk dress, sitting on a rock in a verdant field. She was surrounded by a flock of sheep and her hands were folded in her lap. Her light brown hair fell in waves around her shoulders, and her expression was serene. Savinus explained that she had liked to walk in the countryside and collect flowers, which she would press in her favourite books. Her love of animals was well known in the village, hence the sheep. Her father, a prosperous merchant, commissioned the portrait at the time of their marriage. It was given as a wedding gift in addition to her trousseau.

∞

Excitement of a different kind was building in Antonius as he worked his way through a mountain of vegetables destined for Katerina's soup. It was the full moon and his initiation was to take place that evening. She was often nervous leaving him with a knife when in such a mood. To date, he still had ten fingers. His whole body bristled with energy; he sat upright in a state of heightened awareness. The trouble was that the awareness was not directed towards his current task.

"Antonius! Young man, you have a knife. It is very dangerous. Look at your hands and what you are doing, for the sake of Our Lady."

For a moment he looked at her with a bewildered expression, as if awakened from a deep sleep.

"Oh! Yes, I was thinking about something else. I'm sorry; I've hardly spoken to you today. Has your daughter had her baby yet?"

Katerina gently pried the knife from his hands and led him over to the copper bucket. She motioned to the dishes soaking in oily water.

"Here. This is your job now. Wash these up. Bonita is still waiting for the child to come. She has tried scrubbing the house from top to bottom, walking the streets, and massaging her stomach with patchouli oil. The pains have been coming but not the child. I went to see her last night and tried to distract her with village gossip. It is no good. She just wants to see her baby. So, young man, you're lucky not to be a woman. The trials we have."

He regarded her as if she described life in another country.

"Was having babies difficult for you too?"

"Not so bad. I have the hips, see?"

She placed her hands on her hips and rolled them in a circle with the grace of a much slimmer woman. "My Giorgio, he said when he met me fifty years ago, "Katerina, you have the fertile body of a mama." But Bonita, she's built differently. Two days she was in labour with my first grandchild." She clucked softly and shook her head.

"That's terrible. Is there nothing that can be done?"

"No. Sometimes the only thing to be done is to bring the child into the light and allow the mother to slip into darkness."

He nodded and plunged his hands into the tepid water. On the surface floated a rainbow-coloured oil slick surrounded by bubbles.

Thoughts of Giulia flashed into his mind each day and he let them come and float away. He hoped in time they would dissipate. It seemed the only thing to do was concentrate on his two jobs.

Finishing early, he made his way to the port to go rowing in Timo's father's boat. He hoped it would distract him from the gnawing hunger gripping his stomach. Savinus had instructed him to fast in preparation for the ritual. His mind was also troubled by a dream he had experienced the night before. Looking up from his mattress, he had watched as an eagle flew above him, giant wings flapping like the sails of a ship changing direction. Its amber eyes stared into his as it alighted on the edge of the bed. The charcoal wings came to rest against its sides. A deep voice erupted in his mind.

The time has come for you to awaken into the art of seeing and communing with the spirits. Sleep now and ready yourself for the wisdom awaiting you.

It was only now he realized the voice of the eagle had been that of Savinus.

His friend waited in the shallows, leaning against the paddle. The air was pungent with salt, seaweed, and mackerel blood. A group of fishermen had just arrived with a large haul and were busy knifing those fish that were not yet dead, before cleaning them. They were some distance away, but their uproarious laughter was carried by the wind. Antonius avoided looking at the men as they reminded him of his father. He could remember an occasion when he returned home after a similar haul with a whole pig in the crook of his arm. They had feasted for days.

"I think you're walking differently," remarked Timo.

"What on earth do you mean?"

"Like a noble. You know, gliding along regally."

He rolled his eyes. "Ha! I'm sure that's right. I'd best not be seen with the likes of you then."

"No. Better shove off and have some duck liver paté with your new friends."

"You're an idiot."

"No more than you. Come on. We need to get going before the

tide goes out."

They rolled up their breeches and pushed the vessel into deeper water. Below them, in the pale green depths, tiny rainbow-hued fish darted in all directions. The sky was overcast, with billowing grey clouds low on the horizon. Whilst Antonius held the boat steady, Timo hauled himself inside. Then Timo stuck his paddle in the sand and Antonius clambered on board.

They sat in silence, savouring the feel of the wind playing on their faces and arms, as well as the balm of each other's company. It had been several months since they had last spent time together. Antonius let his friend do the rowing, and leaned on his elbow.

"Something has changed," Timo smiled. "What is it? You look sad but also happy at the same time."

He shrugged. "Nothing. I'm just the same."

"You lie. Mother of God—you're in love! Who is she? No, let me guess; is it the daughter of the seer? I've heard of her beauty."

"She is a beauty. I do love her but it's no good."

"And why not?"

"Because she loves the son of the Conte, the other apprentice."

"Oh. That's not good. Well, I'll take you to the tavern one night soon and you'll see so many attractive girls you will forget about her."

"Timo, the girls who frequent the tavern are not the sort of girls that interest me." He regretted the words as soon as he said them.

Timo bristled. "It's like that is it? You're now too good for the normal village girls?"

"No, it's not that. I like them, but more the ones you meet at weddings or parties. The ones at the tavern are too loud, too flirtatious for me. I'm not smooth with them like you."

"All right then. We'll see if we can get ourselves invited to some weddings and then—"

"Timo, it's not important to me at the moment. I'm learning many things. Tonight there will be a special ritual for me to become a seer. Girls, marriage, there will be plenty of time for all that. I'm becoming what I'm meant to be. Do you understand?"

"Yes, I think so. So you won't even go out with me?"

He smiled. "Yes, I'll go out with you, but we'll do things like this. We'll talk, because I don't see you a lot at the moment. Perhaps we'll even drink a little ale—but not too much as it messes up my abilities."

"Fine. Well, I think this girl is crazy. Shallow probably—just wants to be rich."

"No, that's not true," he frowned. "She has a good heart, a fine mind, and converses kindly with everyone she meets. Please, let's talk of other things."

He could feel tears prickling in the corners of his eyes and looked out to sea, hoping his friend would not notice.

∞

Nichola tidied the workroom, flicking the dust cloth over the surfaces. Glass bottles clattered to their sides and dust swirled into the air and into his nostrils. He sniffed and pushed Savinus's chair into place under his desk. On the top sat a small opened book. The words caught his eye and he leaned closer to read.

The initiate is assisted into the trance state by music, dance, and the burning of the sacred substances. Once there, he is able to communicate with the spirit guides who offer him their protection. It is essential the ritual be performed in communion with nature on the first night of the full moon. On the night before the ritual, the mentor must send a thought message to the initiate. If this is not received, then it is not an auspicious time for the ritual to take place.

Nichola then understood his rival's absence. He kicked the table leg harder than intended and winced at the pain in his shin. It seemed he was often excluded from experiences intended only for the principal apprentice. Had he been asked he would have declined and asserted his place on a higher social plane. To be the victim of subterfuge was an insult. Even the victory of Giulia's affection did not console him.

To the right of the book sat an ornate wooden box. He knew it was full of semi-precious gems. Looking behind to make sure he was not observed, he opened it and took a handful. Their myriad reflections danced in the muted sun, sending multi-coloured arcs of light in all directions. Wrapping the gems with care in a handkerchief, he placed them in his pocket.

CHAPTER 17

After cleaning up the dishes from the evening meal, Antonius was exhausted from nerves and anticipation. He drooped against the copper bucket, hands raw from the scalding water. It was almost time to leave. Katerina knew he was to see his mentor, but was unaware of the meeting's purpose.

"You've worked hard tonight, young man. The time off this afternoon must have revived you." She hesitated for a moment.

"What's it like to work with Signor Valperga? Do you like him?"

He studied her face before answering, his jaw clenched.

"He does not think I'm his equal. We're not friends."

She nodded. "I was friends with his nursemaid. Even as a child he was arrogant. Never mind, Signor di Benevento is a good man. He will support you."

"Thank you. You're kind to me."

He reached over and placed his hand over hers.

"I must go now if it's all right?"

Her round face broke into a smile. "Yes, good boy, off you go. See you at rooster's crow."

Savinus had promised to meet him at the palazzo gates. Slowing from his run down the winding driveway, he tried to control his breathing. The wrought iron gates were higher than three men and he leaned against them for a moment. Craning his head around the corner, he could not see the old man. Then he saw the pale brown rump of a horse backing out from the tall-hedged garden fronting the entrance.

"Signor? Hello?"

Savinus emerged, as did the rest of his mare, Jocanda. What appeared to be at least six saddlebags were strapped to her sides and he carried one more across his body. Antonius's usual mount, a black horse called Horatio, had been led there by means of a long rope.

"Greetings, young man. I thought it best to conceal myself in case our friend Nichola happened to come by. He is unaware of our plans for tonight, you see. Are you ready? Jump on Horatio and we'll be off."

"Thank you, sir."

The animal snorted in irritation as Antonius clambered onto its back. He kicked its flanks and they trotted down the hill, small plumes of dust arcing behind. Savinus rode beside him. He was quiet and rode at a rapid clip. Antonius kicked his steed in order to keep up. Every so often, Savinus would turn to him with a wide grin, his eyes glinting and his cheeks flushed.

"Are you alright, Signor?" he asked, concern creeping into his voice.

Savinus gave a laugh that sounded more like a wheeze.

"I do apologize if I am acting strangely. It's just that I've waited for this moment for many years. It will ease my mind considerably once you've had your initiation. If my health declines any further, it means you're ready to take over at any stage."

"Is it possible for me to fail the initiation?"

"Possibly yes, but likely no. You clearly have all the qualities necessary; this is just a final test. I have every faith in you. Giulia will meet us at the bottom of the hill near the forest. I hope you don't mind, but we need someone trustworthy to assist."

He shook his head. "Not at all. I thought she might come."

They passed a group of workers from the wheat fields as they approached town. Hats were tipped and they regarded the pair with wary expressions. They hunched their shoulders over wiry bodies and their prematurely aged faces looked downwards, as if searching for errant stones that might trip them on the road; a few held sacks of flour, given in lieu of payment.

Antonius felt a wave of melancholy after they passed—he was not sure why. Then he realized men like these were his kin, yet he felt different from them. His life was expanding outwards into unknown territory.

Following his mentor, he saw they had detoured along a dirt track skirting the town fortifications. He had not noticed it before. It was stony in parts and tangled with weeds in others, yet led them in privacy towards the wooded hills to the east of the town. Without asking, he understood the nature of their task demanded secrecy. He also knew that far from being an insignificant journey on horseback, it was a time for quiet reflection before the ritual took place.

Towards the end of the stone fortifications, the path veered right and tall beech trees enclosed them. The melodic song of birds filled his ears and tiny blue flowers and moss covered the forest floor. Horatio hesitated on the pitted ground, eventually coming to a complete stop. At that moment, Giulia appeared from behind a tree, carrying a deep straw basket. Over her shoulder was the strap of a musical instrument, half concealed by her body. She gave a wide smile but her green eyes held the solemnity of the occasion.

"The path finishes here, Papa. I've found a copse where we can tie up the horses."

"Thank you, my dear. You're well prepared, I see. Give Antonius the basket; you are encumbered enough with the lyre."

The two men dismounted and followed Giulia through the trees. They were almost too dense to penetrate, but soon gave way to a mossy glade dotted with wildflowers of every hue. Several beams of dark gold light broke through the trees. Antonius looked at the sky as he tied Horatio to a tree. It was filled with burnt orange, and wisps of red and pink. His eyes met those of Savinus.

We need to hurry to reach the clearing before darkness falls.

Yes, Signor. Please, let me carry some of your bags.

Here, you may take one, and the basket and lyre. It's not my upper body that's the problem, only my knee.

He took the leather bag and asked Giulia for the lyre which he draped over his body. She refused to hand over the basket, declaring she was a woman and not an invalid. Leading the way, she broke twigs from trees and stamped down ferns to clear the path. It meandered at times, used as it was by the forest animals. Antonius noticed an ambling hedgehog and, as they climbed higher, a fleeting glimpse of a red-coated fox as it darted through the thick foliage.

Behind him, Savinus made slow progress. It seemed every time he turned around, the old man was clutching a tree trunk and gasping for breath. In his concern, he spoke aloud.

"Signor, are you all right? Shall we stop?"

Savinus waved a gnarled hand and his eyes were resolute.

"Certainly not. There is not time." His voice was curt. "Please continue."

He took a swig from a metal container and pushed himself forward with a sturdy branch. Antonius understood his frailty was not to be mentioned again. Inhaling deeply, he could discern the fresh scent of pine, tree sap, and damp earth tinged with the sweetness of flowers. The air felt cool on his cheeks.

As the incline grew steeper, his worry deepened and he feigned shortness of breath so that they might pause. He imagined the old man's heart giving up before they reached the top.

"Are we almost there?" he called out to Giulia, who was several yards ahead.

"Yes," she replied. "Only a few minutes now. Is Papa managing?"

"Indeed I am, strong as an ox!" he bellowed, before succumbing to a fit of dry coughs.

Catching her eye, he shook his head and frowned. She pretended to rearrange the contents of her basket until he recovered. The last of the light seeped away, and they continued in moonlit darkness.

As they neared the top of the hill, a clearing came into view. It was large and almost a perfect circle, surrounded by pine and beech trees. At their feet lay soft grass, bathed in the milky light of the full moon. Savinus lowered himself onto the grass and caught his breath, turning his back to them. Antonius gave Giulia a knowing glance and helped her unpack her basket, filled with bottles of herbs and crystals in translucent hues of blue, pink, and green. The lyre was placed against a tree and they set about gathering stones to form a circle. Savinus roused himself to take some stones and arrange them. He waved away offers of assistance. Soon a circle of pale stones lay in the middle of the clearing, reflecting the white light like smooth skulls. Without being asked, Giulia disappeared for several minutes, returning with an armful of twigs, which she placed in the middle of the circle.

Antonius watched Savinus coaxing a fire to life with the aid of a flint and a firesteel. The temperature plummeted and he hugged himself against the chill. He could hear the rustle of animals in the shrubbery, and faintly, the sombre call of an owl. A beating of wings overhead made him jump, and he looked up to see a group of bats cross over the clearing.

He felt a hand on his shoulder and his eyes met those of Savinus. He was smiling, but beneath his expression was a gravity. It was time. He was led to the fire and they stood three abreast, holding hands. In a firm voice, Giulia said an incantation and separated herself from them.

"We ask for the help and protection of the spirit guides in this initiation, those who have gone before and understand the journey of seers. Show yourselves to Antonius. He is open to your knowledge."

The pale light fell on Giulia's face as she stood before the leaping flames, her arms outstretched as if beseeching the sky. Savinus raised his arms and turned his palms upward. Without looking at Antonius, he asked, "Did you have an unusual dream last night?"

"Yes."

"Can I ask what happened?"

"I was visited by an eagle who spoke to me in your voice."

He nodded. "He is ready."

Giulia picked up the lyre and played—the notes were clear and slow, as gentle as a lullaby. They filled the air with their sweetness, circling them and evaporating into the night.

Antonius watched the blue and amber flames as they crackled upwards, repeating the same patterns into infinity. He felt his body move to the rhythms, and realized they all moved in tandem around the fire. The music, the flames, and the night were as much a part of them as the blood coursing through their veins. The pace quickened and they followed, twisting and turning with fluidity.

Antonius's mind was clear and untroubled. At the same time, he watched Giulia's russet hair swing across her back and the long line of her slender white arm as she moved with perfect grace. He felt the eyes of many upon him, but he was not afraid. It was a sense of being held in the embrace of the observation, as if he were returning to the home of a friend that was as familiar as it was strange. Glancing at Giulia, he saw she scattered herbs into the flames. His nose twitched as their combined scent wafted towards him—sage, elderflower, cloves, and others. Three crystals were then released into the fire— purple, white, and gold. Several loud cracks erupted into the air and multi-coloured sparks flew with a hiss and a whine. In a low voice, Savinus chanted. It was the same mellifluous language he had heard during the ritual at the blue cave. He spread his arms in an outward motion, as if clearing away smoke.

Then, as if a cord had abruptly been severed, Antonius was in another place. He was surrounded by pale yellow grass as high as his waist in a field, bathed in sunlight. A low hum, like a swarm of bees, filled his ears. In the distance, a lone figure walked towards him, parting the grass with a gnarled stick. His robes were deep purple, tied at the waist with a gold cord. As he came closer, Antonius could see his deep-set brown eyes and close cropped grey hair. His face was pale with a strong jaw. He smiled and his eyes radiated warmth.

Hello, Antonius.

The voice was assured yet gentle. As soon as it came into his mind he felt at ease.

Who are you? I feel there are others but I cannot see them.

I am Arion. I come to you with ten others, the spirit protectors of Savinus. We thought it best not to overwhelm you. As his original guide, it was decided I should appear. We welcome you to this place, sacred to the followers of the way. The way is all around you—it is in the trees, the stars, the animals, and through your own body. You must keep your mind and body free from impurities and all will be revealed. Spend quiet time in your mind, without distraction. Do not hate those who show ignorance, they too are emanations of the Great Spirit. They are not ready to realize all that is around us. Your powers are great and will only increase with time. Be patient. You have many years to realize your potential. We will be here to guide you. Savinus will teach you the incantation, then you must sit in a quiet place in nature, and we will come.

How did you come to be his guide?

Antonius felt the heat of the sun on his face and the grass tickling his legs. Behind him lay a thick forest of pines. Their rich fragrance filled his nostrils.

We knew of him as soon as he was born. A seer of his calibre is rare and we waited until he was ready before appearing. He had been recognised as talented by another seer, so we introduced ourselves as part of his initiation. Although you are not related to him by blood, we see you as part of his family. There is a strong connection between you, and also with the girl. She does not realize it, but do not despair.

The image of Arion quivered, and he wondered if the sun was obscuring his vision. He began to shake.

The effect of the ritual is weakening. We must allow you to return. You are an initiate now—we wish you all the blessings of the awakened ones. If you are ever afraid, know that we are here at your shoulder. Goodbye.

Goodbye. He mouthed the words and fell into the soft cradle of the grass, his body spent. His vision went black and his senses turned inward.

When he awoke, the flames were still leaping towards the indigo sky. He looked up into the loveliness of Giulia's face. She was frowning and stroking his arm with a tenderness that brought tears to his eyes. For a moment, he pretended to be unwell, hoping to prolong her attentions.

"How do you feel?"

He smiled at her. "Wonderful. I saw him—Arion. Have you met him?"

She sat back and pushed a strand of hair behind her ear.

"Yes—he is our protector along with the others. Papa, he's back."

"Aha, welcome back young man. Our initiate—congratulations. You did everything as if you had practiced this ritual many times before. Where did you go?"

"To a golden field. Are there other places?"

"Yes, all peaceful sanctuaries of one kind or another. I'm sure you will visit more. A word of warning; sometimes when we do these practices you will see things that are not so pleasant. You must remain calm. It is a test of your mettle. I'm surprised you didn't have these experiences this time."

Antonius sat up and rested on his hands. The cold grass prickled against his palms. He was overcome with fatigue.

"Thank you. I don't mind if it's frightening next time. Either way I feel fortunate to go anywhere outside of this world."

Savinus smiled, his eyes almost vanishing beneath deep wrinkles. "Don't thank me. I merely assisted in a natural process—at least, natural for seers. Also, it's not another world. It's an unseen part of this world. Now, can you stand? We must move on before my old bones seize up completely in this awful cold. Giulia, can you help him my dear? Very good."

As the old man sat on his haunches, readying himself for the downward trek, Giulia and Antonius ignored his offers of help. They busied themselves removing each stone, placing them at the foot of a towering beech tree. Giulia explained the circle could be used for more sinister practices if it were not dismantled. This would infect the stones with negative energy and spoil their rituals. He was surprised and discomfited by this revelation.

"Do you mean to say there are practitioners of the satanic arts in Pesaro?"

"Not necessarily. This clearing is used by many, from Pesaro, and other villages. It is known for its free flow of energy. It is a sacred space and has been so for thousands of years. We hope those practicing the dark arts do not know of it, but we can't be sure."

"You two, hurry and pack up or I won't be able to stand up again. You'll have to bring the physician in the morning to break my old bones."

"Sorry, Papa. We're finished. Here, I'll help you up, there, take it slowly."

He grimaced and wheezed as he allowed her to pull him upright. Then he gave a grim nod and they departed. Once under the cover of the trees they were cloaked in darkness. The only light came from Giulia's lamp swinging ahead, beams of gold leading them down the hill. The blackness felt like a thick soup and, for a moment, Antonius struggled to find his breath. He winced as a branch scratched his face and took uneasy steps, his feet crunching the stones. Behind, he could hear the old man's laboured breaths. His jubilant mood ebbed and exhaustion weighed down his limbs. Holding one hand against his cheek, he used the other to feel ahead for obstructions.

"I can see the end." Giulia turned and he saw a flash of white in the gloom, her smile of relief.

He held out his arm to Savinus. "Here sir, let me help you out of here."

His reply was gruff. "I'm all right. Go on and I shall follow."

Antonius could still see the long grass in his mind, and Arion standing before him. He wondered when he might see him again.

CHAPTER 18

Impatience caused Antonius to corner Giulia some days later. He stood in the doorway, watching her. She was embroidering in a corner of the sitting room and Savinus was at the market. He had run out of glass jars for his healing liquid. Antonius had been unable to sleep, his mind aflame with the desire to visit other worlds. It was all he could think about; he was sure it would further his knowledge. She did not hear him approach and pursed her lips as she pulled the thread through the fabric circle.

"I have to go back." His posture was taut and expectant.

She jumped and glanced up, irritated. "Hello, Antonius. Go back where? What are you talking about?"

"To the woods. I wouldn't feel comfortable going to the stone circle without your father, but perhaps we could do a ritual elsewhere. Do you know of other places?"

She smiled and set down her embroidery. "Yes, I do know of another clearing. When did you want to go?"

"What about tonight? I suppose your father will know, as you can't keep secrets from him. Do you think he would mind?"

"No, I think he'll understand you need to explore without him. We could meet at the same place at the bottom of the hill, just after dark."

∞

He walked from the palazzo, the stones crunching under his feet. The air was crisp and a yellow moon hung above the trees in the blue-tinged dark. He followed the same track along the fortifications until he reached the bottom of the hill. Giulia stood wearing a black-hooded cloak, carrying the straw basket.

"We must hurry, the moon has to be in the right position. It has already started to wane, and it makes the ritual more difficult." Her face was a smudge of white beneath the cloak, and he could see the faint pink of her lips.

She walked ahead of him, twigs snapping beneath her feet. Shafts of moonlight penetrated the foliage, illuminating the path. It was different from the one he remembered, climbing right instead of left. Unseen animals scuffled in the undergrowth. The clearing was smaller when it came into view. The trees surrounding it were monumental pines, their needles dense and black.

Giulia placed her basket on the grass and rummaged for crystals.

"Can you please collect some twigs? We need a small fire."

Antonius gathered an armful of twigs beneath the pines. He laid them at her feet and she crouched and rubbed a flint and firesteel together until a spark flew out. The fire was slow to take hold, and they blew on it until the flames licked upwards. She dropped the crystals in the fire and they popped and hissed. Reaching for his hand, she said the incantation. To his surprise, she asked for what he desired.

> "On this night of full moon, we ask to meet our guides
> Those who protect and watch over us
> We honour them and desire to share in their wisdom
> Take us to their world—*Deflagrate muri tempi et intervallia!*"

He felt air rushing past his body at great speed and saw white light in a vortex. All the while, Giulia remained at his side. For a moment there was blackness, then blinding sunlight. He blinked and found himself sitting on a sandstone cliff dotted with olive trees. A vast shimmering ocean stretched to the horizon, the cobalt waters breaking against the shore with rhythmic sighs. To his left, he was relieved to see Giulia. She beamed and rose, standing near the edge. Turning around he saw a Grecian temple, its columns meeting a blue and gold painted frieze.

Arion stood on the marble steps, his feet in leather sandals, white robes fluttering in the breeze. On his head was a crown of gold laurel leaves. Antonius jumped to his feet and almost tripped in his haste to reach him. Giulia followed behind.

"Arion, hello! I need to speak with you."

"Hello, Antonius. Hello, Giulia. Our first meeting was brief and I thought you might visit. I'm pleased you have come."

"Where is this place?"

"The temple of Apollo, at Thera. It is a sacred place. When I lived, this was my home. I was the high priest of this temple. I come here to connect with spirit. It remains the same as when I left it. We perform sacrifices and have rituals as we did when I lived. The only difference is I come and go."

Antonius stared at the intricate painting on the frieze. Young women in white robes cavorted in a circle next to the sacrifice of a bull. Their black hair fanned out behind them. To the left and right of the painting were marble statues of Apollo, standing at the corners of the pediment.

"Sir, how is that possible? It's a time that no longer exists."

"Those who reach the higher levels can choose to be in any time or place they wish. It is true it no longer exists in a physical sense. But all times and places exist simultaneously. I apologize, as I do not wish to confuse you. Savinus travels with me. Understanding different times and places enables him to help others. As you progress, you may join us. Giulia, you are almost ready. Is there somewhere you would like to go?"

Her eyes shone. "To Egypt, to see how the pyramids were built. But I love to come here. Is Agathe serving at the temple today?"

"Yes. I excused her from duties for a while. She will be back soon."

Giulia turned to him. "Agathe is a high priestess. Her powers are so great she's permitted to be a priestess of Apollo."

"Can women not serve male gods?"

"No, it's not customary. She is special."

As if she had heard her name, Agathe emerged from the trees. Her dark hair hung in wet strands on her shoulders, and her white robes clung to her. Water droplets glistened on her pale skin.

"Giulia!" She broke into a run and embraced her.

"I've just been swimming in the stream. It's wonderful to see you!" They kissed each other on both cheeks. Pulling away she fixed large brown eyes on Antonius and smiled.

"A newcomer. I'm Agathe. I've heard about you. Is it Antonius?"

"Yes. It's good to meet you. Does Savinus come here very often?"

Arion answered. "It's his favourite place, aside from his home. He has become quite adept at helping us with sacrifices, but his main role is as an oracle. People come from all over the Cyclades to see him."

"We're performing a ritual now. Will you stay and see it?"

Antonius and Giulia nodded, looking down at a group of young women climbing the hill to the temple. Carrying instruments, they wore fluid white robes, their heads crowned with laurel wreaths. Antonius swallowed and stared. Their limbs were long and they moved with grace, their dark hair curling down their backs.

"It is the Pythia," said Arion. "The attendants of the temple."

Behind them followed a long procession of people: hunched elderly, skipping children, and women with robes covering their hair. A number of men accompanied them, their backs straight and their bodies sinewy. They carried small drawstring bags and Antonius wondered what was inside them. As if reading his mind, Giulia whispered in his ear.

"They're responsible for giving offerings of gold coins. Women can't make the offerings."

All were dressed in white. They stood near the olive trees, their eyes downcast and reverent.

The sun was high as the sweet notes of string instruments filled the air. Some of the Pythia played music and some danced, their slender arms raised to the blue sky. Their steps were careful and delicate, their faces deep in concentration. As the sun rose higher, their movements quickened and their golden skin glistened in the light.

Arion lit a brass brazier with a torch and stood on the steps of the temple. He spoke in mellifluous Greek, his hands making symbolic gestures.

The words calmed Antonius, even though he did not understand them. He felt Giulia's gaze and looked back—her green eyes shone and she took his hand. He blushed and stared down at the sandy earth, then back to Arion and the sinuous dance. The warm breeze flowed through his hair and over his face as Giulia's hand pressed against his. It was almost time to return.

CHAPTER 19

The morning before the banquet, Nichola arrived on the doorstep. Agnese raised an eyebrow and waved him inside, muttering he was early and the master was not expecting him until later.

"Are nobles above announcing themselves?"

"I beg your pardon Agnese?—I didn't hear you."

"Never mind. Come through."

The custom in the Valperga family was to send word of their arrival by way of the butler, who would send a message boy to the house in question. As Nichola was warmly received, whether he followed this custom or not, he had dispensed with it. The only time he bothered with it was if he were in another village and visiting someone of higher status. He nodded at the servant and entered the sitting room, making himself comfortable in an armchair.

"Fetch me some mead, would you? And tell the mistress I'm here to see her."

He picked up a china ornament of a bird from the side table and turned it in his long fingers, admiring the hand-painted, translucent wings. Agnese understood she was dismissed. She gave a small nod and padded towards Giulia's bedchamber, her lips moving as she grumbled under her breath.

She gave a soft knock on Giulia's door.

"Miss Giulia? Master Valperga is here to see you. Can you come out, or do you need some help with your grooming?"

"Thank you, Agnese. I'll be out in a minute. Would you please look after him and get him some mead?"

"Yes, Miss."

Inside her room, Giulia panicked. As she was not expecting visitors, she was dressed in a simple white housedress. Having dismissed Agnese, she realized her inability to remove it on her own. She seized a green embroidered coat from the armoire and pulled it on, fastening the buttons. Picking up a tortoiseshell comb she slotted it into her bun and ran her fingers through the sides to tame stray hairs. She examined her reflection for flaws and turned to the door, taking a few slow breaths.

"Good morning, Nichola. How lovely to see you."

He rose and took her hand, touching his lips to her fingers.

"And you. Agnese is getting mead but you look so ravishing I want to take you to the streets and show you off."

"But Nichola, you know I must wear that silly hat. You'll only be showing off my figure."

"And what a magnificent one it is."

His eyes held a mischievous glint. "Is it too rude to just leave?"

She felt both shaky and elated when his eyes were on her.

"I'll go and tell her. Just a moment."

In the kitchen Agnese was searching for mugs in the storeroom.

"Agnese, I'm sorry, but we have decided to go for a stroll. It's such a beautiful light this morning and the Signor thought it would be a good idea—"

Agnese smiled and held up her hand for silence. "It's all right, Miss Giulia. You don't need to explain. Enjoy your walk. I'll tell the master when he comes out of the workroom." Giulia grinned and dashed from the room, holding her skirts up so as not to trip.

It was the kind of light that inspired Florentine painters to take their brushes, paint, and boards to the fields for the day. The sky was infused with gold that brightened as the sun ascended higher. Nichola took her arm in his as they walked. She blushed, thankful for the veil hiding her magenta cheeks.

"People will think we're engaged or married if you do that."

He suppressed a smile. "And so? Would that be so terrible?"

"It's just that people talk. And we're not engaged. It would create a false rumour."

"People talk. So what? You sound like my mother."

She withdrew her arm.

"It could compromise my honour—as much as I enjoy it. Look at that flock of gulls! There must be one hundred!"

"Yes, perhaps there is a fish carcass at the port for them to feast on."

They walked along the stone wall following the sea. Giulia's nostrils filled with the briny smell of the seaweed and salt water. Passing others, she took pleasure in their reaction to her companion. At first, they would glance at the pair and look away. Then, noticing the fine cut and embellishments of Nichola's clothing, as well as his proud bearing, they would do a double take. As they walked away she could hear ill-disguised chatter about him and musings about who she might be. She imagined walking with him as his wife, her face triumphantly revealed.

At the end of the walkway they were forced to turn into a smaller street. Some illegal vegetable stalls had been set up along the sides, balanced precariously on the cobblestones. Boys who had not yet reached their teens manned the stalls. They set their shoulders back and jutted out their chins, trying to pass as men. A gang of younger boys were huddled in a circle. It was impossible to see their focus, but as a gap formed, Giulia could see Piero, Antonius's brother, with his arms raised against his face and his hands in defensive fists. He squealed with fear. The boys shouted and jostled him with their elbows.

"Moron! Go home. This is our part of town."

"Ha! He thinks he can join us. What an idiot. *Smetta di importunarmi!* Stop bothering us. Go and see your Mama."

A heavyset boy with red cheeks kicked him in the shins, provoking laughter in the others. Piero winced in pain; his eyes squeezed shut as if he hoped to disappear. His face was pale.

"I'm going to help him. I've had enough."

Giulia set her jaw and moved forward. Nichola clasped her forearm.

"Leave them. You might get hurt."

She withdrew her arm and stepped away, positioning herself in front of them and raising her veil.

"*Basta*! Leave him alone! Go and kick a ball if you need to kick something. Get away from him!" Her voice reverberated off the stone walls of the alley.

The boys turned from their quarry and gaped in silence. Then the large one spoke in a low voice.

"He's always in our way, wanting to join our group. We're sick of it."

"Get moving before I find your mothers and tell them of your cruelty. Go!"

They nodded and ran, footsteps echoing on the stones. Piero sat hunched on the ground, sobbing into his hands.

"Are you all right?" She touched his shoulder.

He gave an agonised moan.

Nichola stood stiffly behind her.

"Can we go?"

She glared at him. "Come and help me get him to his feet—we need to take him to his mama."

They escorted him home after asking a few people the whereabouts of his house. Nichola was taciturn. At the door of the house, Fiora was effusive in her gratitude and asked them inside. Giulia declined and patted Piero on the back before leaving.

"He's a good boy. I'm sorry he has such a hard time."

"Yes, Miss. He has a good heart. Thank you for coming to his rescue."

"Anytime. Good day to you."

They continued walking but the incident had changed their mood.

"You know, whoever marries Antonius might end up with an

idiot like that. It's in the blood."

"What nonsense. It's just bad luck."

"Perhaps. But have you ever thought there might be a reason why noble families are so careful with their marriage choices? The family tree must be examined for problems like that."

"It wouldn't hurt to show a little compassion. He may be lacking in intelligence, but his heart contains nothing but love."

Nichola sighed. "My goodness you're sentimental. Come on, let's go and find you a pretty bauble at the market. Something you can wear to the banquet tomorrow."

She smiled despite her irritation and followed him back towards the piazza.

The jewelry stall was heavy with its glittering stock. Almost at once, Giulia spotted a gold pendant from which hung a pear-shaped aquamarine. Blue arcs of reflected sunlight beamed from its surface and she was captivated.

"Well? Do you see anything you like?" He noted her fixed gaze beneath the veil and suppressed a smile.

Pulling her eyes away from the pendant, she pointed at a silver bangle set with lapis lazuli.

"I like that one."

"My dear Giulia. There is no need to be polite. You're the most beautiful girl in Pesaro and deserve a pendant matching your beauty."

He turned to the stallholder, who watched them with growing excitement. He had been trying to sell the pendant for months, and was considering selling it to a merchant from a bigger town. A broad smile pierced his swarthy cheeks and he puffed out his chest.

"Can I assist you, Signor?"

"Indeed. The lady is interested in the aquamarine pendant. How much do you want for it?"

"Ah, yes, a lovely piece. It is 500 florins."

Giulia had to bite her lip to stop from gasping. It was more than her father earned in six months.

"Nichola, let's look somewhere else."

He laughed and withdrew a velvet purse, handing over the

money with a casual air, as if buying a sack of potatoes.

"A good choice, sir. Good day to you."

"And to you."

They walked in the direction of her house. Giulia felt as if it were she who had been bought rather than the necklace.

"Don't you like it?" Nichola was bewildered by her silence.

"I love it. But it's too much. You hardly know me."

"I know enough. Here. Put it on."

"No! People will gossip. Wait until we get inside."

"As you wish."

Agnese ushered them inside before disappearing into the kitchen. Giulia allowed him to fasten the necklace in front of the hall mirror. It made the green of her eyes appear more emerald. Their eyes met in the glass and she smiled into the mirror without looking away.

"Thank you. I will be honoured to wear it tomorrow night."

She glanced around in case Agnese was present, before kissing him firmly on the lips, her fingers enmeshed in his hair. Stepping back, she gave him a teasing glance and skipped away. He touched his fingers to his lips and, for a moment, was unable to move.

The workroom gems were heavy in his pocket. He spotted Antonius's coat on the stand near the door. In a rapid movement, he pulled the pouch out of his pocket and slotted it into the large exterior one on the coat.

∞

The cold weather proved fortuitous for his plans. The workroom was the most frigid room of the villa. Savinus preferred it that way as it kept his mind alert. For the boys, however, it was becoming uncomfortable as autumn took hold. That afternoon, he instructed them to read about geomancy diagrams as well as the properties of different healing liquids. Sitting at the long desk, they hunched over.

Antonius rubbed his upper arms and stamped his feet. It did not work. Excusing himself, he left the room and returned wearing his coat. Savinus looked up from his work.

"Oh, dear, are you boys cold? How selfish of me. Agnese!"

He waited for her to respond, tapping his fingers on his desk.

"Yes, Signor?"

"These boys are cold. Would you please light the fire? I may doze off, but I don't want them to be uncomfortable."

"Yes, Signor."

She returned with an armful of kindling, and set to work. Her torso disappeared into the brick mouth of the fireplace so only her voluminous linen skirts were visible. Before long, she had coaxed an impressive blaze from the kindling and left to fetch some more wood.

As she dropped a log on the flames, the fire blazed higher, crackling and sparking. They thanked her profusely and she beamed.

"My dear papa taught me the skill of fire lighting when I was five. He said it was more important than learning to cook, as how can one cook without the aid of a fire?"

"That's right Agnese. Now, speaking of cooking, is it that delicious salted mackerel for my supper tonight?"

"Yes Signor. I'd best go and attend to it."

As the room heated up, Antonius removed his coat and hung it on the back of a chair, close to Nichola.

"You won't be needing your coat now, let me take it back to the stand for you."

He gave the chair a slight push as he grasped the coat, causing it to fall on its side. The coat was snatched from his hand and tumbled to the floor, spilling the contents of the pockets. The gems clattered on the wood floor.

"What's this?" asked Nichola. He picked up the pouch and opened it. "Goodness Antonius, where did you find such a lot of gems? They really are amazing."

"I've not seen those before." His voice was bewildered.

Savinus watched the scene with a grave expression.

"Bring them here please."

Nichola walked over and handed the pouch to him, suppressing a smug grin.

Savinus shook his head. "There has been a terrible wrongdoing here."

Nichola nodded. "Yes Signor, it is a shocking betrayal of trust—"

"Silence!"

Nichola took a step back, confusion erasing the smile.

"You have tried to bring dishonour onto Antonius. What foolishness, to think you can trick me, a reader of minds. It is disgraceful. You must leave the workroom today. Do not even think of returning until you have found some humility. An abject apology will be the only action that will retain your apprenticeship. I won't tell your father for now, but you must get out of my sight."

"Signor, I—"

"Out! The sight of you is making me want to seize that hot poker and beat you with it! Go home and do not return for at least one week."

"Signor, I am to escort Giulia to a banquet tomorrow night."

"For Giulia's sake, I will let you escort her, but do not enter the villa. You will have to wait at the door. Go!"

With a sigh Nichola turned and left, anger in the staccato tap of his boots.

Savinus turned to Antonius. "I'm sorry. It seems he is trying harder to discredit you. If he were not the Conte's son—"

"It's all right, Signor. I understand you are in a difficult position. You don't need to explain anything to me. If Nichola is my only difficulty, then life is not too bad."

CHAPTER 20

All day Savinus tried to avoid his daughter. Giulia was excited about the banquet and he did not want to bring down her mood. Even if he withheld the incident with Nichola, she would read his mind within seconds. He sat hunched at his desk, trying to look busy.

He need not have worried. She was absorbed in her preparations and more concerned with trying on dresses than conversing with her father.

"Agnese—can you come here please? I need to try on the blue lace. Can you untie me? Agnese!"

Agnese gripped the edge of the kitchen table and took a deep breath. For most of the morning she had been attempting to scale and de-bone a fish for the evening meal. Every time she picked up her knife her mistress summoned her.

Exhaling, she let go of the table and walked to Giulia's bedchamber. Her mistress was flushed, her hair unruly. To her servant's alarm, she was pulling at the buttons on the back of her yellow silk dress, as if she intended to rip it off.

"Miss, let go of that and turn around. I'll help you."

"Agnese, I know you've already helped me put on three dresses but I just can't decide. None of them are right. All those noble girls will be better dressed than me, I'm sure."

"Well perhaps they will, but what of it? They will be less intelligent, less beautiful. Wear something of good cut and colour and little ornamentation. Then they won't look at your dress, only your face and figure. You mark my words."

She made quick work of the thirty buttons, unbuttoning the dress with deft fingers. She led Giulia over to the wardrobe and peered inside. In silence, she scanned the multi-coloured row of silk, chiffon, and brocade, before fixing on something. Her sinewy arm darted out and parted the dresses, her hand seizing a gown of pale green silk.

"This one. Your red hair would be perfect with this, and your eyes. Step in please."

"But Agnese, it is so plain. I didn't even think of it as a possibility."

"Just try it on, Miss. You will see."

Sighing, Giulia did as she was told, and waited whilst the buttons and hooks were fastened. Agnese led her to the full-length mirror and held her hair back from her face.

"You see? Beautiful—once I've done your hair and rouged your cheeks."

The dress had been made by the most skilled tailor in Pesaro and accentuated her curves in the right places. A grateful client of her father's in Rome had sent the fabric. It was a heavy lustrous silk, the green of shallow seawater. The only decoration was a row of seed pearls, which followed the rounded neckline. Savinus gave her the money to have it made for a dance the previous year. Paired with the aquamarine necklace it would be perfect.

"Thank you. I suppose I'm ready then. When will you need to do my hair and face?"

"Not until later. The church bells have only just sounded, and you are being collected at nightfall. You could do some weaving? Or help me in the kitchen?"

"I'll do both. What are you making? I'll help you first."

The rest of the day passed in a blur of baking and threading. After de-boning the fish, Agnese entertained her with stories of her youth in Perugia. They baked and giggled together, the older woman clapping her hands and sending clouds of flour billowing in all directions. Agnese was an excellent baker and showed Giulia how to knead the bread for an even texture.

"You're a complete mess now. Go to the water pump and clean up and then it is time for your weaving. I'll finish up here. Thank you for your help, Miss."

"Ah, but you're helping me Agnese. Who will want to marry me if I can't cook?"

"A nobleman won't need you to cook. You know that. If you marry a merchant you might cook sometimes, for a special occasion. Your beauty is currency enough."

"Well, I like to cook. I like to feel the ingredients on my hands and even on my face."

Agnese smiled. "Miss, your enjoyment is a lovely thing to behold. But you must not speak of it tonight with those nobles. They would think you common."

"Perhaps. It's weaving time. Can you tell me when it's time to get ready? I get so absorbed when I weave."

"I will. Off you go."

The weaving kept her mind from her nerves. She finished eight rows and fell into a meditative state as she pushed the weft shuttle across the warp threads, and alternated the loom levers, row after row. As dusk fell, Agnese tapped her on the shoulder and led her to her bath. The water was fragrant with rose oil and she sank into it, the steam billowing around her face. Agnese sponged her, and dried her with soft cotton towels. Then they set to work before the mirror. Her hair was swept up and fastened with tortoiseshell combs. Powder and rouge were applied, and her lips painted. The necklace was fastened around her long neck with gasps of admiration. The older woman looked pleased with her handiwork. Her eyes were moist as she spoke.

"Such a spectacular girl. Everyone will be looking at you tonight. Be proud. If only your dear mother, rest her soul, could see you now."

"Thank you, dearest Agnese. What would I do without you?"

She coloured. "Go and wait in the sitting room and I'll bring you some warm milk with brandy. It will help your nerves."

Savinus hesitated at the door of the sitting room. The sight of her poised on the edge of an armchair caused him to draw in his breath; she so resembled her mother. Her posture was tightly coiled like a cat, poised to leap at the slightest provocation. She turned and smiled, a shimmering aquamarine pendant glinting beneath her chin. Returning the smile, he sat next to her, taking her hand.

"You have nothing to be nervous about, my dear. You will dazzle them, there's no doubt. If you can't think what to say, ask questions. Flatter, but don't be obsequious. They have servants for that. Have a wonderful evening."

He leant over and kissed her cheek before pushing himself upright.

"I must go and do some charts. Good night, and send my regards to the Conte. Tell him I'll visit next week."

"Yes, Papa, thank you. Good night." She noticed the stiffness of his gait and thought he must be in pain. There was something odd about their exchange. When they spoke there were two parts of the conversation, the spoken and the unspoken. This time, the unspoken was absent. Giulia was not sure why, but he was blocking her.

CHAPTER 21

The bell chimed and Agnese hurried to the door, smoothing down her hair and brushing crumbs from her apron. Nichola stood taut with impatience, craning his neck to catch sight of Giulia. Behind him was a gleaming black carriage, curlicues of gold leaf decorating its edges.

Giulia was on her feet at once, twisting her hands and adjusting her skirt.

"Good evening, Agnese. I won't come in. Could you please fetch the young lady for me?"

The rich sound of his voice caused pains in her stomach. Agnese motioned her to the door, squeezing her hand as she pushed the small of her back.

"Enjoy your evening, Miss."

She watched her mistress's tentative steps towards the carriage, Nichola's gloved hand at her elbow.

Inside, enveloped in the grey velvet seats, Giulia took furtive glimpses of Nichola. His doublet was made of a deep blue silk embellished with gold thread. Catching her eye, he smiled and reached for her hand.

"There's no need to be nervous. I've known everyone there since I was a young boy. They're good people. The necklace suits you very well. Ask the men about their hunting and the women about their daily lives."

He fixed her with such an intense heated look that her stomach flipped over and she reddened.

"My God, you are exquisite."

Pulling her arm, he drew her to him, his face close, and his other hand circling her waist. He pressed his lips to hers. She felt as if she were an unusual dish he was tasting at a banquet, his lips exploring hers with curiosity. Blood rushed to her cheeks. His free hand traversed the line of her body until it reached her breast. He cupped it, then ran his fingers around it lazily. Before she was able to protest, he had slipped his hand beneath her bodice and was stroking her bare skin.

"Please, stop!" She wrenched herself free and adjusted her dress, her breath jagged. To her relief, a curtain was drawn almost to the edge of the window, and their kiss had not been witnessed.

She looked at him sideways and could not suppress a smirk. "You are a very badly behaved man. Do you know that?"

"So I'm told. Is it such a sin to kiss my future wife?"

Stunned into silence, her eyes widened. When she spoke, her voice was a near whisper.

"What are you talking about?"

"You heard me. I want you to be my wife as soon as possible. You're the only girl I have ever met who is strong enough to be married to me. I like the way you know your own mind, and you don't tell me I'm wonderful just to get your hands on my father's money. You are simply the most perfect, beautiful creature I have ever known."

She drew in her breath. "Are you sure? Marry me? But Nichola, there are so many wealthy girls you could choose from. Would your father approve of me?"

"It's you I want. My father will approve. Do you not want to be my wife?" His voice was soft.

"Yes, I do. I will marry you. But please, don't speak of it tonight. I'm nervous enough as it is. If everyone knows we're engaged, then

I won't have a moment of peace."

His face glowed and he kissed her hard on the lips once more, burying his fingers in her hair.

"Dearest Giulia—you will be the most pampered, indolent wife in all of Italy. Your every whim will be granted before you've even had a chance to recognize what it is you want. I must find you an emerald so large your left hand will hang lower than your right."

She laughed as the carriage turned into the palazzo gates.

"Let's just enjoy tonight for now."

They entered through immense double oak doors. Six butlers waited at the threshold, bowing deeply as they passed. One reached out to take her fur capelet. In the distance, Giulia could hear the orchestra of animated voices, the deep male voices like cellos interspersed with the violins of the women.

The head butler addressed a point next to Nichola's ear, whilst motioning with a white-gloved hand.

"Sir, drinks are being served in the sitting room before the banquet. Master Gianni awaits you. Signorina, welcome to the Palazzo Ducal."

The entrance hall was three times the size of her home. On each wall, a blaze of candles shone from wall sconces. Beneath them sat groups of plush burgundy armchairs and mahogany tables. Persian carpets covered the Carrera marble flagstones. Life-sized portraits of Nichola's ancestors hung on many of the walls. Their expressions were impassive, their haughty jaws jutting in much the same way as his.

Nichola held her elbow as they entered the sitting room. There was a lull in the conversation as all eyes turned to them. Giulia could sense the women dissecting every aspect of her appearance, from her hair to the fabric of her shoes. She tried not to blush and stood straighter. Nichola ushered her towards his brother.

"Happy Birthday to you. Gianni, I present Giulia."

She could feel the cold wall of tension between the brothers. It surprised her that Gianni's manner was so different from Nichola's. Although his bearing was proud, she saw humility and sweetness in his smile.

"Well, it is lovely to meet you. Nichola never tells us anything about his life. I think we may have met before, but I think you were only eight at the time."

"Yes, I'm sure we probably have. I'm very pleased to meet you again. Happy Birthday."

Gianni snapped his fingers and a liveried servant brought over a tray of drinks. Tall glasses were filled with a pink liquid with mint leaves decorating the top. Giulia hesitated and the servant spoke.

"It is pomegranate juice, Signorina."

"Thank you."

She brought the drink to her lips—it was delicious and cool.

Soon they were surrounded by people. Nichola was drawn aside into a group of men and several women stood close enough to see her pores. They fired questions at her, not waiting for her reply.

"Are you the seer's daughter?"

"Can you predict our futures?"

"Who made your dress?"

"Nichola never brings anyone to these parties. Are you engaged?"

She wanted them to stand further away. Ignoring her discomfort, she tried to answer their questions.

"Yes, Savinus di Benevento is my father. No, I cannot predict your futures; you would have to see my father for that. Joachim Corelli made my dress; he is very talented. Signor Nichola and I are not engaged. May I ask how you are all connected to the Valperga family?"

It turned out that most of their fathers were connected to the Conte, either as friends or through business dealings. One was a distant relative from Milan. She was asked about her friends and her skills. Could she play an instrument, speak Latin, embroider? After a while, they seemed satisfied that, although not their equal, she was not a threat. They then spoke amongst themselves.

"Did you hear that Giorgiana fell from her horse on Thursday? Terrible, she is still in bed and won't be coming. So, do you think Signor Gianni and Violetta will announce their engagement tonight?"

"No, I think it will be later. The focus is on Signor Gianni and his birthday. Oh, Alessia, I need to ask you about servants. My mother is having trouble with her lady's maid; she is apparently rather free with her favours. She said would you mind asking your mother if she knows of anyone appropriate?"

"Yes, I will tell her of your predicament. It was an awful bore getting ready for this evening. My maid hasn't a clue about adornment and grooming. I practically had to do it all myself. Your mother won't want my Hestia—she is abysmal. In fact, I think I've decided to let her go. Anyone interested in an overweight girl with only one obvious skill, folding clothing?"

The women laughed before moving on to the next topic. Giulia tried not to stare at their necklaces, many of them heavy with diamonds and emeralds. Their dresses were of a fine cut and the silks were of a quality she had not seen before. The skirts hung in perfect folds over their satin shoes. Alessia was the dominant personality in the group. She held their attention with stories of people at other parties, their mishaps and faux pas.

"Did you see Salvatore at the Roselli's luncheon last Friday? I can't see how you could have missed him. He was completely drunk. His cheeks were beet red and his clothing rumpled. I couldn't believe my eyes when he staggered in, his hair on end. It was a disgrace. Fortunately, one of the servants led him outside and sent him home to bed. His poor wife. I don't think he has spent a single night at home since their wedding. She is desperate for a child, you know. A bit difficult to achieve with an absent husband."

Giulia glanced around for Nichola. To her relief, he approached and slipped his hand around her waist. The women looked at her with renewed admiration. To be shown public affection from the Conte's son was the pinnacle of achievement.

"Good evening Alessia, Bianca, Lucia. I trust you are all well. I hope you don't mind if I steal Giulia for a moment. There is someone I would like her to meet."

They nodded, silenced by his good looks and manner. He took her elbow once more and guided her towards his father.

The Conte had not seen her for several years. He took her hand and kissed it, a manoeuvre made awkward by her attempt to curtsey at the same time.

"Papa, I think you have met, but this is the lovely Giulia."

"Please, dear girl, there is no need for that. Rise so I may see you properly."

She blushed deep red and straightened her back, trying to meet his eyes.

"Ah, yes, I think you resemble your mother. She was quite ravishing. Such a tragedy for your father. Still, at least he has consolation in you. It is typical that my son has kept you a secret. He's very private about these matters. Tell me, what are your interests?"

"I enjoy weaving, playing the lyre, dancing, and horse riding, Your Eminence."

"You may address me as 'Sir'. 'Your Eminence' is for the servants. All very worthy pursuits. If you are to get to know my family, you must take up card games and embroidery. Singing is also useful. I am also aware you have some skill with fortune telling. You may use this with my immediate family. Don't worry, I won't tell anyone. Nichola, has she told you she is quite gifted like her Papa?"

He nodded and frowned.

"Sir, I'm flattered, but I have never used my skills outside my home. It's dangerous. What if one of your servants were to talk about it? I would rather not practice fortune telling here, if you don't mind."

"Very well. I won't force you to do anything you're not comfortable with."

A butler stood at the door and announced in a resonant voice that the banquet was served. The Conte nodded to Nichola and Giulia and excused himself. The conversation lulled and everyone watched as he led the way. After a short pause, Nichola and Giulia trailed behind him through a long hallway, its curved ceiling decorated with intricate paintings of nymphs and flowers. The guests waited until all the Valpergas left before exiting.

The banquet room glowed pale orange from the wall sconces and multiple candelabras lining the table. Giulia followed Nichola to the end of the room, and stood behind a red velvet chair whilst the guests filed in. The Conte's status meant he was able to dispense with this courtesy. He sat at the head of the table in an ornate wing-backed chair, embellished enough to be a throne. His fingers thrummed on the white linen tablecloth and he appeared bored. Ilaria Valperga entered through the door behind Giulia and glided over to her husband. He half rose as she sat to his right and touched his lips to her rouged cheek. Giulia felt her sharp blue eyes on her and stared down at her feet. For some reason, she felt unprepared to meet his mother.

When everyone stood behind their chairs, their eyes turned to the Conte and the room fell quiet. He nodded and the liveried servants standing behind each guest dashed forward to help them into their chairs.

Giulia found the courage to smile at Ilaria Valperga and received a curt nod in response. Although stung, her senses reeled from the decadence of the room. She inhaled the scent of the roses and lilies which filled crystal bowls along the length of the table. The smoke from the candles was impregnated with sandalwood. Place settings were crammed with enough silver and glittering crystal to feed a family in the town for a year. She examined the adornment of the guests. The women wore heavy silks in pastel shades. She imagined this was a deliberate ploy to avoid detracting from the splendour of their ruby, emerald and diamond jewelery. The servants wore a uniform of navy wool breeches and matching doublets. Their hair was pulled back into neat ponytails tied with black velvet ribbons. Nichola leaned over and her nose filled with his woody scent.

"You are staring, but as you are so beautiful I don't think anyone will care."

She laughed. His full lips turned up at the corners and she fought off the urge to kiss them. As if he were reading her mind she felt his hand on her thigh and her dress inching upwards. Sipping her red wine, she considered pushing it away but his touch was gentle and soothed her nerves. After a few minutes the skirt was high enough that his fingers caressed her bare skin, giving her goose bumps.

"You're being naughty again, you'd better stop before someone notices or I start to blush."

With a sigh, Nichola did as he was told and responded to a question from his father. Opposite sat Gianni and Violetta, their heads bent close. Gianni whispered something in her ear.

To the left was a silver-haired matron, her neck glittering with multiple strands of diamonds. They looked heavy and Giulia wondered if it was difficult for her to hold herself upright. The lady turned to her and with every slight movement, the diamonds reflected the candlelight in colourful arcs. She tried to keep her gaze fixed on her face and not the dazzling display.

"What gorgeous hair you have. My husband has a similar colour red and I was hoping it would be passed to one of our four children, but alas, it wasn't to be. They're all blond. I'm Signora Testoni; the Contessa is my niece. I see she is ignoring you. Don't worry; I do believe no one would be good enough for her Nichola. He's clearly besotted with you and I can see why. *Bella, bella*! Now, where on earth are the antipasti? I have been starving myself all day for this meal."

Nichola's hand was on her thigh again. She gave up on reprimanding him. His head was inclined forward as he attempted to listen in on their conversation.

"Zia Carlotta, what are you gossiping about?"

"Nothing that would interest you, dear boy. Now, why did you not tell me about this divine girl? Introduce us, please."

"Giulia, this is my great aunt, Signora Testoni. Zia, this is Giulia. Prepare yourself for an ear bashing; Zia knows everything there is to know about this family."

"Scandalous to speak to your old aunt that way! And it's not true, at least not these days. I've lost some hearing, which prevents me from overhearing conversations. However, I have started to teach myself to lip-read and it's already paying off. You two give me a thrill, I can see the chemistry a mile away. It takes me back to the days when I was young and had my first lover."

"Zio Giuseppe?"

She tittered, her gnarled and bejewelled hand covering her mouth. "I'm afraid not, dear. His name was Carlos, I believe."

Nichola smirked. "Zia, you are the scandalous one. I trust my great uncle was not yet on the scene?"

"You know, my memory is becoming a little hazy about the order of things. Perhaps, perhaps not. Anyway, it is not really your business. Nichola, can you please wave over a servant? If I don't eat something soon I will be face down on the table."

Nichola gave a small wave to the servant closest to them whose eyes were settled on a fixed point in the distance.

"Oh, it's useless, he doesn't see you. I'll try waving my diamond hand."

She half stood and waved her hand so her diamond-encrusted fingers caught the light. In seconds a servant was standing to attention at her side.

"Madam, may I be of service?"

"Yes, and I wish you had been of service some time ago. I'd like to know how long I must wait for the first dish to arrive?"

"I'm terribly sorry, Madam, but the fire is too low in the kitchen and we are awaiting more firewood. The platters should be served shortly."

"I beg your pardon, did you say shortly? That is simply unacceptable. If I don't eat something immediately I will have a fainting spell. I'm seventy years old. You must do something."

The young servant pushed a stray hair behind his ear and his cheeks flushed. He stammered.

"I do understand, Madam. Would a plate of goat's cheese with fennel help? I saw some in the kitchen."

She sighed. "Well, it does sound quite rustic but I suppose it will have to do. Thank you."

He bowed his head and scurried away. Giulia was in awe. In her family, servants were treated as near equals. To wield power over others was not something she had been taught. She wondered if she would be expected to learn this skill when she married Nichola.

Signora Testoni received her dish of goat's cheese. She ate with delicate intensity, savouring each mouthful. Giulia felt awkward and tried to follow Nichola's conversation with his father. They were discussing their latest hunting expedition. There seemed to be some contention as to who was first to arrive at the kill. They had followed their pack of hounds for hours, the servants sending out smoke and shouting. In the end, Nichola conceded his father had beaten him to it by some minutes. They then dispatched the pigs and deer at their leisure. The idea of a killing spree sickened her, particularly as she was about to consume a meal. Gianni chimed in and declared they had arrived at the same time. Then, losing interest, he turned back to Violetta, kissing the inside of her wrist.

Without warning, the Conte broke off from the conversation and smacked his palm three times on the tabletop. The babble of conversation came to a halt and all heads swivelled towards him. He stood and held his wine glass aloft.

"Good evening and welcome to Palazzo Ducal. As you are well aware, we are here to celebrate the birthday of my eldest son, Gianni. If you would all please stand, and raise your glasses in a toast."

There was a shuffling and groan of chairs scraping backwards as everyone rose.

"Gianni, you're an excellent son and member of this community. Your mother and I are extremely proud. Happy Birthday!"

"Hear, hear," bellowed an elderly man at the far end of the table.

"A fine young man," added Zia Testoni.

"Salute!"

A pure bell-like sound of many notes rang out as the guests reached over the table to touch their glasses.

Gianni rose from his chair, swallowed and smiled, his gaze sweeping the length of the table.

"Thank you all for coming this evening. I'm very fortunate so many people wish to mark my birthday in such a grand fashion. Thank you, Papa, for insisting on a banquet, I do feel very special. I would also like to take the opportunity to make an announcement."

At this, there was a mass intake of breath.

"I have asked Signorina Violetta Bonacci to be my wife, and thankfully, she has accepted. I would like to propose another toast to our impending nuptials."

"Mother of God," exclaimed Zia Testoni. "I am surely going to have a heart attack! Too much excitement for an old lady."

The women squealed with delight and the men within Gianni's vicinity clapped him on the back. The noise level rose to a fever pitch. The song of clinking glasses resumed beneath the hubbub.

When the noise died down, Nichola leaned towards her and whispered, his cheek brushing against hers.

"Imagine if I announced our engagement now—all the oldies would have a fit."

She giggled, her spine tingling at the closeness of him.

As if reading their minds, Giorgio raised his glass and voice.

"I wonder who will be next? Perhaps a relative of Gianni's?"

Nichola responded to the whispers and guffaws by snapping his fingers at the daydreaming servant. He appeared unruffled, and gave Giulia's thigh a squeeze. She interpreted this as: they are right, but we must wait our turn.

"Excuse me, but are the fires stoked yet? I'm famished. Can you bring out some bread at least?"

"I do believe the soup is about to be served, Signor Nichola. Just a moment and I will check for you."

He made for the door just as a waft of porcini mushrooms met Giulia's nose, and a line of servants entered bearing steaming trays of soup. She realized she was weak with hunger. The gold-rimmed plate was placed before her and she found it a challenge to wait until everyone was served. Her hand lingered on her spoon, ready for action.

Nichola noticed her eagerness and smiled.

"A woman with a healthy appetite. Some say it's a sign of other things."

She gave him an indignant shove under the table. "Honestly, must you insist on being so crude? Save those comments for your cronies, Giorgio and Matteo."

"Giorgio would appreciate it but not Matteo, he's a prude."

"Is that so? Be silent now. I must eat."

The final guest was served and she immersed her spoon in the thick soup. Scented plumes of steam curled towards the ceiling as she swallowed her first mouthful. The delicate flavour of the mushrooms was balanced with tarragon and oregano. She decided it was the best mushroom soup she had tasted and consumed the entire bowl within minutes. Nichola watched in astonishment.

"If the theory is true, then I would like to take you back to the stables later this evening. You are a marvel."

She rolled her eyes and whispered in his ear. "The theory is male gossip. I'm simply hungry, that's all. And furthermore, as your betrothed, I will not be going anywhere near your stables before our wedding. Now eat your soup before it gets cold. It's delicious."

Pheasant with root vegetables and creamy baked potato followed the soup—the dishes were perfectly seasoned. Giulia consumed them with rapid enthusiasm. She wondered if Nichola ate this well all the time. Zia Testoni raised an eyebrow, as did Nichola's mother. The latter asked.

"Does your family not feed you? You poor waif. Visit us more often and you will become accustomed to having your fill. Perhaps it will slow you down somewhat. What's your name, child?"

Nichola responded for her. "Mama, this is Giulia di Benevento. Giulia, may I present my mother, Contessa Valperga. You should be pleased to make the acquaintance of someone who enjoys cuisine as much as you. Luckily for her, it doesn't show on her figure."

Ilaria ignored the dig. She stared at Giulia for a long minute, causing her to fidget with her napkin and drop her gaze.

"Di Benevento. Ah yes, I met your mother once; she was very lovely. You resemble her."

A girlish smile spread on her face, and Giulia saw a remnant of past beauty.

"Oh really? What was she like? My father has told me she liked to talk."

The older woman smiled. "He's right about that." She took a small mouthful of her pheasant and chewed with care. "She spoke to me about many things. She was just married and was enjoying going to the market without covering her face. Nature was another thing—she was always going for long walks in the mountains, picking armloads of flowers. I remember she offered to bring some flowers to the palazzo. A sweet girl, but also strong natured. I'm sure she was not pushed around. It was scarcely a year later that I heard of her passing. Terribly sad. Please, eat some more, it is very good."

Giulia was grateful for the description of her mother. Whenever she heard about her she was greedy for more. It never seemed enough. It was always a matter of viewing her through the prism of other peoples' perceptions. Then joining the pieces together to form an impression. She would never know her scent, the sound of her laughter, or the warmth of her voice.

Most of the guests had finished their main course. There followed a selection of savoury dishes—crisp cheese-filled pastries, spiced boiled eggs, steamed asparagus with parmesan. Giulia was amazed by the variety of ingredients and spices and tried everything, despite her hunger having dissipated.

Many of the guests had swapped seats in order to catch up with friends. Nichola stayed by her side but looked pleased when Giorgio made his way over.

"Well, well, aren't you the lovebirds? I've heard about you but we've not met. I'm Giorgio Rinaldi."

He was almost as handsome as Nichola, but without the same polish. The son of a merchant, he had spent his childhood in Venice. His wavy hair was jet black and reached his shoulders.

"Delighted to meet you," she smiled, turning in her chair.

Nichola sighed. "Giorgio is a terrible flirt, do forgive him. I am sure he practices in front of the mirror. In fact, I caught him trying out facial expressions once."

Giorgio looked stricken. "Don't condemn me before I've even begun. The facial expressions were due to a part in the town play, during the festival. And I only flirt with the prettiest girls as it would be an insult not to. My friend, she is ravishing. So, I will have to oblige."

He pulled over a chair and sat next to them. "Tell me about your father. I have heard he is a master of fortune telling. I think I may need to consult him soon. My father wants me to join him in his business and I have other ideas. I need a fresh slant on things. Perhaps I should be stealing you from Nichola before it's too late?"

"Smooth, Giorgio, very smooth. I must start taking pointers from you." Nichola shook his head.

"Well, I had to work it in somehow, otherwise my reputation would be ruined."

Giulia ignored both the flirtation and Nichola's response. "My father is a complex man. What is it you would like to know about him?"

"Is it possible to have any secrets from him?"

"Not really. But we are very close so I don't mind."

∞

Whilst Giulia conversed with his friend, Nichola turned to see his Uncle Domenico at his shoulder. He had made his approach by stealth, giving him a fright. He was a grave and pious man, determined to make his mark working for the community. His bald head shone in the candlelight and his chin was spiked with grey stubble. His slate-coloured eyes were bulbous and lined with dark circles. His mother was assiduous in her avoidance of him, calling him a self-righteous bore.

"Good evening, Dom, I trust you are enjoying yourself?"

"I would if indigestion had not set my belly on fire. A spectacular night though, to be sure. You have a lady here I see, good for you."

"The last time we met you were a guild member. Is that still keeping you busy?"

"I'm afraid not. The disputes between the members were driving me to distraction. I've taken over the administration of the asylum. It's been six months now and it's going as well as can be expected. I feel I'm making a difference to the poor souls."

"That sounds like a challenging post. Do you think it's better for them to be at the asylum?"

Domenico regarded him as if he were a potential candidate. "Nichola, are you really that ignorant? They are tormented by the devil and must be kept in a controlled environment. They are a danger to both themselves and others. Depending on the level of disturbance, we keep them in their beds or tie them up. They are fed at regular intervals and the nuns come and read them tracts of the Bible."

"It's very noble of you to take the position. Do you ever feel as if they might attack you?"

"Yes, at times. I wear a metal vest with the worst ones so I can't feel their punches. I do not think I'm noble, merely a humble servant of God. One of his many soldiers. When I must correct the worst cases, I say the catechism and it sanctifies the punishment."

Nichola grimaced. "What, may I ask, is the punishment?"

Domenico sighed and scratched the corner of his eye. He wore a dour black frock coat that resembled a priest's habit.

"We have a number of things at our disposal. The spiked mask, the stretching ropes, the small black room. All effective in most cases."

"I'm glad to hear it." Nichola shifted on his feet, peering over his uncle's shoulder to check on his betrothed.

∞

Giulia was hearing about several generations of the Testoni family, from which Ilaria had descended. Zia Testoni enjoyed having a captive audience. It had begun with her great-grandfather, Giuseppe, who imported fabric, spices and other goods from the Far East. They were transported all over Italy for consumption by the upper classes. These days, their fortunes meant they no longer needed to be enterprising. When the Testoni family joined with the Valpergas, news of their combined wealth travelled as far as Rome. As a result, all manner of salesmen, shysters, and conmen had appeared at the gates of the Palazzo Ducal. All were deflected by expert butlers.

"Ilaria was a beauty in her day, she still has lovely bones, don't you think? She had many suitors but none were as charming as the Conte. He rode a white stallion right up to the copper-plated doors of her father's palazzo in Urbino. He wore a red cloak, which he swished around him each time he departed. It almost makes me swoon to remember. I was always visiting her mother, so I often saw him come and go. When I look at your Nichola, it takes me back. He is every bit as dashing as his Papa. Well, you must also know there is a tendency for plumpness on the Testoni side. Luckily, I have avoided it, but I must always watch what I eat."

"Zia Carlotta! Are you boring Giulia to death? Really, she does not need to know every detail about our family. Goodness, I suppose you'll be onto the Valpergas next. I've come to rescue you."

Zia Testoni straightened her spine with indignation. "I've been doing no such thing. She is interested in you, and therefore I'm confident she would be interested in your family. She is a woman, and women like to know background information. Am I not right, dear girl?"

"She's right, Nichola. I am interested. I'm afraid my family history is not nearly as colourful, nor as glamorous."

He touched his great aunt's sinewy hand as he sat down. "I'm sorry Zia, you really are an expert on our history. We must get you to write it all down one of these days."

The dessert was served. It was a mascarpone confection with layers of sponge cake, dusted with icing sugar. Trays of different flavoured chocolates were placed down the length of the table. Giulia had never eaten such a large supper. She knew she had consumed more than enough, but the cake looked enticing. In the end she took two mouthfuls, which she savoured for as long as possible. Nichola was bemused by her absorption.

"I'm getting jealous of your meal. You're giving it more attention than me. Do I need to be naughty again?"

"I'm all yours, I can't eat any more. This is the best meal I have ever had. What happens now?"

"There are musicians in the ballroom. We will dance for a while, then the celebrations will finish around midnight."

Giulia twisted her napkin in her lap. The only dance she knew was the brando, which involved dancing in a circle with others. No one looked at the way you were moving, and everyone just laughed and trod on each other's feet. She was sure the upper class would perform more elaborate dances.

The Conte's chair scraping the floor as he rose was the signal for the party to move to the ballroom. "And now for the dancing!" he declared in a booming voice.

The conversations increased in volume as the guests weaved towards the ballroom. Many were unsteady on their feet and there were bursts of laughter as well as the clatter of footsteps on the marble floor.

The musicians could be heard tuning their violins and flutes so those staying to dance followed their ears. The warmth of Nichola's palm on her forearm soothed Giulia's nerves.

"I only know one dance," she whispered to him.

"What is it?"

"The brando."

"Oh. Don't worry, just follow my lead and try not to step on my feet. You have such grace that no one will notice."

She did not believe him for a second.

The Conte stood near the five musicians, smoothing his beard and waiting for everyone to file in. When they stood before him and the noise had dissipated, he spoke.

"This evening we will begin with the pavane. Then when you're all warmed up, we shall dance the galliard, a favourite in this family."

A single sonorous note emanated from a flute before being joined by the staccato notes of three violins. The Conte took the hand of his wife and they glided onto the floor, their spines straight. Their relaxed manner showed they were used to being watched.

Giulia observed them from the sidelines. Every few minutes, other couples joined them. There seemed to be a protocol for the order in which people started to dance. The senior members were first, followed by the middle-aged, then the young.

Nichola gave her a pointed look and took her hand, leading her towards the centre of the parquetry floor. She was aghast; from the middle, everyone would witness her ineptitude. With great concentration, she held Nichola's hand as he guided her through the rapid steps. The music was fast, almost frantic, and she struggled to keep up. She could feel his eyes seeking out hers but was unable to meet them, as the effort of moving her feet at such a pace meant she had to look down. The vertiginous heels of her satin shoes made it even more difficult.

By some miracle, she managed to stay upright and the musicians reached their finale. The head violinist stood to perform the final notes as a riotous solo. Applause broke out and she grinned with relief at Nichola. She could feel the approving looks of the guests surrounding her. They murmured in surprise. The pavane took a great deal of practice and she had done well for a first-timer.

The effort had exhausted her. Leaning her head close to Nichola, she whispered that she wished to stand aside for the next dance. He nodded and followed her to the far wall, where gilt chairs had been placed for weary dancers.

The dancing continued for another hour. After encouraging Nichola back to the floor, she was beckoned over by Alessia and her friends. She did not contribute much to their discussion about weddings. There had only been one occasion where she had attended one. Listening to them describe the lavish nuptials of several of their relatives, she realized the one she had attended was akin to a small garden party.

The Conte thanked the musicians and guests before bidding them good night. Once he had left, everyone darted around kissing each other on both cheeks, promising to meet again soon.

Noticing her drooping shoulders, Nichola spared her the endless goodbyes and spirited her towards the entrance hall and imposing doors. Her capelet was placed around her shoulders and she was wished good night by several of the butlers. A footman helped her into the waiting carriage. She allowed herself to relax back into the padded seat and gave Nichola a wan smile.

"Thank you for this evening. I enjoyed it all so much."

"A pleasure. I will pass on your thanks and goodbyes to Gianni."

She was stricken. "Oh, how rude of me, I should have said goodbye to him, and to your parents! They will think I have terrible manners."

"Not at all. I will tell them how the pavane was tiring for you, and that your shoes made it difficult to walk, making goodbyes impossible."

"Thank you. You're very kind."

They were silent for the rest of the journey. Giulia had achieved the performance of her lifetime and there was no conversation left in her. Nichola understood and let her rest.

She allowed him a chaste kiss, holding her body away so he would not take liberties with her thighs. Although she enjoyed his touch, she did not want him to think he could do as he pleased.

"I'll see you soon."

"Giulia?"

"Yes?"

"You were incredible tonight. Everyone was so impressed with you. Tomorrow, the whole of Pesaro will know of your success. Have some rest now."

"I think you're biased. I was adequate and avoided embarrassment. Good night."

"Good night."

The footman opened the carriage door and took her hand to help her down. He tipped his hat, wished her good night and clambered up to his seat at the front. Something unintelligible was said to the horses before he cracked his whip through the air and struck their flanks. She listened to the sound of their hooves on the cobblestones as they clipped away at a steady pace. She was home.

Agnese sat on a ladder-back chair in the hallway. Her head was tipped to one side and she snored with a slight whistle. Her hands were folded over her starched apron. She had waited for her mistress, well past her bedtime. Giulia shook her arm and she sprang to life, confusion etched around her eyes.

"Dear Giulia, you're back! How was it, child?"

"Agnese, it was wonderful. Thank you. Go to sleep now and I'll tell you about it at breakfast."

CHAPTER 22

By the time Giulia had eaten her strawberries and sipped her tea, she knew about the gemstones. Savinus had asked her about her night, with less eagerness than Agnese. The latter stood by the table, her eyes wide as she listened to the description of the palazzo and the finery of the nobles. Wiping a tear from the corner of her eye she declared, "I knew you would charm them all. Brains and beauty, not many girls have those two things together. A triumph! Have some bread with your strawberries, I made it this morning."

Savinus sat and ate without enjoyment. He looked at her and sent her images of what had happened. He did not wish to spoil her happiness, but thought she should be armed with knowledge. She dropped her fork and returned his look, her eyes a darker shade of green and her mouth set in a thin line.

I don't believe you. It must have been a misunderstanding.

His shoulders drooped and he stopped eating.

It was nothing of the sort. There is no one else who could have put the gems in his pocket. Besides, he's shown nothing but dislike for Antonius, right from the start. He wishes to discredit him so he may be the primary apprentice.

I think it's possible Antonius took them. Perhaps his family cannot eat at the moment, they could be desperate. I don't want to hear about it, Papa. I'm going to marry Nichola.

He stiffened and sat up in his chair, his mouth agape. In his agitation, he knocked over a glass of water. Agnese ran to fetch a cloth and mopped up the mess, clucking her tongue.

"Oh dear, what a mess. It must be your eyes, Signor."

Recovering his composure, he met her gaze.

You will need my permission.

How can you refuse? The Conte is your most important client. To refuse would cost you everything.

He did not have an answer and this made him furious. He slapped his napkin on the table and rose. She noticed a tremor in his hand as he turned towards his workroom, muttering under his breath.

Agnese was accustomed to their silent conversations. She frowned and pressed her cloth to the flooded table.

"What in the world were you talking about, Miss?"

"Never mind, Agnese. He'll calm down soon."

∞

He did not. Pacing the workroom, he ran his fingers through his hair and felt the thudding of his heart. His breath was shallow and he knew he would be unable to work. She was right. A proposal from the Valpergas would not, could not be turned down. There was a long history. A staggering amount of money had changed hands. He was in a tight corner of his own making. He could only hope Nichola's true nature would reveal itself to her before it was too late.

∞

Antonius arrived at ten o'clock. Piero had suffered another beating and he had been called home for the night. His brother was in pain and he held him close, whispering to him and stroking his head. Sleep was impossible.

With stinging eyes, he greeted Savinus, noticing his pallor and gruff voice.

The older man ushered him into the workroom, closing the door behind them. They sat down on the ladder-back chairs facing the fire.

172

"Are you aware Nichola won't be coming for a week? After the incident the other day I needed some distance from him."

"Yes, I heard you say that."

"I'm sorry it happened. How do you feel about it?"

"I'm not surprised. He has hated me from the start. If anything, it was ill-considered given you can read minds. It was hardly going to escape you that the gems were planted."

"Yes, for an intelligent boy he can be remarkably stupid. Now, we have more important things to discuss. His absence means I can share my findings with you. Since Lorenzo di Montefiore visited, I have been experimenting with some methods to access the First Matter. It involves solitary time, communion with the spirit guides, and purification. I've actually succeeded in changing my shape to that of an eagle. I want to use this time to teach you these methods. The guides have warned of difficult times ahead and shapeshifting will be useful."

Antonius frowned. "What do they mean by difficult times?"

"Don't concern yourself with that now. All I know is the troubles stem from our friend Nichola. The important thing is to be prepared. You must not eat or drink ale for two days. For the next two nights, spend half an hour being still in your mind and try and connect with the guides. Ask them to assist you with changing form. When you return on Thursday morning, we will attempt to shapeshift together."

"Is there a ritual first?"

"Yes, it involves fire and incantation. You must also decide what form to take. A bird of some kind is useful, due to its ability to fly and navigate small spaces. It's up to you."

Antonius smiled. "I'm honoured, Signor, that you think I'm ready for the secret practices."

The seer shrugged and spread his weathered fingers wide, palms facing upwards. "I don't wish to take the wind from your sails, young man. It's merely the taking of an opportunity when it presents itself. Whether you're ready or not, it is time."

∞

A statue of Apollo, god of the sun, crowned the fountain in the piazza. He was lithe and muscular, his graceful form shaped from Carrera marble. In one hand he held the sun, in the other a small harp. From his circular base the water flowed into a low trough, filled with coins. Nichola sat on the edge, trying to ignore the small boys daring each other to jump in. He was filled with blackness. Not even thoughts of Giulia could lift his mood. No one in his family had ever been banished. They were feted and celebrated, not shunned. He imagined Savinus and Antonius laughing about his foolishness, pleased to be free of him. He kicked the base of the fountain with his heel, then suppressed a yelp of pain.

One of the boys sidled up to him. He was short for his age with a smattering of freckles across his wide nose. Shuffling on his feet, he cleared his throat.

"Is that rabbit fur on your cape?"

"No, it's the fur from my dog. He was barking too much, so I clubbed him."

The boy gasped. "Do nobles club their dogs?"

"Nobles do whatever they like. Now leave me alone."

Chastened, the boy slunk back to his friends, who had managed to collect several coins from the bottom of the fountain. Nichola's thoughts returned to Antonius. The image of him sitting beside Savinus, basking in his attention, flitted into his mind. They were hunched over an enormous book. He knew his limited psychic powers had given him one meagre insight. It was enough to cause a wave of nausea.

A boy rounded the corner of the piazza, chasing a ball. He was heavyset, with thin blond hair and bulbous cheeks. He half-ran, half-walked as if he thought the ball had a mind and would wait for him. It was Piero. Nichola watched him, noticing the way his limbs seemed to have a ten-second delay before responding to his brain. The boy had not seen him, but it was only a matter of time. It was a gift. He rose from the fountain and walked over. At his feet lay the cloth ball, striped with lurid colours. He scooped it up and tossed it from hand to hand. Piero looked startled, then reached out with sausage fingers.

"Mine," he said in a soft voice. Nichola looked over his head and flung the ball high into the air before catching it.

"Mine," he said again, with more urgency.

Nichola walked backwards, holding the ball high over his head, smiling. His mood was lifting.

"It's my ball now, go home to your Mama."

Piero reddened and panted, his eyes narrowing.

"Give it! My ball, mine!"

Nichola shook his head. "No moron, it's mine now. Go home."

"No home! My ball, need it now!"

Nichola held the ball out, his eyes contemptuous.

"Take it then."

Piero smiled and reached forward. Just as his fingers had almost closed around the ball, Nichola whisked it above his head again.

"Like I said before, go home."

He gave the boy a shove. It was too much for Piero. He gave an anguished cry and looked up at his persecutor. The ball was still held aloft. His gaze then fell on Nichola's face, filled with satisfaction and malice. Fury gripped him and his body took over from his impotent brain. He charged Nichola with all his strength, knocking him to the ground and pummelling him with his fists.

Nichola shielded his face with his hands, then seized the boy by the wrists and pushed him off. He stood over him, and dusted himself down.

"Calm down idiot, I just wanted a turn of playing with your ball."

He glanced around and was pleased to see a small crowd had formed.

"Are you all right, Signor?" Several women fussed around him, their brows knotted.

His expression was perplexed. "I'm not sure how it happened. One minute I was standing here, and the next I was being charged by this young bull."

"Scandalous."

"The Conte's son, too. Unacceptable behaviour. Are you injured?"

"Thank you for your concern, but I'm fine. The boy may need to be accompanied home, though. I believe he's a bit simple."

"Yes, Signor, you're right. You poor thing, being attacked."

His face was solemn as he walked away, averting his eyes from the sight of Piero. He sat on the cobblestones, keening and swaying, his face screwed up in pain.

As he turned the corner, he allowed a smile to emerge.

In the piazza, a few feet away from the crowd stood Agnese. She blinked away tears, and waited for the crowd to disperse. On her way to the market, the sight of a noble playing with a ball had been enough to stop her in her tracks. Making her way towards Piero, she crouched down and stroked his hair.

"You're Fiora's boy, is that right? You are safe now. Come on, give me your hand and I'll help you up."

CHAPTER 23

It was icy in the chapel that morning. The window at the front would not close, and despite numerous requests, none of the servants had arrived to repair it. Cardinal Costa wrapped his cloak around his shoulders and lit the candles on the altar table. Stained-glass windows cast vivid patterns on the tiled floor. His nephew was quiet and withdrawn as he took his place beside him for the mass. Although Matteo was never at ease, his uncle had noticed an increase in his anxiety over the past weeks. He ate even less than usual and would not meet his eyes when he spoke.

Once the incense was lit, it was time to begin.

"The grace of our Lord Jesus Christ and the love of God and the fellowship of the Holy Spirit be with you."

"And also with you," said Matteo, crossing himself whilst trying to stop his teeth from chattering. His breath emerged as a fog.

The mass progressed slowly. Matteo was too distracted by the cold to draw comfort from the ritual—the flickering candles, the waft of incense into his nose, and the calm reverence of the words. He rubbed his arms with stiff hands when his uncle was not looking and was relieved when they came to the penitential rite, signaling they were halfway through. The words fell from his lips without effort, as he had said them since he was a small boy.

"I confess to almighty God, and to you, my brothers and sisters, that I have sinned through my own fault, in my thoughts and in my words, in what I have done, and in what I have failed to do, and I ask blessed Mary, ever virgin, all the angels and saints, to pray for me to the Lord, our God."

The Cardinal nodded with approval at his pious tone of voice.

"May almighty God have mercy on us, forgive us our sins, and bring us to everlasting life."

"Amen."

After the communion and concluding rite, they strolled back to the villa in silence. Matteo was accustomed to this. His uncle liked to "commune with spirit" for at least ten minutes after the mass. To Matteo's relief, the villa was warm as the servants were instructed to light the fires at dawn. His uncle's quarters were at the side of the main villa. The church gave him a generous stipend every year. This was reflected in the opulence of his rooms, furnished with velvet armchairs and paintings of various saints. Matteo enjoyed the deep purple colour of the gilt-legged furniture and the sweet aroma of cut flowers.

In front of the crackling fire they sipped mead brought by Franco, the manservant sent by the Vatican to look after the Cardinal. He was expected to return to Rome several times a year, and Franco always accompanied him. Franco had a serious face, as chiselled and beautiful as a male Madonna.

The Cardinal stared for a long time at the curls of steam rising from his mead.

"What's troubling you? You haven't been yourself for weeks."

Matteo was relieved his uncle had noticed his suffering and answered in a rush, his voice agitated.

"It is Nichola, Zio. He is mixed up with the seer, Signor di Benevento. From what he has told me, the old man engages in evil practices."

The Cardinal frowned. "What sort of practices, dear boy?"

"Changing his form to that of a bird."

His uncle coughed, choking on his mead.

"A bird? Goodness, that sounds like the work of Satan. Has he tried any of these things?"

"No, he was frightened by them. It's the seer and his friend from Genoa, I don't remember his name, but he's quite well known."

"Would it be Lorenzo di Montefiore?"

"Yes! How did you know Zio?"

"The Vatican keeps me informed about a number of things. Heretics are a problem I like to keep in touch with. Thank you for telling me, I shall ask some questions and see what I can do about it. It looks like you have been anxious, it's good you have unburdened yourself."

"Thank you, Zio. I do feel better. Ever since Nichola told me I have had pains in my stomach and can't sleep at night."

"It's true, just hearing about the work of Satan can have an adverse effect on one's constitution. I feel a little queasy myself. Finish your mead and go and check on your mother. She was upset this morning, I believe."

Matteo's father had died some years earlier after falling from his horse. His mother had never emerged from mourning and was incapable of leaving the villa. Even the sight of a crowd was enough to send her into a panic. She wore a long black chiffon veil at all times, and survived on a pear and two spoonfuls of polenta each day.

After one year of intense mourning, it was obvious to his relatives she was incapable of giving Matteo the attention he needed. He had become ill and depressed, and was being looked after by a reluctant maid. A request was made to his uncle in Rome for him to come to Pesaro and live at the villa. To everyone's relief he accepted, on the condition he receive a small allowance from the family estate in addition to the stipend he collected from the church.

They had become close and were on equal footing in their devotion to God.

After Matteo had left his quarters, the Cardinal sat at his desk and composed a letter. He addressed it to the head of the Inquiry, Monsignor Tomas di Ignacio, whom he had met the previous spring. He was sure that, as a respected practitioner, the Signor would not be tortured, only warned against such practices. If it became apparent he was continuing his heresy, then more invasive measures would need to be applied.

∞

It was difficult for them to get started that morning. Twice, Nichola had come to the door and been told by an embarrassed Agnese to go away. When he returned just before lunch, Savinus confronted him.

"Young man, you must desist from this behaviour. I've made it clear you are not to return until next week. If you continue to disobey me, I will have to extend it to the week after."

"Signor, surely as your daughter is betrothed to me, I may enter, at the very least to see her?"

"That in itself is an outrage. At what point did you come to me to ask for her hand?"

He dropped his gaze to his feet and shuffled for a moment. A muscle in his jaw tightened.

"I'm sorry, Signor. You're right to be angry. I was swept away by the moment, seeing her there in the carriage looking so lovely. It does not make the proposal any less serious, and I ask you now—do you object to her marrying me?"

Savinus could not meet his eyes. He stared at a fixed point, somewhere behind Nichola's ear.

"If my daughter is happy, then I am happy. I give my permission."

He winced and clutched his chest with one hand as he spoke.

Nichola smiled with relief. "That's wonderful, Signor. Is she here? I would love to see her."

The scent of lilies announced her presence as she crept up behind her father.

"Here I am. Hello, Nichola."

Nichola blushed at the sight of her, his face lighting up with pleasure.

"Signor, I know I am not allowed past the door. But could I perhaps take Giulia for a stroll?"

Savinus sighed. "If you must. But please be back soon. She is to accompany Agnese to the market before lunch."

He watched them walk up the path, arms intertwined. *I am too old for this,* he thought. *Carmen, I need you. What am I meant to do here?*

∞

Antonius was watching from behind a pillar in the hallway. He now knew about the engagement. It was hard to believe Giulia still loved Nichola, even after finding out about the gemstones. Only one conclusion could be drawn—she thought less of him than a stranger. A pain thrummed behind his temples. Nichola's attractiveness and riches had rendered him invisible to her. He felt the weight of his family's low status like a suit of armour, dragging him into apathy. There was only one solution—to immerse himself in learning.

"Signor, I'm sorry about what's happening. I know you are upset." He did not add that he was more upset. "But I think we must get back to work. We have a lot to do before he comes back."

"As always, you're right, young man. Work will be our salvation. Now, have you been fasting and being quiet in your mind like I advised?"

"Yes, Signor. When I smell food I start foaming at the mouth like a crazed animal. And my mind feels as clear as a church bell."

Savinus chuckled; it sounded like a dry cough. "Good, good. To the workroom, then."

They sat down at the long workbench with the vials, alembics, and dust-covered stacks of books. Savinus stared out of the window for a minute, trying to collect his thoughts.

"Did you contact the spirit guides as I asked?"

"I did, Signor. I told Arion I was nervous about changing form."

"Why are you nervous?"

"I'm worried I'll not be able to change back to human form. That I'll be trapped as a bird."

He shook his head. "That won't happen. It's impossible for the elements of our human form to stay in the bird shape for more than a few hours at a time. Did you decide what sort of bird you would like to be?"

"A starling. They are quick and don't take up too much space."

"Very good. I think you've chosen well. Before we begin, I need to explain some more concepts to you. As you may have noticed, in my alchemical work, I do not utilize the alembics very often. I observe the alchemical processes with my higher powers of perception —in nature. The First Matter is an all-pervading element, which flows, has currents and presents itself to the physical eye as the sun and the moon. In order to change our shape we must have the sun or moon on us and we must light a fire. Fire is the key that locks and opens; it reveals whatever is hidden. It is the primal matter. Am I making sense to you?"

"I think so. So how do we begin?"

"We must perform the ritual in the courtyard, so the sun can fall on our faces. We burn salt, the root of water, sulphur, the root of fire, and mercury, the root of air. These are the primary aspects and facilitate our connection with the First Matter. You saw Lorenzo de Montefiori perform a shorter version of this ritual when he visited us, without the fire. At least you will have some familiarity."

His mentor rose and walked towards the courtyard where a large fire had been lit in a brazier. He smiled at Antonius.

"Don't be afraid. Just follow my lead and we can fly together. As rituals go it's quite short—the power is in the elements and the intention."

The sun was high and unobscured by cloud. For a winter's day, it was warm. Its position was ideal.

He chanted in the ritual language. It was a brief invocation, charging the space with the atmosphere Antonius remembered from other rituals. It was as if the courtyard had been wiped clean of impurities and hummed with lightness and warmth.

"Repeat after me, I ask the spirit guides to help me change shape, *delios, deleus et delit.*"

"I ask the spirit guides to help me change shape, *delios, deleus, et delit.*"

"I ask that they protect me whilst I am in unfamiliar form, that negative forces cannot harm me."

Antonius repeated the words. The flames danced and flickered as Savinus withdrew several packages from the folds of his robe. He scattered the sulphur, mercury, and salt into the flames, which popped and sparked in response.

"I give mercury, the root of air, salt, the root of water and sulphur the root of fire. May they conjoin to form the First Matter—the great oneness which transforms all."

The fire rose higher, and the heat burned Antonius's cheeks. The smoke caught in the back of his throat, and he coughed. He was transfixed by the colours of the flames—amber, red, and vibrant blue. At the same time, he could feel the sun's rays on his face, and he looked into the sky. It shimmered with heat from the fire at eye level then flattened to a dense blue, endless and calm.

"Change me," intoned Savinus, opening his arms wide and tipping back his head to look above.

"Change me," repeated Antonius, keeping his gaze fixed on the heavens.

CHAPTER 24

At first nothing happened. They continued to gaze upwards and wait. Antonius felt a tingling sensation in his hands and feet and a wave of cool energy swept through his body. Looking down, he saw he was translucent, the image of his body rippled and swayed. He noticed Savinus was the same, as if he were viewing him through water. The next moment, his viewpoint was altogether different. He was almost level with the flagstones and his sight was muted, as if tinted with grey. Across from him stood an eagle, resplendent with glossy black wings, white head, and a deep yellow beak. It cocked its head and adjusted its wings before speaking.

It's a pity you can't see yourself—you make a very handsome starling. Your colourings are black, purple and emerald green. How does it feel to have changed so much?

Very strange. Wings feel rather odd, don't they? How do we use them?

As you would expect, you wave them up and down and jump off. Are you ready to try?

I suppose so. Is Arion watching this? I'm sure I will embarrass myself.

Savinus laughed. It was discomfiting to hear his voice in his head and see an eagle in his place. It did not feel real and his mind found it hard to accept.

He's here, yes. Just to ensure our safety. You will not see him. Let's go then—I have something I need to show you.

Antonius, the starling, was almost blown backwards by the air generated from Savinus, the eagle's, wings. When he stretched them out they were vast and intimidating. He was hovering in the air before Antonius had worked out how to extend his small wings.

Don't think so much; just beat them up and down.

It's all right for you; your wings are much bigger.

You're being churlish. Now hurry up, we may not have much time.

He beat his wings as hard as he could, to no avail. The flagstones were as close as ever and he was sure he looked foolish to his mentor.

He made a silent plea to Arion to lift him into the air. Within seconds, a gust of wind whipped through the courtyard under his wings and he was aloft, as high as the wall enclosing the villa. He discovered it was not necessary to beat his wings. All he had to do was angle his small body to catch the breeze, keeping them stretched out.

Well done, I knew you could do it. Perhaps you should have chosen a larger species, it certainly helps with flying. Follow me, we'll go and look at the town. It's fascinating from the air.

Being in the air was astounding. He could feel different currents supporting him, ready to carry him in any direction he chose. There were moments when he had to use his wings, but more often he floated.

Savinus guided him towards the centre of town and they hovered above, observing the strange spectacle of Pesaro in miniature. Antonius felt dizzy with the shock of flight, his brain unable to accept he was not about to plummet to the ground.

The market is just below; can you see the striped awnings? To the left you can see the road leading to the wheat fields, then the palazzo. I had a vision last night that I needed to show you the mental asylum. It's at the base of the mountains, to the east, and has a grey-tiled roof. Can you see it? It's a large building.

Yes, I think so. Is it set apart a little, with a small road leading up?

Yes, that's right. We will come back for a closer look.

My villa has an orange-tiled roof and is to the right of the market; see if you can locate that too.

Next to the well? There it is.

Good. Have you seen enough? Follow me and we will go further. Beyond the mountains, the landscape is very beautiful. In some fields, the lupines have started to come out. This way. Flap a little, let the current carry you, then flap again.

He was right. Once they cleared the snow-capped mountains, the fields were dotted with blue and pink lupines. He saw a lithe brown animal dart into the surrounding forest. He stretched his wings as far as they could go and allowed the air to carry him.

A flock of geese shared the current with them, eyeing them as if they suspected something was amiss. Their brown wings were dusted with green and gold and their call was urgent and incomprehensible. They arced away, joining a different path of air.

Savinus's laughter filled his mind. *They were trying to communicate with us, but my skills don't run to animal languages. I think we were quite disturbing to them, birds unable to speak.*

Signor, I'm finding it hard enough to adjust to flying. If I were communing with geese as well, it would all be too much for me.

You're right. One thing at a time.

At such a height, Antonius could feel the heat of the sun on his back, unobscured by clouds. Every time he looked to the side, he felt a jolt to see his wings stretched out. Below them, fields of flowers changed to wheat fields and then forest, criss-crossed by ribbons of silver streams. The wind rippled the tops of the trees, like a wave moving across a body of water. The clouds were sparse and low.

It was quiet. The air stream buffeted them and they could hear a low whoosh as it passed. Antonius was filled with lightness and a strange joy to share this experience with his mentor. He did not want to speak and ruin the peace.

The current took them on a diagonal towards the coast, where another town came into view. *Fano,* Savinus said, his eagle's body tilting as he caught the air stream.

It appeared larger than Pesaro, laid out in a pattern like a wheel, with the cathedral in the centre. White specks of boats dotted the harbour.

You need to turn yourself, like me, or else the current will take you in the opposite direction.

Where are we headed?

Back to the mental asylum. Turn around and we will head towards Pesaro.

It was difficult to turn—the wind had picked up and seemed determined to carry him further south.

Don't stop beating your wings as you turn! There, that's right, it's just a question of the right angle.

Once he had made the turn, he was lower down and the air was still. He beat his wings in a rapid motion to remain aloft.

Startled, he spoke aloud. "Signor, where is the current? I don't know how long I can keep this up."

I think it's a bit lower. Don't panic just follow me.

He allowed himself to drop down and continued to beat his wings. To his relief, they landed on another stream. It was faster and carried them at great speed towards Pesaro.

In half the time of their journey the other way, they saw the terracotta brick cathedral of their town. Antonius stared at its bell tower. The mental asylum came into view as they flew closer to the mountains. It was a squat building of red brick, a sober construction without embellishments. Antonius wondered if the architect had been advised that decoration might incite the inmates. Narrow windows punctuated the front, like wary eyes.

Here it is. Remember it, and how to find it. I wish I could explain to you why, but the information has not come to me yet.

Yes, Signor.

It was time to return to the villa. The wind had dropped and it took all of their energy to propel themselves in the right direction. Antonius was relieved to see the high walls of the villa courtyard, and almost forgot to beat his wings. They descended onto the flagstones just as the power of the ritual was weakening.

CHAPTER 25

The spell was in the book Savinus used for the flying ritual—a book of transformations into birds, beasts, and invisibility. Antonius studied the illustration of a beast: a cobalt face with round black eyes. An inky blue torso sprouting long red wings sat upon the legs of a goat. A chuckle emerged from his throat. Glancing around, he committed the incantation to memory, along with the one for invisibility.

Antonius was tired of being a passive recipient of Nichola's hostility. As well as giving him something back, it was a good opportunity to practice his new skills. He thought about the wind caressing his wings as he flew. There would be many new experiences to come.

Ignoring stabs of guilt, he left the workroom and accomplished a solid afternoon's work with Katerina. It was a long wait before the villa was quiet. Stretched out on his straw mattress next to Luca, he tapped his fingers on the sheet. He could hear the horses settling down in the stables, Katerina putting vessels away in the storeroom, and the crunch of stones outside as a servant extinguished the torches. All that was left was Luca's snuffling and snoring. He rose and made his way to the main building.

Ignatio remained awake in the immense hallway, a security

measure against intruders. He muttered the spell for invisibility at the entrance, watching his arm disappear, then the rest of his body. It felt like water running over his limbs as they vanished.

It was important to take care with his footfalls and he walked placing his toes down on the carpet before his heels. He edged past the antique chairs and sombre portraits lining the hallway. Creeping past Ignatio, he gave him a mock salute, before continuing towards the oak door of Nichola's rooms.

With a gentle movement, he pressed down the gilt handle of the door and pushed it open, controlling it in case of a squeaking hinge.

He mouthed the words of the spell:
> "From human form I change
> With will, heart, and body
> Into a beast of wing and hoof
> *Licet mei commuto!*"

Within seconds he felt a wrenching in his chest, as if it were being split apart. His head was full of blinding light, and his legs shook with violence. Looking down he saw the brown legs of a goat, covered with coarse hair, the mottled hooves sinking into a Persian rug. He ran a hand over his chest—smooth, hairless and deep blue. His hand went to his face. It was flat, with a small mouth, but his eye sockets felt enormous. To his left was a gilt mirror, and he turned and peered at himself in the candlelight.

His face was the same blue as his torso, and his large eyes had black irises. His ape-like forehead was wide and protruded. Scarlet and orange wings hung down behind him, almost to his ankles. The feathers tickled his arms. He found he could extend them by contracting his shoulder blades. Shuddering he turned away, and tried to manoeuvre his goat legs towards the bed. They were stiff and unyielding. With difficulty, he managed to raise a leg and place a hoof onto Nichola's chest. The weight stirred him and he opened one eye. Both eyes snapped open and Nichola attempted to sit up, then fell back on his pillows as Antonius applied pressure.

His voice was hoarse. "What are you? What is it you want of me?"

"You must cease harming Antonius. If you continue your hostilities, this will be the result."

Antonius had created the image as he strolled to the villa that afternoon. It tumbled into Nichola's mind, vivid enough to place him in the nightmare.

He was seated at a wooden table, wearing a coarse brown monk's habit. The fabric prickled his skin and he scratched himself. Across from him sat his Uncle Domenico, making the sign of the cross before picking up a knife and fork. He gestured for Nichola to eat. A rotten smell drifted up his nose, and he looked down at a skinned pigeon on a clay plate. Its flesh looked flayed pink, with dots of black mould flowering at the edges. His stomach heaved and he pushed away from the table, the chair screeching on the wood floor. Understanding filled him. He was cast out and Domenico was the only person prepared to have him. Another image came. In the bedroom of the cottage, a corpulent priest pinioned him against a wall, lifting his habit and running rough hands over his body, his fish-like mouth wet against his neck. Nichola thrashed from side to side, trying to rid himself of the images, smells, and sounds. Vomit burned the back of his throat.

Antonius lifted his hoof and placed it back on the ground. He was about to speak when the wrenching sensation started in his legs. The spell was weakening and he needed to get out. White light filled his head once more and he was immobile.

He stood before Nichola, fighting back the urge to run. Their eyes locked.

Nichola swallowed and gripped the bedsheet before launching himself forward. He seized him by the collar and rammed him against the wall. His voice was low but Antonius understood every word.

"You did this—put those things in my mind. If I had a knife I would plunge it in your stomach. Come with me."

He yanked him towards the door and glancing around, saw Ignatio was not there.

"Where are we going?"

"You'll see."

They made slow progress along the hallway and outside, as Antonius elbowed his captor and kicked him in the shins. Dust billowed behind them as they scuffled. Reaching the entrance of a stone structure, Nichola opened the door with one hand.

"Stop fighting or I will take you straight to the Conte. You won't keep your job by practicing witchcraft on his son."

Antonius ceased his blows and hung his head. Nichola picked up the candle in the wall sconce and led the way down a steep granite staircase. The candlelight cast an orange glow on the walls.

Their footfalls echoed on the narrow staircase, winding down to a cavernous room. In the muted light, Antonius could see endless rows of wine barrels, stacked to the ceiling.

"Sit down. I will be locking you in here for a while. If you get thirsty, help yourself to some wine." He walked over to a barrel and pried it open with a metal rod, then pointed to a stack of wooden cups nearby.

"Quite the host." Antonius sneered.

"Mind your mouth. You're lucky to be alive after what you just did—peasant."

He spat the last word, as if it were bad food, and placed the candle in a holder on the floor.

Antonius watched him as he turned and climbed back up the stairs. He heard a key rattle in the lock.
Picking up a wooden cup, he dipped it in the barrel of wine and brought it to his mouth. An owl called out as the liquid flowed down his throat, the warmth spreading in his chest. Antonius watched the candle burn lower, casting long flickering shadows on the wall.

∞

The vision woke Savinus at dawn. Antonius, barrels towering above him, a wooden cup in his hand. Darkness. He rose and dressed, before waking Agnese and instructing her to saddle up Jocanda.

The light was still feeble as he tied up his mare at the gates. He hastened to the servants' quarters and kitchen and knocked on the mottled glass window. Katerina emerged in her lace, sleeping cap, rubbing her eyes.

They could hear singing as they came down the stairs, off-key and slurred. He was leaning against a barrel, waving his arms to the rhythm of his song. He did not seem aware of their presence until they stood before him. Katerina held the candle near his face.

Savinus held out his hand. "Get up, Antonius, I'm taking you home."

He gave a lop-sided smile, his eyes hooded, the contours of his face yellow and shadowed in the candlelight.

"I'm drunk."

"I can see that. Take my arm, for goodness sake."

CHAPTER 26

On the return journey, Antonius almost tumbled from the horse. He let go of his mentor's waist and sang, swinging his arms. Agnese rushed to the door as they arrived, helping Savinus drag him to the older man's bed. He slept for the rest of the day. The light was turning to gold as he woke and saw Savinus hunched on the edge of the bed.

He swallowed and pushed himself up, dizzy with the movement. "Sir, will you be able to forgive me? What I did was foolish." He was unable to look him in the eye and kept his gaze fixed on the wool blanket.

A long silence followed. "Antonius, I have taken you into my home, into my trust, and shared the wisdom of generations of seers. You have been privileged. I'm disappointed you have gone behind my back; using an incantation I've not yet taught you. I understand you were excited after we went flying and it gave you the confidence to experiment. However, you must take things slowly, and use your powers for good. If Nichola locked you in the cellar, you must have frightened him. This is a misuse of power. You will not be banished, but I must caution you, if anything like this happens again, I may not be as lenient."

"Thank you, sir. I am most grateful."

∞

The engagement party was scheduled for the middle of February. Giulia had been riding a wave of excitement since the announcement. Everyone she spoke to asked endless questions about the wedding date, the Valpergas and her ring. It was a flawless emerald of gigantic proportions. She found she was taking it off just to give her hand a rest. Weaving, helping Agnese, and life in general were challenging with the impractical bauble.

Nichola continued to escort her around town of an evening. They also went horse riding; she chose a russet-coloured mare from the Valperga stables who ran faster than she had anticipated. Near the woods, she was almost pitched over her head. Pulling hard on the reins, she managed to come to a halt. Her mare let out a crazed whinny, surprised to be interrupted. Nichola laughed and offered to swap.

She kept her distance from her father. Despite his acceptance of the engagement, his displeasure simmered beneath the surface and made her uneasy. Their meals together were a strained, silent affair.

Over supper one night she became exasperated. "Papa, are you going to be cold towards me for the rest of my life? You're upsetting me so much."

He barely glanced up from his meal and wiped his mouth on his linen napkin. "My dear, I'm acquainting myself with the concept of having a disagreeable son-in-law. It may take me some time, but I'll get there. In the meantime, just let us be silent."

His reply left her mute. She could not argue with it. Retiring to her bedchamber, she shifted positions many times before finding sleep. In the middle of the night, she sat upright in bed, tears soaking her nightdress. She sobbed until her chest hurt and it was difficult to breathe. A poisonous dream had visited her. In it, her betrothed had been paddling with her father and Antonius. He had risen from the boat and struck Antonius on the back with a paddle, sending him over the side. Having experienced many prophetic dreams, she was certain the scene would occur.

She lay awake for the rest of the night. In the shaft of white moonlight coursing through her window, she stared at her engagement ring on the bedside table, sparkling with treacherous beauty.

In the servants' quarters at the palazzo, Antonius sat up on his mattress, his nightshirt drenched with perspiration. He gasped for air and clutched his rigid body. Clenching his fists, he told himself it was a nightmare. The boats, the impact of the paddle on his back, the frigid water, Nichola's contemptuous eyes. Once he was able to breathe, he allowed himself the truth. It was his future.

∞

The dirt road leading up the hill to the mental asylum was potholed and uneven. Weeds sprouted at its edges. Nichola walked with his eyes cast downwards, to avoid tripping. He sensed the building before he saw it. A shadow fell over his feet and he looked up to a red brick facade with narrow barred windows. His throat felt tight and he hesitated before reaching for the brass knocker on the door. The memory of the hoof on his chest spurred him on.

It took several minutes for someone to respond to his three loud raps. A harried man with greasy hair appeared and stared at him. On his white tunic there was a dark stain, which looked like dried blood.

"What is it?"

His eyes were narrow slits and he half turned away, as if ready to dismiss him.

Nichola ignored his rudeness. "Good day. I am here to see the administrator, Signor Valperga."

"What is your name?"

"I'm Nichola Valperga—his nephew."

He nodded without interest. "You will have to be quick. We have three new patients arriving today, and I need the Signor's help. This way please."

The reception room was large and spartan, with pale floorboards and a circular staircase of black painted metal. Two brown goatskin armchairs sat by the window, facing each other. Nichola had a sense they were rarely used. A stained-glass window let in long coloured plumes of light. Behind the staircase was a hallway with studded

196

iron doors. The man led him in that direction at a rapid pace, his footsteps echoing. From a distance he could hear a piercing shriek, then a thud. He imagined someone was banging his head against a wall. His uncle's office was the last door on the left. Unlike the others, its door was made of thin wood, without a padlock.

Nichola's mouth was dry as he approached the door. Domenico lived alone in a small cottage on the outskirts of town. Surviving on polenta and the occasional rabbit sent from the palazzo, he shunned his family's riches. Years before he had tried to join the priesthood and been rebuffed. No one was sure why. Nichola guessed it was something to do with his lack of compassion. He spouted the correct words and platitudes without his heart behind them.

"Your nephew, Signor," the sallow man announced, after a small knock on the open door.

"Thank you, Joachim. Ah, Nichola, what a pleasant surprise. Do come in."

"Hello, Zio Domenico. How are you today?"

The office contained a large mahogany desk with a gleaming surface. Behind his uncle hung a crucifix with Jesus near death, his limbs blinding white, his wounds leaking copious amounts of vivid blood. Domenico sat in a red leather chair and motioned his nephew towards a spindly wooden one, facing the desk.

"I'm quite well, young man. Do sit down. Now, what brings you here today? I'm sure you're not here for pleasure."

"Indeed I'm not. There has been an incident I thought you should be made aware of."

Domenico sat forward in his chair, his hands clasped together on his desk as if he were praying. His chin was grey with stubble beneath the skin.

"And what might that be?"

"Well, I was walking the other day and I came across a boy, Piero Sardi. I'm not sure if you know of him? He is a simpleton. He was playing with a ball in the street and I took pity on him. I thought it might be kind to play with him. We were throwing the ball and I think I had it for longer than he expected. All of a sudden he charged me and punched me. I'm sure you can imagine what a shock that was. Terrible. To try to help someone and be repaid by an attack. There was a large group of townspeople who witnessed the attack, one of them was Signor Rosetti, the shoemaker, if you wish to verify my account."

"There will be no need for that; you are my nephew, so of course I believe you. How awful. Yet I'm confused. What has this to do with me?"

"Zio, I'm concerned not only for my own safety, but for that of the other townspeople. They are uneasy about what happened, and suggested I bring it to your attention. In my opinion, the boy is unbalanced and should be brought here as soon as possible. Who knows who else could be harmed? What if he attacked a child?"

"Goodness, you're quite right. I will send Joachim to examine him just to make sure."

"No! I mean I'm certain he needs treatment. He was almost foaming at the mouth; such was his aggression towards me. I no longer feel relaxed when I walk around Pesaro. I think he now sees me as an enemy."

Domenico looked thoughtful for a moment, leaning back in his chair and glancing out the window. His eyes were rimmed with dark circles, contrasting with the pallor of his skin.

"I'm impressed with your sense of civic responsibility, Nichola. I have not noticed this about you before. It must be a sign of your maturity. I will be sure to let your father know of this. He will be reassured you are developing into a fine young man."

Nichola felt a pain jolt near his heart. "I don't need my father to know of my actions, Zio. I prefer to do good works in an anonymous capacity. I feel like a braggart otherwise. Do you understand?"

"Indeed, I do. Humility is the mark of those who are close to God. I will send Joachim and some others to collect the boy in the next few days. We have some new inmates and must settle them in first. Good day, I must go and do my rounds now. I hope to see you again soon. Feel free to visit me at my cottage when you have some free time."

He rose and walked around his desk to clasp Nichola's hands and kiss him on both cheeks.

"Good day, Zio. I'll be sure to visit soon. Thank you so much for helping me."

Domenico smiled without revealing his teeth, and turned to the door.

"Nichola?"

"Yes?"

"I have not seen you at church the last few Sundays. Do not neglect your spiritual side; the devil is always on the lookout for weaknesses in the soul. He likes to sneak in when we are looking the other way."

"Yes, Zio. I will come next Sunday. Good day to you."

∞

Just after sunrise Antonius left the palazzo and walked to the villa. He waited in the workroom after being allowed inside by a bewildered Agnese. She had not yet pinned her grey hair into a bun and her buttons were fastened wrongly. It seemed his knock had dragged her from her quarters in great haste.

"The master has not yet emerged. I never disturb him before seven. Would you like to wait in the workroom?"

He flicked through the heavy tome about Hermeticism as he waited. It smelt musty and the words were small and hard to decipher. They flickered in front of his eyes. His mind bombarded him with images from his nightmare and he stood up and paced the room, rubbing his forehead with the back of his hand.

Savinus's rich voice was a welcome intrusion.

"What on earth is the matter? You were not meant to come until later."

"Signor, I had a terrible dream. About Nichola. I believe he will try to harm me."

Savinus frowned. "Sit down. You need to try to relax. What happened in the dream?"

Antonius realized there were tears over his eyes and he blinked them away.

"We were at the salt marshes in the boats. He was paddling and he stopped. He stood up and hit me on the back with a paddle, sending me into the water."

The old man looked at his gnarled hands, his expression morose. "It is as the guides told me. But don't panic. We'll all play our part to make the best of it. For my part, I must jump in after you and pretend to search."

Antonius stared out of the window, considering his predicament.

"Play our part. I suppose I must learn to swim."

His mentor nodded and smiled. "Now you're on the right track. And what else? How will you stop him from seeing you once you reach the other side?"

"I must stay underwater, holding my breath for as long as possible."

"Good, good. I knew there were many reasons why I chose you. Now go to the salt marshes today. Spend as long as you require. Try to swim. You may take Horatio. I've saddled him up."

"Yes, Signor. I will leave now."

"Don't be silly. Have some breakfast with us."

"No. I need to go now. Thank you. I'll see you later today."

Savinus looked at his grave face, his pallor and clenched jaw.

"Antonius?"

"Yes?"

"Please be careful. Stay in the shallows to begin with."

"I will, Signor."

At the breakfast table, Savinus waited for Giulia to emerge. She was never late and he wondered if she were ill. He ate buttered bread and jam and sipped his milk. At eight thirty she opened her door and shuffled out, her hair askew.

"Good morning, dearest. Are you all right?"

Her face was devoid of colour and her eyes rimmed with dark circles.

"No, Papa. I need to find Antonius. I had a nightmare about him last night."

"I'm sorry to hear that. I will tell you where he is, but first you must eat. It will help with your fatigue."

"Papa, it's a matter of great urgency. I must see him now. Where is he? I'll eat later."

Savinus let out a sigh and pushed back his chair. "This is not a good morning. He's at the salt marshes. Go then. Don't forget your hat. An emergency does not mean we forget decorum."

"Yes, Papa. Eat your bread and don't fret. I'll bring him back by lunchtime." She kissed the top of his head and walked towards the door.

CHAPTER 27

Jocanda meandered along the dirt road, ignoring Giulia's kicks to her flanks and stopping to chew wildflowers. As there was no one to witness her rancour, Giulia cursed the mare in a multitude of ways. She imagined the animal was her betrothed and kicked harder. Disbelief filled her as her mind replayed the dream. She passed wheat fields where the workers had been toiling for several hours. They did not glance up from their labours. Jocanda whinnied and trotted faster. Giulia's throat felt closed and a film of tears obscured her vision. She imagined breaking off the engagement, trying out different words in her mind. The thought of living with a man who was capable of such violence sickened her. Yet he had shown tenderness and seemed to love her. The two extremes, of his behaviour with her and towards Antonius, were difficult to reconcile. Her mind could not make sense of them. She wondered how kindness and cruelty could exist so closely in one person, battling each other like hostile neighbours.

Tears flowed unabated as she pulled the reins to the right and followed the veering path. She had dressed too warmly, and perspiration collected underneath her bodice. Her veiled hat felt stifling and she glanced around before tearing it off.

You're a fool, a love-struck idiot. Anyone could have told you he was at the very least arrogant. He is detestable. Silly, greedy girl.

As she berated herself, she almost passed the marshes. Jocanda jolted to a stop, out of habit, and whinnied again.

Dismounting in haste, she tied the mare to a tree and climbed up the embankment, pushing the reeds aside. Antonius sat hunched over on the shore, his face in his hands. A short distance further, Horatio stood amongst the reeds, tied to a post. He snorted and pawed the ground with his hooves.

Frowning, she walked over and touched his shoulder.

"Antonius? Are you all right?"

He jumped and turned to her. A strained smile contrasted with his red-rimmed eyes.

"Giulia. I'm glad to see you. I have a small problem, you see."

"What is it?"

"I need to learn to swim. The trouble is, I'm too much of a coward to go in the water."

"I know how to swim a little. Perhaps I can teach you?"

"Thank you. I would like that very much. How do we start?"

She blushed. "Well, you need to take off your shirt."

He obliged and she turned away, unbuttoning her skirt. Beneath it she wore bloomers that covered her to the knees. Although they did not reveal anything, she waded into the shallows to conceal herself. She looked at him. He stood tall, with broad shoulders and a strong chest. His skin was honeyed from the sun. He met her gaze and his eyes held the question: *Well, what do I do now?*

She heard the question in her head. It felt odd to communicate with him in a manner reserved for her father.

She held out her hand. *Just walk over here, I'm going to take you in slowly.*

The water eddied around his shins as he made his way over to her, grasping her hand.

There is a ledge just in front of me. We will step over it and be in the deep. I'll hold you and the water will hold you too.

Can't we just do this in the shallows?

Antonius, the deep is what you are going to have to confront. So why not do it now?

He nodded and they walked two more steps before the sand vanished beneath them. She wound her arms around his chest and under his arms. With vigorous kicks, she kept them afloat. The cool water lapped at his chin. Warm currents flowed around his knees and icy ones around his upper body. He shivered.

Kick your legs, that's it. You're doing a great job. Isn't the water lovely?

Under her hands, she could feel his muscles rippling with exertion.

They stayed like that for some minutes. Antonius kept his eyes averted, ignoring the heat flushing his cheeks. Then, to his panic, she said aloud, "Antonius? I'm going to let you swim on your own. I'll be right here if you get into trouble. Just kick your legs and extend your arms out like this."

She let go. He kicked and stretched his arms out, but kept going under and swallowing mouthfuls of silt-laden water.

Giulia! This is not working!

Her long arms snaked around him and she pulled him to her chest. He relaxed against her, coughing into his hand. He felt the scratch of a stick against his leg, and the slimy caress of a reed.

All right. That's enough for today. I'll take you back now. Well done.

At the ledge, he was able to find his footing and they stood, extricating themselves from the strange embrace. Their eyes met and held. Giulia's stomach contracted, as the look contained his feelings from the preceding months and the present. Their eyes dropped and they waded towards the bank. Sitting down, Antonius's chest heaved and he tried to slow his breathing.

"Thank you."

"You don't need to thank me. You did very well for a first-timer. So, are you going to tell me what's really bothering you?"

Antonius stared at her before glancing away. He hesitated, hugging his knees as if they might protect him. "Well, I had a premonition, a dream that someone will try to drown me, right here."

"I had the same dream last night. Did you dream it was Nichola?"

His eyes widened in surprise. "Yes. If you had the dream last night it can only mean one thing."

"What is that?"

"That I sent it to you, as it was happening to me."

Giulia frowned. "Why would that happen?"

Embarrassed, he pulled a reed from the ground, twisting it in his hands. Only twin souls sent their dreams to each other, he had read about it in one of Savinus's books.

"I'm not sure. Perhaps the guides wanted to warn you of his character."

"I feel so ridiculous. You must think me shallow. He's not what I thought he was. Or at least, I saw him as he was at first and was persuaded to think better of him."

"You're only human."

They sat in silence for some minutes, watching the herons take flight. The water rippled in their wake, the sun glistening on its surface.

Giulia touched his hand. "I can teach you some more. We could meet here every few days. Who knows how much time you have."

"Thank you, that's the trouble. It could be in several days or several months. Can you come here again on Friday? At this time?"

"Yes. I will be here."

CHAPTER 28

Savinus felt odd to be alone in the workroom. Agnese was visiting her daughter, Giulia and Antonius were at the salt marshes, and Nichola was banished. The window was ajar and a frigid draft chilled him as he pored over his calculations. He pulled his jacket around his frame and rubbed his hands together to no avail. Sighing, he stood and approached the window. The stuffy room was preferable to being cold.

He had woken that morning with a premonition and it continued to make him uneasy. He did not want to analyse why, as he knew it would not make him feel any better. The only remedy was work. The Conte had requested a reading in order to set a date for Gianni's wedding. Outside the window, a robin had been building her nest for some weeks. She was joyful about the imminent arrival of her chicks and trilled a loud melody. Three weeks earlier, Savinus had found it charming. Jamming his quill in the inkpot he pushed himself upright and paced the room, cursing under his breath.

Three loud raps sounded on the door, harder than necessary. He jumped and froze, unsure what to do. Then, resigned, he made his way out of the workroom, towards the entrance. With a deep breath, he opened the door. Standing before him were two men in black habits. One was portly and of small stature. His priest's habit was unadorned. The taller man wore a magenta square hat and a matching silk sash around his waist. His face was gaunt with deep hollows under his cheekbones. Black eyes were deep set above a curved nose—the dominant feature of his face.

Savinus stared at his nose for some seconds before remembering to speak.

"Good day, how can I help you Monsignor, Padre?"

"Good day, Signor di Benevento. My name is Monsignor Tomas di Ignacio and this is my assistant, Padre Franco. I am in charge of an inquiry into occult practices and witchcraft. I've come to inspect your premises. There is no need to be alarmed, as I'm sure you have nothing to hide. May we enter?"

Savinus's mouth went dry. He mentally scanned his workroom for offending items. There were texts on shapeshifting that were difficult to understand if untrained, books of incantations and spells, dried snakes, bones and sacred stones. It was impossible to know which items would offend. He waved the two men inside, his heart thudding. Padre Franco gave him an apologetic glance as he followed the Monsignor.

The Monsignor whispered something in his assistant's ear as they entered. Then both men examined each book, object, and sheet of parchment. The older man frowned as he flicked through pages of the book on Hermetic Alchemy. Savinus cringed. It was the first thing he would have hidden if prepared for their visit. Monsignor di Ignacio swept objects off tables with his forearm, taking pleasure in the havoc. Stones, glass ornaments, and test tubes clattered and smashed. He picked up a rose quartz crystal, turned it in his hand and flung it at the wall, a smile playing on his lips. It disintegrated into sharp fragments on the floor. Padre Franco picked up a glass alembic and, under his superior's penetrating gaze, threw it without enthusiasm against the same wall.

"Monsignor! Please show some respect—this is where I work. There is no need for destruction! Stop that!"

A withering look was shot in his direction.

"I have my methods, just as you have yours. In any case, I've seen enough. You are engaging in dark practices and must cease. I will return in four weeks' time. If I find the alchemical texts here, they will be burnt. You must clear out the crystals and ritual objects. The only practices acceptable to the Church are geomancy and basic seeing. Everything else, particularly the shapeshifting, is the work of the devil. Clear it all out, or you will be incarcerated and tried for heresy. Have I made myself understood?"

Savinus's mouth opened and closed but he could not produce speech. Then something emerged, with resonant clarity.

"Monsignor, I have admiration for your faith but I think you are misled. I am well known in Pesaro and have been practicing alchemy for most of my life. I have faith in God and have never been interested in witchcraft. All my practices are to aid others in their quest for happiness. I feel God himself looks over my shoulder and blesses my work. To be accused of seeking the dark, well, it's just unthinkable to me. May I ask from where you have received such erroneous information?"

The Monsignor laughed, a humourless wheeze into his black-gloved hand. "God himself looking over your shoulder? Watch and learn, Padre Franco. This is how the devil reveals himself, by masquerading as God. The arrogance! You have forgotten, Signor, the essence of faith is humility under God. Black magic influences people to change their actions. Their lives evolve in a different direction to the one ordained by God. That is the essence of the evil you are perpetrating."

"As I said, black magic is not part of my repertoire. I work with positive forces. But I can see you have made up your mind to disbelieve me, so I will desist."

"A wise move, Signor. I trust you will adjust your practices as I advised. You are fortunate to be associated with Conte Valperga; otherwise we would take you, and your books with us. Good day to you."

"Monsignor, may I have some warning before you come calling next time? I do like to be prepared for my guests."

Monsignor di Ignacio narrowed his eyes before curving his lips into something resembling a smile.

"I'm afraid not. If we were to warn the subjects of our inspections, it would provide them with ample time to hide evidence of their wrongdoing. I'm sure you understand. Good day to you."

With a supercilious nod and a final sneer, he surveyed the room for the last time, dusting down his habit as if he feared contamination from the devil. His subordinate reddened and nodded at Savinus, before following his master with a bowed head.

∞

A week had passed and Nichola had seen Giulia twice. They strolled around the town at dusk, conversed about light topics and she allowed him to take her arm. He brought up their wedding plans several times, asking her if she had visited their family dressmaker as he had instructed. She responded with a vague description of helping her father and being occupied. At the doorway to her home, she had brushed her lips over his cheek before disappearing inside. Although she was pleasant, he sensed something was amiss. The emotional intensity marking their earlier encounters had subsided. It had been replaced with something amiable but bland.

He replayed their conversations in his mind, examining his words to find a misstep. One afternoon he was sitting in the library, attempting to concentrate on a book about the history of Umbria. His spine straightened as the thought came to him—there was someone else. It was difficult to imagine how she could have met another man, but he supposed it was possible. His body was tightly coiled as he hurled the book at the wall with as much force as he could muster. It made a gratifying thud as it hit the floor.

He had promised to call on her in two days. Subtle questioning might yield some information. At the very least, he would be able to read her face and body language. He decided women were, on the whole, faithless and without substance. His stomach churned with bitter nausea. Rising from his chair, he walked over to the window and gazed out at the row of immaculate hedges. It was just after dawn, and a haze of greyish-blue mist hovered above them. The low sun broke though the cloud, illuminating tiny drops of water on the grass so it seemed dusted with jewels. His eye twitched with sudden violence and he cupped his hand over it.

CHAPTER 29

It had been a happy day for Piero. He played with a litter of puppies belonging to the fruit vendor, kicked a ball with the four-year-old son of a neighbour and was given a boiled sweet by his mother. Afterwards, he sat at the kitchen table, finishing a bowl of pasta with gorgonzola.

Fiora smiled at him as he recounted the pleasures of his day.

"Mama, I kicked ball so far, Roberto laugh at me. The puppies lick me on my face and on my knees. I want puppy, Mama. Can we have puppy?"

"I'll think about it, *caro*. Eat your pasta before it gets cold. Use your fork."

Fiora's hands were slimy with potato skins. Theresa was helping her peel them to make gnocchi for supper. Plumes of steam curled towards the ceiling from the potatoes, just taken from the boiling water.

"Mama, Federico asked if he might come and visit next Thursday? I'd love it if Antonius could come too."

"Yes, I'm sure Antonius would like to meet him. He wants to play the role of your dear Papa, I think. Making sure that Federico is worthy of you."

Theresa mashed the potatoes and Fiora slid them over with a

cupped hand to mix them with flour and eggs. They often worked in this way and it was not necessary to think. Falling silent, they became absorbed in their tasks. Piero rapped his fork on the table and sang the San Terenzio song. He was finished. Theresa collected his plate.

There was an abrupt series of bangs on the door, as if someone were using their palm. They both jumped on hearing the noise. The women were hesitant as they made their way to the door. Fiora opened it a crack and peered into the darkness.

"Good evening, who is it?" She could barely make out three shapes of varying sizes and heights.

"Signora Sardi?"

"Yes?"

"May we come in? I am Joachim Conti from the mental asylum. We have been instructed to examine your son. There is concern for his health based on recent reports of his behaviour."

Fiora froze and blocked the door. A stab of pain shot across her heart.

"What behaviour are you talking about? My son is not a bother to anyone."

"I'm sure you're probably right, Signora. However, I must see the boy and come to my own conclusions. If you could please step aside, I would be most appreciative."

"Come in." Her voice was quiet and she waved them through.

Piero remained at the table. His mother's tension had not escaped him and he looked at the men with a wary expression.

Joachim approached him without a word. He lifted his chin with an index finger and turned his face left and right. Piero's blue eyes were wide and fearful.

"Is this the boy?" he asked.

Fiora nodded.

"How old is he?"

He did not look at her as he asked the question.

"He is ten years old this month."

"This boy assaulted the son of Conte Valperga."

She inhaled sharply, "That's not possible. Piero is a gentle boy. He must have been provoked."

Joachim shook his head and turned his gaze on her. "I'm afraid not, Signora. Signor Valperga was trying to play ball with him and was charged. It was quite unexpected and shows impulsive, violent tendencies. There is no point in me questioning the boy. He wouldn't understand."

Fiora wrung her hands. "So if you're not going to examine him, why are you here?"

Joachim gave the other two men an almost imperceptible nod. They stepped forward and took each of Piero's arms. One was thick set with red hair like stubble on his large head. The other was of a wiry build.

Theresa stood in the corner frowning, her body rigid with tension. When she saw what they were doing, she lunged forward and pummelled her fists against the chest of the smaller man.

"Leave him alone! He's just a simpleton who's never hurt anyone. Shame on you!"

The wiry man stiffened and averted his eyes, as if she were an annoying insect. He pushed her away with his elbow so as not to lose his grip on Piero.

Joachim stepped forward. "It's in Piero's interest for you to stay calm. He must be taken to the asylum now. I realize this is upsetting for you, but it will be less traumatic for him if you don't make a fuss."

"You bastard! Let him go! This is wrong. A mistake has been made. He must stay here with his family." Tears streamed down her reddened cheeks as she spoke, her voice trembling.

Fiora spoke. "My daughter is right, Signor. What you suggest is impossible. My boy is kind-hearted and would never hurt someone. The only possibility is that he was teased and he charged the Signor in defence."

"I know it's difficult for you to believe, but there were witnesses. We must go now, Signora. Say your goodbyes."

Piero looked from his mother to his sister, their anguish washing over him. The men tightened their grip on his upper arms as they hoisted him out of the chair. He was not sure why, but he knew he was in danger. A sound emanated from his throat, halfway between a groan and a shriek.

"I want stay Mama, stay Mama. Here!"

In an attempt to elbow the larger man he upended his bowl. It clattered to the floor, turning around in loud circles like an oversized spinning top. Piero continued to wail and shake his head as they dragged him by the armpits across the room. He alternated between allowing his feet to drag on the floor and trying to kick his persecutors.

The women were unable to speak and were engulfed with tears. As they approached the door, Fiora was jolted by a sudden anger and picked up a broom. Her face turned deep red and she gave chase, the broom held above her head like a battle flag.

"Let him go! I will give you both a beating. Leave my son alone!"

Joachim turned to her with an unruffled, resigned expression.

"Feel free, Signora. I would then be within my rights to commit you to the asylum along with your idiot."

At this, her whole body drooped, as if she were a sail on a boat that has just lost the momentum of wind.

There were no more words left to say. There was not money with which to bribe, a man of the house to defend, or powerful connections to enlist. All that remained was defeat.

Noticing this, Joachim waved her forward.

"You may say goodbye. You will be permitted to visit him once every month."

Fiora grasped her son's head and pulled it to her breast, stroking his blond hair with her free hand. His tears moistened her skin.

She felt some of the tension leave his body as he allowed himself to be held. The men stood at his back, wary of escape. His voice was soft.

"Stay Mama, stay here."

Fiora's tears welled up again. "No, son. You must go with these men; they are taking you to a new place. Mama, Theresa, and Antonius will visit you there. It won't be forever. Be a good boy."

"No, Mama. No new place. Stay here." His eyes were resolute.

Theresa kissed her brother and patted his head. "Goodbye, my dear brother. We'll see you soon. It will be all right."

The men seized him and dragged him out the door to a waiting horse and cart. He sobbed, shouted, and kicked. Joachim struck him across the cheek, leaving a red welt. Some of the neighbours had emerged to watch the spectacle. A man yelled out.

"Monsters! Leave the boy!"

"An outrage! Where are they taking him?"

The women gathered around Fiora, their arms around her shoulders as she shook with tears. They watched the men tie Piero to the cart with what seemed like an endless coil of rope. Theresa held her mother's hand and stood with a straight back.

"I hope you sleep well tonight! God punishes the heartless, you'll see!"

She spat the words as the cart rolled away carrying the struggling form of her brother, tied from his neck to his ankles.

∞

Just after helping Katerina prepare the luncheon, Antonius was taken aback to see the rotund shape of his mother at the door to the kitchen. In the past, she sent notes to him through Katerina when she saw her at the market. There had never been any need for her to visit the palazzo.

Opening the door, he took in her dishevelled appearance and red-rimmed eyes. She was panting from the exertion of walking up the steep road. Wisps of grey hair escaped from her bun, and her eyes were clouded with anguish.

"What is it Mama?"

"Son, Piero has been taken, last night. The asylum."

She was unable to speak further. Stumbling forward, she grasped him to her and sobbed, her large frame shaking.

He led her to a chair and sat her down, trying to lull her with comforting words. Katerina took in the scene and picked up the kettle. She rushed to the courtyard to fill it at the well, then returned to the kitchen and placed it on the hearth, over leaping flames.

"Mama, you need to try to calm down so you can tell me what happened. Take some breaths. Start from the beginning."

Fiora sat up in the chair and wiped away her tears with the back of her hand. It was almost impossible for her to speak without crying. She inhaled and let out a shaky breath.

"We were just finishing Piero's supper when they came; three men from the asylum. The main one was called Joachim. I've forgotten his second name. They tricked us into letting them in, saying there had been an incident and they needed to examine him. I was foolish, trusting them. All they wanted was to take him away. He's gone now, to that awful place. He probably thinks we've betrayed him."

Antonius gripped her hand, feeling the blood drain from his face. He tried to keep his expression calm, but his body was rigid. He could hear his rapid heartbeat in his ears. "Now Mama, you mustn't say that. There was nothing you could do. I just don't understand why they would single him out."

"The man, he said that Piero charged the Conte's son when he was trying to play ball with him."

Antonius sighed, pressing his thumb and index finger against his forehead. "That can't be true. First of all, Nichola wouldn't want to play ball with anyone, least of all Piero. And Piero wouldn't be aggressive unless someone provoked him." He felt the ache of raw emotion in his throat, and avoided her eyes.

Fiora's eyes widened and she squeezed his hand. "That's right son! That's what I told them, at least, the part about Piero not being aggressive."

"I will find a solution, Mama. I think this has been initiated by Nichola to hurt me. I haven't told you this before, but he despises me. I can't do anything straight away, but I will figure it out. In the meantime, we must visit him and keep his spirits up."

Fiora's voice was despondent. "We may only see him once a month."

"We must make the best of it. I'm so sorry Mama, I feel this is my fault somehow."

"Nonsense. It was important for you to take the opportunity. If the boy is jealous, it's not your doing."

"How is Theresa?"

"Not good. She's taken to her bed today. Like me, she's angry and sad."

"I'll visit later, when I finish."

Katerina placed a mug of steaming barley tea in front of Fiora, who gave her a grateful smile.

"Thank you, Katerina, I need something warm in my stomach."

"A pleasure. I'm sorry if Signor Nichola has played a part in this. Pardon me for overhearing."

Antonius let go of his mother's hand. "I'm not sure of it, but I'll check later."

Katerina raised an eyebrow. "How do you do that?"

"It's hard to explain. I find a stillness in my mind, and the answers come to me."

"That's impressive. I have a lost necklace you may be able to help me with?"

"Perhaps. Mama, I need to get back to work. Take your time with the tea."

Fiora nodded and gazed with swollen eyes at the curls of steam wafting out of her mug.

Without meaning to, she had sent her memory of the night to her son. Antonius tried to blink away the image of his brother, ropes cutting into his skin on the back of a cart.

CHAPTER 30

The white brick wall did not yield to the chain clattering against it. It was late afternoon, and the chain, attached to Piero's arm, had not ceased its movement since morning. A wide metal cuff circled his wrist and the chain was bolted to the wall. There were four more beds in the room, set aside for difficult cases.

He had stopped crying, as his voice was almost gone. From time to time he let out a moan, which emerged as a rasping noise. With his free hand, he beat his chest. The man in the next bed tried to calm him.

"It's no good. They're not coming. Try to rest, boy. Save your energy."

Piero looked at the man, his large blue eyes glassy with despair. "Want go home. Mama and Theresa."

"What's your name, boy?"

"Piero."

"I'm Gregor. We're not going home. Not for a while. If you keep that up you will get sick. If you get sick here then you die. Why did they bring you here?"

Piero regarded him without comprehension, then rattled the chain once more, his knuckles bloody from hitting the bricks.

"I'm here because I said to my wife that perhaps God didn't

exist. We had lost our four children to the plague. I thought, how is this possible if there is a loving God? Well, my neighbour overheard my remark and he has always disliked me. He told the priest, who told his friend who runs this place. That was the end of my freedom."

"Home. Want go home. See Mama."

"You're a simpleton, aren't you? I suppose you can't even answer that. You like to play ball? Stay home with Mama?"

"Yes. Play ball. Mama give cuddles. Love Mama."

"Thought so, you poor thing. Not many cuddles going around in this place. Make sure you eat the gruel and drink the water. Only comes once a day. If not, well, like I said, you must not get sick here. Stop rattling, please. I really will turn into a crazy bugger if I hear that for much longer. Good boy, just rest, please."

Piero's arm stilled. He fell back onto the sheets streaked with grime, holding his wrist with his free hand. A red welt had formed from the metal band. He imagined his Mama washing it with rosewater and dressing it with clean rags. Kissing it before returning it to his lap. The thought comforted him and he dozed for some minutes.

The iron door's metallic groan startled him awake. The man who had taken him entered with a tray of gruel. Behind him followed another man he did not recognize. He was bald and dressed in a starched black gown, like a priest.

"Is this our new patient?" He asked the other man.

"Yes, sir. Piero Sardi. Brain of a four-year-old."

"Ah, looks like he's calmed down somewhat. Hello, there."

Piero gave him a suspicious stare, riveted by the prickly stubble on his chin.

"Hello."

"How are you feeling today?"

"Want go home." The words were just above a whisper.

"Speak up boy, I can't hear you."

He coughed and tried to find his voice. A sound like a wood saw came from his throat.

"Want. Go. Home."

"Yes. I'm sure you do. But the best place for you is right here. Chin up and eat your gruel. I will be back later to read to you from the Book of Job."

Gregor sneered. "He doesn't need your preaching; he needs his mother. How can you call yourself a believer? Untie him. He's calmed down now."

Domenico Valperga bristled. "If I wanted your advice, I would have asked for it. If you were more open to the purity of our God and his teachings, perhaps you might be released. Don't try to drag the boy down to your level. I believe Joachim has only just taken off your restraint. Don't make me order him to put it back on."

Gregor sat back on his bed, arms folded. His eyes were dark with fury and his mouth pressed together to prevent insults from spewing forth.

Piero looked down at the tepid bowl of gruel. It was grey and lumpy. He picked up his spoon with his free hand and immersed it, bringing the spoonful to his lips. It smelt like old perspiration. His stomach flipped over—he forced it into his mouth and swallowed hard to avoid tasting it. He was not successful. The taste was similar to the smell and he gagged, specks of grit sticking to the roof of his mouth. Domenico was bemused.

"No good? Unfortunately, we don't have enough benefactors to provide anything better. Besides, simple food is good for the soul as well as the digestion. You will become accustomed to it."

Gregor glared at him, his face screwed into itself. Such was the effort to restrain himself, he was biting his lip.

The two men left the room. Piero was about to take another mouthful, his stomach lurching. His roommate kicked the end of his bed and the iron rail twanged in response. The three other inhabitants of the beds were either asleep or catatonic.

"They are vile. Be polite to them and they will release you from your restraint in a couple of days. I'm unable to do that, but you, well, you seem like a nice boy."

Piero tasted the gruel and his mouth puckered. He was speechless with disgust. His vision blurred with sudden tears as he thought of his Mama's ragú.

"I be sick."

"No, you won't. Like they said, you'll get used to it along with the Bible reading and the torture. Welcome to hell on earth, my friend."

∞

The salt marshes were quiet that morning. The herons had migrated south, and the only sound was the gentle susurration of the reeds as they were parted by the wind. Larks warbled in the cypress trees at the edge of the marshes. The sun was low on the horizon as Antonius waited for Giulia. He twisted a reed in his hands until it drew blood. Her hand on his shoulder jolted him from his thoughts.

"Hello. You look like you were far away. Are you ready for your lesson?"

He turned to her. His mouth smiled but his eyes were grim. "Good morning. Yes, I'm ready."

"What is it? Something is wrong."

"It's Piero. Some men came to the house and took him away. To the mental asylum."

Giulia shook her head in disbelief. "But why would they do such a thing?"

"They said he's dangerous because he attacked Nichola."

She snorted. "Piero? Dangerous? That's completely ridiculous. He's a loving boy, isn't he? Such a sweet nature; I don't understand. It sounds like there is something else going on."

"I haven't seen him yet so I can't be sure, but I think it's Nichola trying to undermine me again. There is a good chance he's set this up. He just never stops making trouble, I can't stand him."

"Yes, the trouble does seem never-ending, and I think you're right. If it's true, it's a horrible thing for him to do. When can you see Piero?"

"In about three weeks. It feels like a long time."

"You poor thing. Do you think you can swim or are you too upset?"

"No, that's fine. It will take my mind off things. Let's start."

A routine had developed. They would strip to as few clothes as modesty allowed, and wade into the cool ripples. Antonius was no longer frightened to cross into the deep, knowing she was beside him.

The red-gold curtain of her hair fanned out on the surface of the water as she swam, and she turned to him and smiled.

"Come on, you need to swim faster or I won't be close enough to rescue you if you sink. That's right, hands need to be as if you are pushing through tall grass and legs kicking all the time. Are you all right? You're getting very red in the face."

"I'm fine. Just trying to stay afloat." He cringed as he felt something frigid and smooth brush past his thigh. A fish? Seaweed? The water was an opaque, deep green. He decided swimming was an unnatural activity for a human. It was odd that some people swam for pleasure. The one consolation was watching Giulia at close quarters, and semi-clad. Her skin was almost translucent in its pallor, shimmering with moisture. The apples of her cheeks were flushed pink and her wet hair made her green eyes appear larger. The top of her dress had slipped down her arm, revealing the perfection of a white shoulder.

He pedalled his legs at a frantic pace as he attempted to keep up. It was hard to decide which was worse—staying in the water as his legs weakened, or returning to the shore and trying to disguise his arousal. Deciding on the latter he turned for the shallows, alerting her with a croaky voice.

"My legs have had enough. Take your time and I'll see you back there."

She arched an eyebrow. "So soon? But we've just started. Oh, well, I'll come too."

"Please, don't hurry. Enjoy your swim—it's such a lovely morning for it."

"No. You might get a cramp or something. Wait for me."

He cursed under his breath and tried to think of ugly things.

As he found his feet and walked in the shallows, his clothes pulled him to the earth with their weight. He reached down and squeezed out the legs of his breeches before collapsing onto the shore. The musings on fish guts and corpulence had not diminished his arousal and he folded his arms as she approached. He reddened when he saw her nipples beneath her soaked bodice. He seized a twig and drew patterns in the sand, noticing the way the silt made patterns through it like veins. Turning his head from her, he focused on his hand, desperate to calm down.

"What's wrong with you? You're acting strangely. Did I say something wrong?"

"No, it's not you. I...I guess I'm just apprehensive about whether I'll be able to swim when the time comes."

She nodded. "You'll be fine. You just need to keep practicing, that's all."

Giulia knew he was not telling the whole truth and wanted to kiss her. Her mind turned the thought over, along with those of Nichola and his dark side—the ring, life at the Palazzo Ducal, and her father. Antonius—his goodness, his easy smile, and his serious grey blue eyes. These thoughts, and many others, weaved through her mind as quickly as the tiny fish that swam in the marshes.

She placed her hand on his forearm, her touch light and hesitant, waiting for him to look at her. When he did, his expression was bewildered. Beneath his confusion, she could see what had been there for a long time and she inclined her head towards him. In an instant, his mouth was on hers, gentle and inquisitive, his tongue finding hers. They became a single entity of arms and legs and torsos. She felt his warmth radiate through her body as she buried her fingers in his hair, sinking into their oneness. With reluctance, they stopped to breathe, staying in the embrace. They were panting and devoid of words. His gaze did not waver from her, as if he feared she might dematerialise.

"Do you understand now? What I feel?"

"Yes." She sobbed, her chest heaving, and buried her face in his neck.

"Why are you crying?"

"Because I feel the same. What am I to do?"

"We'll figure it out. I won't be able to stay here, though. You know that, don't you?"

"Yes. Neither will I."

He ran his finger down the side of her face, his eyes unwavering.

"You don't have to do this, Giulia. Your life could be so..."

"So what?"

"The palazzo, the servants, the jewels. All that."

"Yes, and sharing it with someone who has a problem with morals. No, Antonius, I'm not sure how this is going to play out, but I am with you. I made a mistake."

"An easy one to make. He is very charming to everyone but me."

Giulia brushed away her tears and stared out at the horizon. The water reflected both the sky and the reeds, the wind distorting them into diagonal patterns.

Turning to him, she placed her hand on his shoulder. "Come here."

"Why?"

"Because I want to kiss you again."

CHAPTER 31

The clear crystal point emitted purple and green shafts of reflected light onto the wooden desk. Savinus had been holding it for several minutes, trying to gain clarity of thought. Plans had to be made, set in place. Often he achieved guidance from this specimen, found at a market in Genoa several years before. One word kept surfacing in his mind: escape.

Fair enough, he thought, *but how? When?*

He had summoned his daughter and Antonius to come to the workroom that afternoon. There were only a few more days before Nichola returned, and discussions would become impossible. He laid down the crystal and picked up his quill, dipping it in the inkpot. The diagrams emerged in rapid succession down the page. For whatever reason, this was to be the method of divination. *Aha,* he smiled to himself, *transmutation and flight on the fifteenth day, disguise for one, horse-drawn vehicle to town of safety, friend welcomes travellers.*

It was all there. The guides had instructed him through his hand and now only minor details would need to be addressed. Agnese had been told not to disturb him, but she gave a tentative knock at the door.

"Signor, Giulia and Antonius have arrived and are ready to see you. And if you don't mind, there is something I need to tell you."

"Certainly, Agnese. What is it?"

"It's about Antonius's brother. I heard he has been put in the asylum and I think it's related to something I saw."

"What was that?"

"I was returning from the market a few weeks ago and saw Signor Nichola teasing him. He took his ball away and was trying to upset him, on purpose I believe. Then the boy lost his temper and threw himself at him. Everyone else thought it came from nowhere, but it's not true. The Conte's son provoked him."

Savinus frowned as he took in the information, sitting forward with his hands resting on his knees.

"Thank you, Agnese. This is indeed very useful. You may show them in now."

Antonius and Giulia had been eavesdropping at the door, giggling like naughty school children until they heard Agnese's words. Their faces clouded with worry as they entered the room.

They sat on the stools Savinus had placed in front of his chair and looked at him with grave faces. Although they were focused on the meeting, he noticed the filaments of light travelling between their heads, a spiderweb of psychic connection. He knew they were together, and this fact filled him with equal parts of joy and fear.

"Sorry, Papa," said Giulia. "I know we weren't meant to hear that, but it's terrible and as we suspected."

"Yes, it's not good, but just another example of his hatred and jealousy. There is no point in examining it. What we must now do is plan our escape."

They tried to conceal their surprise; if he was planning an escape for them all, then he knew of their relationship. Giulia had never given up trying to have secrets from her father, despite his abilities.

"My diagrams tell me that at the time of the half moon, around the fifteenth day of the month, Nichola will attack you on the boat. You must free your brother the day before the attack, on the fourteenth. He must be hidden here in my storage room until our escape. Your mother can then come and retrieve him from Agnese."

"How do you suggest I free him?"

"By using the technique of shapeshifting. You will fly into the asylum, free him, and lead him back here, by going around the perimeter of the town. You can approach the villa from the back, so as not to be seen."

In the weeks following the dream, they had flown together three more times, following the same route as before. Antonius learned to angle his wings to catch the currents of air, controlling his direction. He was able to swoop down, but also to glide. The idea of flying to rescue his brother felt less daunting.

Giulia and Antonius were quiet for some moments, absorbing the information. Then Giulia spoke.

"Papa, how do you propose we escape? Will you both shapeshift to fly away?"

"No. Antonius can only maintain bird form for about an hour. I can keep it for several hours. Our new home is to be in Genoa, where Lorenzo di Montefiore will aid us in our resettlement. I will fly, and you two will hitch a ride with a vegetable seller. I have a friend at the market who will be happy to assist us. Giulia, you will need to dress as a boy. Agnese will purchase the garments as soon as possible. You will hide under a sheet on the vegetable cart."

Antonius frowned. "But Signor, what is to stop the authorities from chasing us to Genoa, and seizing Piero again once he has returned home?"

The old man smiled. "Young man, you must understand reputation is everything in this town. If I write a letter to the Conte, explaining his fine son is nothing but a thug and a manipulator; he will be forced to protect us all. Or I could threaten Nichola with exposure once he thinks he has murdered you. He would have to explain what happened with Piero to the head of the asylum, and the boy would be left in peace. We could set up our new lives."

Giulia was not convinced. "Does the Conte really hold that much sway with the religious authorities, Papa? Would they not still try and find you?"

"My dear, the nobility can pull any string they desire. Gold has more influence on the clergy than salvation."

"And our Agnese? What will become of her?"

"She is free to choose. She may follow us to Genoa, or remain here and find another family. I do hope she joins us. Either way, I will need her to assist in the transport of my most precious tools, books, and talismans to Genoa. Eagles do not generally take baggage."

"Signor, that's very thorough and I feel reassured," added Antonius. "But how will I shapeshift without the elaborate ritual? Surely there will not be time for that? Nichola will be around, watching our every move."

Savinus sat forward in his chair. His eyes shone with excitement and he clutched his hands together.

"Aha, good thinking. That is why I have an abbreviated version of the ritual, without the fire, using only a candle and incantations. An answer to everything, my boy."

"Can we try it out beforehand? What if I make a mistake?"

"If we try it out you will be a starling at the wrong time. I'll give you a parchment with the instructions, and Arion will help you with the rest."

They waited while Savinus looked out the window, his eyes glazed over, staring at a fixed point. Both knew this as a sign he was considering an important point.

Her turned back, his eyes alert once more. "How is your swimming going?"

"Not bad, although I hope to get better. I've been thinking about what I need to do...when it happens."

"Good, I was hoping you were thinking about it. What have you come up with?"

"When I fall overboard, I must swim underwater to the shallows near the island. I'll wait for a minute underwater, holding my breath. Then I'll emerge in the reeds and continue to wait until you are both gone. I suppose I must then spend the night in the blue cave."

"Yes, that's precisely what I have been imagining. The next morning, Giulia should meet you there. My vegetable seller friend, Bruno, can meet you at the marshes later that morning and take you to Genoa. In addition to swimming, you must practice holding your breath until you can hold it for a full minute. Do you think you can manage that?"

"Yes, Signor."

"Good. You're both dismissed. Oh, and one more thing. Do not be seen together, you look like you're in love and someone will notice. Or at least, try and cultivate an air of neutrality."

They smiled and nodded, leaning into one another.

∞

The next day, Nichola arrived at the villa to see his betrothed. He was surprised when she opened the door herself, as if waiting for him. After greeting him in a soft voice, she waved him inside. Avoiding his eyes as he kissed her on both cheeks, she motioned for him to follow and walked with a heavy tread to the sitting room. They sat in opposite chairs near the fireplace, and she held her head, as if she were in pain. Her face was pallid and drawn, and he noticed her hands shook as she smoothed the fabric on her dress. A pain thudded in his stomach, the same pain that always alerted him to trouble. He examined her face. Her eyes darted around the room, landing everywhere except on him.

"You don't seem yourself. What is it, Giulia?"

She shook her head, as if trying to dislodge an unwelcome thought. "Nothing."

He cocked his head. "Come on, I'm not silly. Something's bothering you. Tell me."

"Nichola, I…I have some bad news. I cannot marry you. It's too rushed, and I don't feel it's right."

He reared back into the chair, as if from a blow.

"I knew it. How could you fool me like this? This is humiliating. Who do you think you are, turning me down?"

Giulia blinked back tears and stood, pacing in front of him. She raked her hair with her hands, her face flushed red.

"I'm sorry. I'm so sorry, I just can't, Nichola. I wish I could explain it to you. You know how sometimes things seem like the

229

right decision, then the situation changes?"

"No, I don't. I don't know at all and I don't understand."

He rose and stood in front of her, grabbing her wrists. Tears spilled down her face, and she stiffened, her eyes on her feet. Nichola realized he had been holding his breath as she spoke; his breathing was laboured, as if he had been running. He loosened his grip on her wrists, and reached out to touch the side of her face. His voice was low and desperate.

"Is it something I did? Haven't I done everything in my power to make you happy?"

Her lips trembled, and as she met his eyes, she looked as vulnerable as a small child.

"Yes. You've been the perfect gentleman. But I thought you were better than the person who tried to discredit Antonius. You're not who I thought you were."

"I am, Giulia. You've got me wrong. Please."

"You'd better go."

He grimaced. "There's someone else, I know it. Tell me who it is." He lunged forward and seized her shoulders. "Tell me!"

She shook her head, her cheeks awash with tears, and wrenched herself from his grip.

"Please go, I need you to go now."

He stood, with his clenched fists stiff at his side. "I will find out, Giulia. You cannot keep it from me."

CHAPTER 32

If ever there was a time he needed psychic abilities, this was it. Nichola sat on his bed. He had staggered home, his throat blocked and his legs unsteady. It was the middle of the night and he was unable to sleep, tormented by thoughts of who might be involved with Giulia. With his eyes closed, he attempted to clear the space in front of his forehead, to allow images to emerge. Strange, linear shapes formed, green-hued. They swayed in the breeze, revealing a stretch of water. The marshes. The ashen clouds hung low overhead, reflected in the water. Satisfied he had seen something useful, he climbed back under the blankets and was soon asleep.

The screech of curtains being pulled back woke him just after dawn. It was Paolo, his valet. It was the same every morning; the man was incapable of carrying out his duties in silence.

"Paolo!" he grumbled, sitting upright. "Must you wake me with that infernal racket? Pull the curtains slowly, and walk with soft footsteps. I like to be woken gently."

He turned to his master, his tone contemptuous. "Sorry, Signor. I did not realize you were asleep."

"Insolence. When someone is lying down with their eyes closed, it's the obvious conclusion. And it's not just the curtains and your footfalls. I expect my breakfast to be brought to my chamber at this time. Every morning you seem to forget this fact. Hurry to the kitchen and ask the cook to prepare it immediately."

Paolo stood immobile, staring at Nichola as if he wished to set him on fire.

"Are you deaf? Go!"

Taking his time, the valet ambled to the door. In the doorframe, he turned around with a supercilious smile.

"Will that be all, Signor?"

Nichola's voice was low but incensed. "Go to the kitchen before I wring your stringy neck."

The man had the good sense to send Lucia with his breakfast. She was a curvaceous blonde whom he had conquered the previous summer. Placing his sardines and sourdough bread on a table near the window, she lowered her eyes in a way that was both coquettish and demure.

"Good morning, Signor. I do apologize for the delay in your breakfast. You must be ravenous."

He made his way over to the silk upholstered armchair, inhaling the aroma of yeast. As she leaned close to place his napkin on his lap, she gave off a pleasing scent of lilac.

"Thank you, Lucia, you're quite right. I have a large appetite this morning."

In the past, he would have brushed his hand over her backside as she moved away. Since meeting Giulia, he was unable to derive pleasure from other women, and so left her alone. Lucia hid her disappointment as she took her leave.

He ate with relish, spreading his bread with glistening yellow butter. The image of the marshes remained in his mind's eye. Paolo returned some time later to help him get dressed. They both cringed as the older man buttoned his shirt and pulled up his breeches. Nichola held out his arms and gazed out the window at the team of hedge-trimmers, wishing him gone. He turned his head as his hair was brushed, and coughed as he was dabbed with strong cologne. His boots were laced as he sat on a stool. As a final touch, an emerald pin was attached to his coat. Aware of Paolo's dislike, this step filled him with trepidation. He wondered how many times he would have to be stabbed with the pin to cause serious damage.

Nodding his thanks, Nichola waved him away and waited until he could no longer hear his footsteps in the corridor. Then he made his way to the stables to find his father's best stallion, Blackheath.

The animal watched him with suspicion. Nichola had been allowed to ride him only once, on a hunt with the Conte's close supervision. He was instructed to avoid jumps, as a broken leg would reduce his value. The stallion's ebony coat glowed with health, rippling as he pawed the ground. He stroked Blackheath's nose, whispering near his ear.

"Good boy, Blackheath, we are going for a little ride."

∞

"57, 58, 59, 60. You can come up now! Antonius, can you hear me? You're finished."

He burst through the surface of the water, and shook his head, sending droplets of water in all directions. Hunching over, he clutched his chest and gulped in air, wheezing.

"Are you all right? Come here, darling, you did it! One minute."

"You'll...get...wet." His voice was hoarse.

"I don't care. I want to give you a congratulatory kiss."

He laughed despite himself. "Not enough air. For a kiss. Need to breathe."

She pulled him to her, placing his head on her shoulder, his wet hair clinging to her hand. Her other hand rested on his waist, his skin beaded with moisture.

"Just rest then."

"Thank you."

"What for?"

He found her eyes, reaching over to push away a stray red-gold hair.

"For helping me with all this." *For loving me.*

His chest stopped heaving and his breath returned to normal.

"I think I'm ready now."

She smiled. "Yes, you're ready to be attacked. And for a kiss."

His lips were salty and warm, pressing hard against hers. The sun warmed their cheeks as they wrapped themselves around one another. The distinction between his limbs and hers became blurred. He traced his finger up her inner thigh, moving his lips to her neck.

∞

The reins were stretched taut as he pulled back—they passed the large boulder Nichola thought he remembered as a landmark, just before the marshes. He peered at it, and decided it was the one. As he rode on, Blackheath's hooves crunched the tiny stones beneath, the noise reverberating in the stillness. He realized he would have to walk the rest of the way.

He dismounted and led the stallion to an olive tree, noticing his hand shook as he tied a knot around a thick branch.

"Stay here and I'll be back soon."

He patted the horse's nose and, giving a cursory glance to the knot, walked up the road. Some larks flew overhead; their melodic calls the only sound apart from his footfalls. As the reeds came into view, the murmur of voices met his ears. Laughter. He slowed down, placing his feet with care to avoid making noise.

His hand went to his face; it was hot and flushed with emotion. He felt confused, unsure whether he was furious or desolate. He clenched his fist, filled with the sudden desire to punch the tree trunk near him, his eyes brimming with tears. Drawing closer, he crouched down behind the reeds and parted them. Despite having sought them out, he was unprepared. They were wrapped around one another, kissing and conversing. Enmeshed, as if they had been lovers for years. Their voices were low and tender. Antonius reached over and stroked her hair. They were entranced. Bile rose in Nichola's throat, and the tears spilled onto his flaming cheeks. He felt giddy, and swayed on his haunches before reaching his hand out to the sandy mud to steady himself.

For the first time in his life, he felt insignificant. A servant who collected his chamber pots had usurped him. Grief held him still.

Part of him had been certain the expedition would be folly, and he would see only the calm waters of the marsh. His chest thudded as he wiped his dripping nose with the back of his hand. Wrenching his eyes away, he rose and lurched off down the road.

Blackheath was gone. He looked over the fields towards the forest and could not see him. The larks continued to circle overhead and he kicked the ground, sending dust flying into his nose. He coughed into his mud-speckled hand, and ran, dust clouds spiralling behind him. Nausea swirled in his stomach at the thought of his father's rage. The horse was from Persia, from an exceptional bloodline. As he ran, taking lungfuls of air, he found himself praying to the Virgin that he be found.

Reaching the bottom of the hill, his vision became monochrome. His limbs felt like they were no longer his own, like the strange appendages of a puppet. Standing still, he tried to collect himself. He swayed in a circle before crumpling to the ground.

∞

He woke ensconced in fluid white sheets, his head cradled in a mountain of feather pillows. By his side sat Ilaria, dabbing at her nose with an embroidered handkerchief. The moment she saw his eyes squint open, she flew at him, pressing her face into his chest.

"My sweet darling! What on earth happened? Thank goodness you're awake."

"Mama. How did I get here?"

"Antonius Sardi from the kitchen found you. He was riding along the road where you must have fainted. You poor thing. He's a kind soul—he carried you back on his horse."

Nichola clenched his teeth. "Reprobate. I would have rather been left there than helped by him."

"Now, son, that is unkind. You're very fortunate he came across you when he did. The sun has been harsh today."

"Was he alone? When he brought me here?"

Ilaria looked confused. "Yes. Why do you ask?"

He turned his head to the window. "No reason. Do you know

I've lost Papa's horse? Blackheath."

She inhaled sharply. "No, dearest, I didn't know. We must send out a search party for him. I'm sorry, but I'd best go and tell your father. I'll be right back."

She left with an abrupt swish of silk skirts, the door clicking shut behind her.

Nichola turned on his side and found his entire body ached. He felt devoid of both energy and emotion, erased clean. His anger had morphed into a calm reckoning. He tallied up his grievances, culminating in the theft of his betrothed. He thought about his ancestors, and the concept of honour. They had not thought twice about retribution when their name had been sullied. This was one of the reasons why the house of Valperga was respected and powerful.

That afternoon, his mother announced that Signorina di Benevento had arrived to see him. He took a sip of water and said he felt too ill for visitors. In truth, he had not decided how to deal with her, whether or not to make her misdemeanour public.

Ilaria was embarrassed. "Nicky! She is your betrothed, not just a visitor. She's worried about you, my love. Let her in. She looks so pale and drawn."

"No, Mama. I'm not well; it's difficult even to speak to you. And I would prefer Giulia see me at my best. Please send her home."

He could not bring himself to tell her the truth.

Giulia was worried, but for reasons unrelated to Nichola's health. She and Antonius understood why he had been on the road, and wondered how much he had seen. It was essential her reputation be kept intact, irrespective of their escape plans. A woman's reputation was her most valuable asset. It was something that travelled with her, even when she moved to another town. Nichola would assume the affair started before she broke off the engagement, and he was right.

They decided to keep their distance until the plan was in motion.

CHAPTER 33

Fiora cried all the way home, Theresa supporting her with her arm around her waist.

They had spent part of the morning at the asylum. Antonius had been impressed by her self-containment, but now understood the effort it had taken. Arriving mid-morning, Joachim had escorted them in silence to the room where Piero was held.

Piero lay on his side, his eyes unwavering from a fixed point on the wall, his face thin and pinched. Angry red welts circled his wrists. He wore a white gown and smelt sour. He brightened on seeing them, but seemed unable to rouse himself from the supine position.

"You have half an hour," announced Joachim, avoiding their eyes. They sat on the edge of his bed, nodding to the man next to him, who observed them with curiosity. Theresa pulled her brother to her, stroking his hair. He remained impassive.

Before they were able to speak to Piero, the man's deep voice filled the room.

"Get him out of here. He's not doing very well. Go to the authorities, plead his case. I'm Gregor. I've been keeping an eye on him but there's not much I can do."

Fiora looked up, startled. "Why is he like this? What have they been doing to him?"

"He's had a few stints in the dark room. Wouldn't eat or listen to the readings so they punished him. It would be funny if it weren't so dangerous for him. He makes a humming noise when they read to him, to drown them out. Infuriates them."

Fiora stared for a long while at her hands, folded in her lap. Antonius wondered if she had heard him.

"Thank you. I'm very grateful you're looking out for him. He is like a small child." Her voice shook. She turned to her son, taking his hands in hers.

"How is my sweet boy today? Come here." Theresa relinquished him and Fiora enfolded him in her bosom, clutching his head.

Antonius reached over and stroked his arm. "Piero. Look at me."

The boy met his eyes and Antonius saw the primal fear in them. "You need to eat, Piero. Otherwise you will die, like those pigeons we saw, when the boys stoned them to death. Do you remember?"

Piero gave a small nod.

"We need you, Piero. You just have to hold on for a little longer."

Then he leaned close and whispered in his ear. "I will come for you and I will look like a bird. You must follow me. All right?"

His eyes widened and his mouth curled into a smile. "Antonius come for me?"

"Yes, but you must not speak of it to anyone. Understand?"

Another grave nod.

Antonius rose and went to Gregor, lowering his voice as he spoke. "Thank you for being kind to my brother. Very soon I will return to free him, and you. I'm a seer's apprentice, and we can change form. I will come as a starling and I need you to help me."

Gregor raised an eyebrow. "A starling? What a strange world. But yes, I will help you."

They passed the remaining time in near silence; aware their presence was enough comfort for him. Theresa whispered endearments in his ear. The room was infused with the smell of unwashed bodies, grime, and urine. Streams of feeble light pooled on the wood floor from the window.

Joachim entered and cleared his throat. "The visit is over. Say your goodbyes."

They squeezed Piero to their chests, one by one, as if the contact would press life into him.

On his bed many hours later, Antonius was filled with apprehension and grief like a cold weight, pinning him down. He asked for help, pleading for Arion, but instead, saw the transparent grey outline of a man, a shadow, almost black in the centre and lighter at the edges. He shook his head, thinking his mind was tricking him, but it remained. It pulsated and came closer, its edges undulating.

What do you want? he asked.

No response, but blinding white eye sockets appeared in the shadow's head. As it inched closer, he could feel pressure in his stomach, as if it were trying to enter his body. A frigid draft blew over him, and he sat up. He held up his hand, palm out.

I call on my spirit guides to send white light and make you go back to the place you are from. You do not frighten me.

He tried to remember the incantation Savinus had taught him, but it did not come. A blow to his stomach sent him flailing backwards, and he was pinned to the bed, looking into a face so malevolent he gasped, throwing his head from side to side in panic. The face was as white as bone, with a crimson slash of a mouth, and pointed teeth. Its red-rimmed eyes were black and glistening. He tried to clear his mind, and kept his gaze averted from the creature. As if a gift were placed in his mind, the incantation he needed came.

Liberius shanach, liberius mellar, aquina. He hoped he said the words like his mentor.

The apparition reared back, faded, then disappeared. In its place came a vision of Arion, radiating calm, loving energy. Surrounding him was the golden field, and his robes undulated in the breeze. Antonius went slack with relief and greeted him.

Arion. Thank goodness you are visiting me. I just saw a horrible apparition, I don't understand why.

Arion nodded. *You have been tested. Every seer, as they ascend the levels of knowing, must confront the darkness. They must show strength in the face of it, as you have done. It may not be the last time he visits you. But I think you now understand what to do. You have the greatest test still to come, which will require more courage.*

Antonius was confused. *Did you send him to me?*

No, but I knew he would come. I did not prevent him, as I felt you needed the challenge to build strength for what lies ahead.

Are you normally there, protecting me from these things?

Not protecting, just guiding. I placed the incantation in your mind. You had truly forgotten it.

Thank you.

You do not need to thank me. Tomorrow you must save your brother. I will be near you. Has Savinus taught you how to shapeshift without the ritual?

Yes, it is a lit candle and an incantation.

Good. I will go now.

Antonius sat up, stunned by both the visitation and the appearance of his guide. His sudden departure left him feeling disoriented. Despite this, he realized the negative emotions had lifted, leaving him with a sensation of lightness and hope.

He dreamt of Giulia, wearing a flowing white dress that covered a rounded stomach, sitting on the terrace of a villa facing a glittering sea.

∞

When he woke at dawn in the servants' quarters, he was alert and calm. He jumped up and approached Luca, asleep on his back and snoring. He shook his shoulder hard.

"Luca! I need your help. Wake up!"

"Hmm?"

"Luca, I have to go out this morning. You must tell Katerina it's urgent family business. I will explain when I return."

Luca rubbed his eyes and pushed himself up onto his elbow. His red hair was as stiff as the worn murush Antonius used to clean the fireplace.

"What is it you say? You'll be out this morning? You want me to explain to that crazy woman?"

"Yes, Luca. Tell her I'm sorry but it's something I have to do."

"All right, friend. I hope you still have a job when you get back. See you later."

Luca collapsed onto the bed, burying his head under the pillow.

In the corner of the room, Antonius had set up a small table with some artifacts given to him by Savinus. There were several books, some healing liquid, feathers, mineral stones, and candles. He stilled his mind, and asked the guides the location of the key to Piero's window. The response was an image of the key hanging outside the door. He was ready. Waiting until Luca was snoring; he lit a candle with a flint stone and said the incantation.

At first, nothing happened. He worried he had not said it the right way. Then, stretching out his hand, he saw a wavering, then translucence. He felt the presence of Arion as the wave of energy spread through the rest of his body. It was a hot tingling, like drinking a large quantity of hard liquor. He found himself on the floor, looking up at the table, with the muted grey eyesight of a starling. Savinus's words echoed in his mind: *To change back, say the same incantation but add 'sequimur alt' to the end.*

He made a fervent wish he would not remain a member of the avian world and flew onto the window ledge. It had been left open a crack to stop the room becoming stuffy overnight. Once through the opening, he gazed up at the broad expanse of blue sky.

Courage. Have courage and all will be well. Think of that squalid place, imagine if it were you.

He beat his wings and was in flight sooner than expected. The practice had been more useful than he had realized. Darting through wisps of clouds, he felt buoyant, forgetting for a moment the reason he was there. Looking down, he searched for the mountains, and below them, the forest at the edge of the town's eastern walls. Nearby was the grey-tiled roof of the asylum.

Swooping down, he flew around the perimeter, looking for an open window. All of them were closed. He lingered at the main wooden door, hoping someone would exit. He did not have to wait long. Joachim flung it open, carrying two pails of excrement. He waddled over to a ditch near the trees, flinging the foul contents into it. Coughing into his hand, he walked over to the well and wound the brass handle. Seizing the wooden container of water, he rinsed out the pails before making his way back inside. Antonius flew behind him, at a safe distance, then darted through the crack just as the door swung back.

He waited for Joachim to disappear into Domenico Valperga's office, then fluttered to the door he remembered as Piero's. Through an inset window, he could see his brother's bed, but it was empty. He remembered the dark room and swooped to the hallway. He spied a low iron door, no more than a metre tall, beneath the staircase. It had a small barred window, and the lock appeared identical to the other doors.

Piero had been inside for two days. He was curled in a foetal position, tapping his hands in a rhythm on his thighs. The darkness alternated between caressing his body like velvet, and pricking him with spikes. He could hear rats scuffling behind the thick walls, and imagined them before his eyes, their sharp teeth bared, their coarse fur prickling his skin. He was sure they would make a hole in the wall, slide in and gnaw at his body. He pressed his fist into his mouth to stop from screaming, praying for unconsciousness.

Antonius perched on the edge of the inset window, letting out a small trill.

Piero looked up in surprise, and smiled at the sight of him. He pushed himself into a sitting position.

"Antonius! You come for me. We go now?"

Antonius trilled again to indicate the affirmative. As the guides had indicated, the key hung on a nail, above a wooden crucifix. He picked it up with his claw and darted into Piero and Gregor's room. He remembered the man on the last bed being kind to his brother and glided towards him.

Gregor was emaciated, with black stringy hair reaching to his shoulders. His cheekbones jutted out from sunken eyes, the bones almost visible beneath the skin. Staring at the bird, he held out his hand. Antonius landed on his finger.

"Ah, you have come as you said, unless I've gone mad. What have you got there, feathery friend?" He took the key and followed the bird to the window, where it alighted on the lock. Understanding lit up his features. He inserted the key in the mechanism, turned it, and flung open the window. The three other inmates were impassive. They remained still on their beds, staring at the wall or the ceiling.

Gregor levered himself onto the ledge, then jumped out of the window onto the soft grass below.

Antonius stayed near his face, his wings making a humming sound.

"What is it you wish me to do now, my friend?" asked the older man.Antonius led him to the unlocked front door, hovering as he caught up. Gregor twisted the handle and opened the door without letting go. They could not risk a squeaking hinge. He crept behind the bird down the hallway, placing his bare feet with care on the wood floor. Antonius stopped in front of the dark room. A small painting of the crucifixion hung above the door, and Antonius felt sure the key to the dark room lay behind it. He pecked it with his beak, and Gregor understood, swivelling it to the right. Behind was a small alcove, the size of a fist, and a key. Gregor picked it up with a nervous smile. His hand shook with a slight tremor as he turned the key in the lock, swinging the door open. The hinges let out a low groan and both bird and man startled. From the far end of the building, footsteps could be heard, and low voices. Gregor placed his finger over his lips and held out a hand for Piero. The boy squinted at them, before taking his hand and scrambling out of the tiny space. It was tall enough for a man to sit in, but not stand. They padded back down the hallway, Antonius fluttering behind them, and out the front door. Behind them, the sound of footsteps quickened and grew louder.

Piero beamed at the bird and Gregor. "Thank you, thank you. Free now."

He shook the hand of the boy. "It's nothing. Thank you for helping me too. Good luck, my friend. I'll be off now."

He sprinted up the hill and soon disappeared into the forest gloom, hidden by the wide trunks of the pines. Raised voices erupted from inside the asylum. They had found the open door to the dark room.

Antonius flew down the hill and Piero understood the need to follow his brother. They hurried along the path skirting the town, obscured by a high wall. When they reached the part nearest to Savinus's villa, Antonius stopped, hovering in the air.

"I climb here?" Piero asked.

Antonius landed on the top of the wall and said the incantation in his mind. The rush of energy coursed through him once more and he looked down to see his human form, his muscled legs dangling over the side of the wall. He held out his hand for his brother.

"Come, Piero, I will pull you up."

His brother was lighter than he expected, having lost weight at the asylum. He hefted him up holding his wrists, then seized his waist and brought him to the top of the wall.

"Are you ready? We just have to jump down now, it's not far. I'll count to three and then we go. One, two, three, jump!"

They collided as they hit the ground.

Antonius rubbed his hurt shoulder. "I said to jump with me, not on me. Come on, it's this way. You must stay with Signor di Benevento for a little while."

"But I go home now?" Tears sprung into his pale eyes.

"No, you can't yet. It will be the first place they will go to look for you. You are safer with the Signor. Signorina Giulia lives there, have you met her?"

"I don't know. Want to go home."

"You can't, Piero. Hurry now, we don't want anyone to see you. There's no time to look at the moss."

Piero's nose almost touched the wall as he examined the mossy growth. He reached out his hand to stroke it and his brother yanked him away.

Antonius had practiced which streets he would take. At this time of the morning, the streets in that part of town were deserted. Despite this, he did not take any risks, and followed the narrow laneways to reach the back door of the villa. Agnese waited at the window, her face brightening as she spotted them.

CHAPTER 34

Agnese had heard them coming and ushered them to the table. It held some bread and a pitcher of water. She clucked over Piero's dishevelled state.

"Poor little mite, sit down and have a drink." She patted him on the shoulder before turning to Antonius.

"I've set up the storeroom for him. There is a straw pallet, and some blankets. I moved some vessels and it's quite spacious in there now."

"Thank you, Agnese. You are very kind. I think he misses home a lot."

She frowned. "This is all right for now, but what about when the Signor leaves? Where will he go then?"

Antonius's eyes widened.

"How did you know?"

"There was the visit from the Church people, then Signor started saying a lot of strange things. I put it all together."

"Well, I'm not really sure. I imagine he will contact the Conte, and ask that he be left alone. Or he and my mother might want to come to Genoa. It was Nichola who arranged to imprison him there and it was a grave injustice."

"That's right. I saw what happened. The boy hadn't done

anything wrong."

Savinus pushed open the door to the kitchen and took in Piero's appearance. He came over and bent down, taking his hand.

"So you are Antonius's brother. I have heard much about you, young man. Welcome to Villa Porto. You need to have a big supper tonight and get your strength back. Your Mama will visit soon. I will send word to her that you're here. Good boy." He smiled, before rising with difficulty. Antonius heard his joints crack.

"I'd better get back to work. I think we're having fish for supper tonight. Antonius, will you join us?"

"I would love to Signor, but Katerina will be wondering where I am. I had to leave very early today. I'm sorry."

"No need to apologize. I wouldn't want you to incur her wrath. Don't worry about Piero, I'll enlist Giulia to look after him."

"Thank you. I really have to go."

"Yes, yes, off you go now. See you tomorrow. Be prepared, I feel that our friend Nichola will rejoin us."

"Yes, Signor. I'll be ready for him."

Antonius strode out, his face troubled.

Savinus turned to Agnese. "You know we are leaving, don't you, Agnese?"

She looked down at her apron. "Yes, sir."

"Do you understand why?"

"A little, sir."

"I cannot explain it all to you, but if you were able to find a way to follow us to Genoa, I would be very pleased. I'll give you the money you need to make the journey."

"Thank you. I—"

Savinus cut her short. "No need to give me an answer now. I realize it's a big decision. But if you could please get some boy's clothing that would fit Giulia, it would be very helpful."

"Yes, I will do that tomorrow."

Savinus's eyes clouded with tears as he reached over and patted her on the shoulder. As she met his gaze, her eyes also filled with tears, so they could only see blurred versions of each other.

"I remember the day you came to us. Carmen spoke to you for a long time in the sitting room, then told me you were the ideal person for the job. And here we are, twenty years later."

"Yes, sometimes I feel like I'm Giulia's aunt as well as a servant."

"In truth, you have been more like a mother to her, particularly since my wife left us. I do hope you come to Genoa."

"I'm not sure. I must speak to my family. My daughter may not like me to be far away."

"Yes, I understand you have your family to consider and those grandchildren of yours. I'm going to the workroom." His voice croaked.

She nodded and turned to Piero, who was drawing patterns on the windowpane.

She swallowed hard before speaking. "Come on, let's go and find Giulia. She might have a game for you."

∞

After ten days of languishing in bed, Nichola was restless and rang the bell for his valet. Paolo arrived at the foot of his bed, shifting his weight from one foot to the other.

"Good morning, Signor. How may I help you?" Beneath the obsequious tone, Nichola could hear his contempt.

"Paolo, how very kind of you to turn up when summoned. You are such a friendly servant and I don't know what I would do without you. Please fetch my doublet and breeches, I need you to dress me, as I think I'm getting bedsores."

He submitted to his valet's belligerent handling as he prodded, pulled, and buttoned his clothing. He manipulated his limbs as if he were a puppet. The last step was his boots, with thirty hooks each. As he watched the detested valet's balding head bent over his feet, he imagined how easy it would be to kick his face.

"Are you almost finished? I have a great deal to do today, you know."

"One more minute, Signor."

"Well, hurry up about it."

Paolo rose and gave him a burning glare, before exiting with a stiff gait.

Nichola decided to leave without alerting his mother. She had been driving him to distraction with her bedside vigil, tending him as if he were a child.

Once through the side door, the cool breeze touched his face and he gulped it in. It dawned on him that staying indoors had not helped his mental state. This realisation was not enough to deter him from his plan, or reduce his outrage.

In his haste to reach the bottom of the hill, he strode too fast, and his body weakened. He was forced to stand still for a moment, catching his breath.

As he walked, he talked to himself.

"They will have been having a wonderful time without you, imagine how annoyed they will be when you show up. That cuckolding idiot, simpering bitch, old arrogant wizard. You show them where the power lies."

He felt hatred bubbling up his throat like acid and imagined it like green liquid inside him, ready to spill out at the slightest provocation. At the same time, tears lurked at the back of his eyes and he felt a stabbing pain in his chest. Images of Giulia flashed into his mind, rendering him helpless and disoriented.

Pausing at the town walls, he clutched the rough brick and willed himself to be stronger. His feeble legs appalled him. Emotion wedged in his throat and behind his eyes.

Arriving at the entrance to the villa, he gave a sharp rap on the door and waited. The image of the lovers beside the marsh gave him the strength he needed and he allowed it to play in his mind.

Agnese's face fell when she saw him. The warmth evaporated from her eyes and she waved him inside with a greeting he could not make out.

"Agnese, lovely to see you too. Now where can I find your boss and his charge?"

"This way, Signor." She kept her gaze fixed on the wood floor as she led him to the workroom.

"I am feeling much better, thank you," he said in an amused tone. "Kind of you to ask."

She ignored him and opened the workroom door.

"Sir, Signor Valperga is here."

Both Savinus and Antonius started, their concentration broken. They were absorbed in a complicated formula written out by Antonius. He was attempting to explain it to his mentor. At the sight of Nichola, the younger man stood up and glared in his direction. Savinus remained seated, his face impassive.

"Good day, Nichola. I see you have decided it's time to return to work. It's just as well, as it is the half moon ritual this evening. I do hope you can remember the ritual from my books, given your extended absence?"

"I remember it well, sir. It is no accident I've arrived at this auspicious time. You mentioned we'd be performing the half moon ritual. I've been practicing the incantations and hope to be of assistance."

"Very good. Be seated Antonius. We need to continue with our geomancy for the remainder of the day. Our clients are waiting for the results and do not care whether we have rituals or not."

∞

Antonius found it difficult to conceal his agitation. That morning, Savinus had explained the ritual would go ahead as planned. They had both predicted Nichola would return that day.

He had argued with his mentor. "But sir, we could just avoid the whole thing. Stay away from the marshes. Why must we go through with it? Perhaps the situation might just go away."

"No, Antonius. It is ordained to happen, I've consulted my guides and interfering with what is destined will only delay it to a later point in time. I must leave soon; the Church inquisitors are coming for me. So delaying is not an option. More importantly, you and Giulia must have a chance to be together. That will not be possible here in Pesaro. Do you understand?"

Antonius hung his head and gave a morose nod. His appetite had been absent for some days and sleep was impossible. Katerina had been trying to entice him with leftovers—prosciutto, small slivers of fish, almond biscuits. It was no use. The potent combination of lovesickness and fear had deprived him of an appetite.

He recoiled as Nichola sat on the stool next to him. He forced his mouth to say, "Good day," and averted his gaze, staring at the formula. His brain was unable to decipher the numbers, the connections between them and the symbols obscured. Rubbing his eyes, he looked to the ground, struggling to regain his equilibrium.

Nichola sensed his discomfort. He spoke in a low voice. "What's wrong? Lost your gift, have you? Maybe it's time you gave it up and went back to scrubbing floors. You might stay out of trouble that way."

"What are you talking about?"

"Getting involved with other mens' future wives, for a start. Getting above your station."

"A man's merit is not based merely on his station."

Nichola snorted. "You don't seem to understand. She might enjoy having some fun with you, but she's not going to marry a peasant. She's a lady, Antonius. Men of your class sell her things, wait on her, and help her into carriages. Delusion is a strange thing. Time to start looking at reality."

Antonius clenched his jaw. "You are the one who doesn't understand. I really don't feel like enlightening you either. There is no point. You're nothing more than a spoilt brat who can't cope when something does not go your way."

Nichola narrowed his eyes and inched closer, his face almost touching the other boy. "I have had enough of your insolence, pretending to be someone you're not."

He reached out and pressed his palm on his chest. "Show some respect, or you will soon regret it. Incidentally, how is that cretin brother of yours?"

Antonius shoved him off with his shoulder and hissed. "Get off me. So you admit you had something to do with it?"

"I had everything to do with it. Idiots like that are a hazard on the streets, a nuisance. Besides, he attacked me."

They both rose, holding their arms stiffly by their sides, crimson-faced.

Savinus marched over. "Boys, that is quite enough. It's obvious that you're not going to be able to work together. Nichola, go back to the palazzo and return after supper for the ritual. Antonius, you too. Try and cool down, both of you."

∞

When they had gone, he sat down and cradled his head in his hands. After a while, he forced himself to work, picking up a sheaf of parchment and sitting at his desk. The boys had just started the formulas and the page mocked him with its near emptiness. He completed several pages of calculations and looked around his workroom, the tall bookcases heavy with thick tomes, the collection of crystals in a glass case, the vials of rare liquids. Breathing in the familiar musty smell he blinked away tears. Sentimental old fool, he chided himself. Pushing out of his chair, he swayed for a moment then shuffled out to find Agnese and ask for his lunch.

∞

Fiora sat at the kitchen table, devoid of her usual bustle and energy. She rested her elbows on the gnarled wood and looked sideways at Antonius, who held her forearm.

"Mama, you can come and join us, although it would be wise to wait a few months. Someone might figure it out if you come too soon. I'll send money for you and Piero as soon as I can. Theresa, I know you can't come."

Theresa sat on the other side of the table. She was engaged to Federico and their wedding was to take place in the summer. Her eyes were swollen from crying.

"So I will never see you again? Genoa is a long way from here and you can't visit Pesaro since everyone will think you're dead."

"I'm sorry. This is the only way. I have to save myself, as well as find a way to be with Giulia. She has broken her engagement to Nichola."

She nodded and wiped her nose with the corner of her apron, her eyes widening in surprise.

"She has rejected the Conte's son to be with you?"

He gave an awkward smile. "It seems so."

His mother shook her head; she was finding it difficult to speak. The life she knew was deconstructing and reforming in ways she did not understand.

"I will come to Genoa. Theresa, don't be offended, but Piero and I need to be with your brother."

Theresa traced a pattern in the wood with her finger. "Mama, I understand. Perhaps I can convince Federico to leave Pesaro too. Cobblers are needed in every town."

CHAPTER 35

The moon shone through the mottled glass. It cast a milky glow over the gnarled surface of Savinus's desk. Piero sat next to him, chewing noisily on a bread roll. He said something indecipherable.

"Swallow Piero, I can't understand you."

"Want more please?"

"The boy you don't like is about to come. There is no time for that. Go to your room and remember to keep very quiet. There have been people from the asylum out looking for you. Have you heard them, shouting your name?"

"Yes, sir. I heard and I scared. I be quiet like a mouse."

"Exactly. You did a great job last time, didn't you? Off you go."

Moments later, he could hear Nichola at the door, followed by a terse exchange with Agnese. Without knocking, he burst in and nodded at Savinus.

"Good evening, Signor. I'm ready. Where is the latecomer?" He flicked back a lock of hair and gave him an expectant stare.

"Good evening. He's not late; you are early. Take a seat and we will wait. I don't imagine he's far away."

"I certainly hope not. Don't we have to get there at an exact time?"

"I would not say exact, more approximate."

"And Giulia—is she joining us?"

"Not this time. She is occupied this evening."

Nichola hesitated for a moment, looking down at his boots. When he raised his head, Savinus was discomfited by the hostility in his eyes.

"Do you realize your daughter is not as virtuous as you might expect? She has broken our engagement and I find it suspicious. It would only take me one day to ruin her name in this town. And the peasant you insist on employing; that would take even less time."

Savinus let out a long exhalation. "What are you saying Nichola? If you are going to make a threat, you need to be more specific. Your cryptic words are annoying me."

"It's not a threat. I am making you aware that I am being gracious."

"How dare you cast doubt on my daughter's reputation! Please desist. Your bitterness is giving me a headache."

Nichola scowled but said no more. Seconds later, Antonius appeared, flushed from a rapid walk.

He flinched at the sight of Nichola. "Good evening. Is it time to go?"

"Good evening, Antonius. Yes, it is. Nichola, please gather up those water bottles near the door. Antonius, could you please saddle up the horses? We won't need lamps, the moon is particularly bright and will show us the way to the marshes."

Both the young men did as they were told, whilst Savinus said goodbye to Giulia. She was hiding in her bedchamber, unwilling to see Nichola.

"Papa, what if he really kills Antonius? I can't bear this. Sitting here waiting for everything to happen."

He touched her arm, pale against the deep red coverlet of her bed. "It is not ordained that he should die. Trust in the guides and in the strength of Antonius. He has prepared well and will be unharmed."

"Yes, Papa. You know I told Nichola I can't marry him?"

"Yes. I read your thoughts the day you did it. You were very brave."

She glanced over at the small bag she had packed, the most she could carry on a vegetable cart. On top of it sat the folded boy's clothing Agnese had bought at the market.

"He will not pursue us, you can be certain of that."

"How do you know?"

"Because I will make sure of it. Now, do some reading and weaving and I'll see you in the morning. Check on Piero once we've left."

"Yes, Papa. Good luck with your swimming."

"Goodbye, my dear." He reached out and drew her to him for a brief embrace.

∞

The moon illuminated their path as they began their journey. Unseen creatures rustled through the bushes and undergrowth lining the road.

They did not speak. Nichola watched the grey silhouettes of the others and his trembling hands on the reins. The air was cool on his cheeks and he tried to breathe it in. The dust caught in his throat and he coughed. He knew he had to focus his hatred into a sharp point, without distractions, as hard as the glimmering tip of a sword. His stomach felt like a trapped animal, twisting and lurching.

For a moment, he wondered if they knew, given their powers. Then he dismissed the idea. They could not know everything. His horse quickened her pace, as if sensing his thoughts.

The road ascended an incline and he saw the large boulder that signalled the beginning of the marshes. He shuddered, and for the first time, doubt flooded his mind. Looking down at his hands, he questioned their strength. Examining his heart and mind, other questions followed. With great effort, he pushed them aside, trying to shut down thought and feeling. A trapdoor of indifference fell into place, setting his jaw. His stomach and hands stilled. Second place; all his life he had felt it. His father, the old man, both relegated him to impotence. And Giulia. His knuckles showed white as he clutched the reins. A muscle twitched in his jaw.

Savinus spoke as they approached the reeds.

"You may dismount now. Antonius, could you please load the herbs and crystals into one of the boats? Nichola, you can untie that boat over there and bring it over please. Tie up your horses."

The boys obeyed him in silence. After placing all the items necessary for the ritual in a boat, Antonius untied it and looked up at Savinus.

"I am ready, sir."

"Good. Nichola, you can row Antonius, I know you've been wanting to practice."

Antonius sneered. "We might see you tomorrow then."

Nichola did not hear him. He was in another place, his mind sharpened to his task.

Antonius shrugged and helped his mentor into the other boat. *I could just ride with you and avoid all this, what do you think?*

Savinus frowned. *You must not shirk your destiny. You are ready for this, and for your new life.*

He nodded and climbed into the boat, sitting at the back. As if in a daydream, Nichola sat at the front and picked up the paddle.

In Nichola's mind, all feeling was gone. All that existed was a fog of red hatred, and a determination to fulfill his task. He would wait until they were halfway to the island. As he rowed, he watched the ripples of moonlight on the water and sensed behind him the presence of his enemy. A small smile formed on his lips as he anticipated his fall.

As he stood and lifted the paddle, images flicked through his mind—Giulia laughing, her head thrown back, Antonius and Savinus poring over a large book, Gianni regaling his father with an amusing story. Drops of water sprayed him in the eyes and he was blinded. Blinking, he regained his sight, turned and swung the paddle behind. The movement seemed interminable, the wood heavy in his hands. His legs felt weak and he almost fell backwards. Antonius swung around and it made contact with his back, sending him overboard, his mouth agape and his arms reaching forward. As he hit the water, Nichola watched transfixed as it swallowed him, the dark shape of his head in the middle of the splash. Moments later, he bobbed up and wheezed in air before being submerged again. This continued several times and then slowed, his head coming up half way, and his hand bursting out before disappearing. Nothing. He scanned the water as it stilled. His mouth was dry and a sharp pain pulsed near his heart.

Remembering Savinus, he looked over and saw him jump overboard, followed by another splash. Panicked, he plunged the paddle into the water, gliding towards the other boat. The old man was paddling on his stomach, pausing every minute or so to take a gulp of air, then turning his face downwards, scanning the depths. Nichola watched him, then, growing impatient, called out.

"Signor. Signor! There is no use; he is gone. Let me help you out!"

Savinus lifted his head halfway out, so only one eye could be seen, before his whole head rose from the surface.

"I can get out myself. I do not trust the hands of a murderer."

He turned his head and swam towards his boat, reaching up and grasping the side. Panting and cursing, he pushed himself up, lost his grip, and tumbled back into the water.

"Signor, please! I can help you. It's too hard."

Savinus ignored him and tried again, this time succeeding in throwing his leg over the side and hoisting himself into the boat, which gave a violent sway as he collapsed into it. He yelled out in pain before sitting up, his chest heaving. Nichola could hear his laboured breath as he waited.

It took several long minutes before the old man picked up his paddle, dipped it in the water, and pushed the vessel forward, his breath rasping into the night air. Nichola followed at a respectful distance.

Reaching the shore, they dragged their boats through the shallows, before tying them to stakes. As they stepped onto the sand, Savinus turned to him, his eyes bloodshot and wild. His hair stuck to his forehead in wet clumps.

"Unworthy. To think I took you as an apprentice. Murderer. He is gone. You are lower than the scum that lines these marshes."

"But Signor, I—"

He held up a hand. "Do not speak. Listen very carefully. You will never speak to my daughter again. She will be leaving Pesaro. Antonius had a brother, Piero. Do you know him?"

"I do not."

"Liar. You had him committed. He has escaped and you will ensure he is not committed again. If necessary, you will plead his case to the head of the asylum and explain what you did. I will also be departing and you will convince your father not to pursue me. If you do not follow my instructions, I will tell your father what you have done. As a man of principles, I am sure he would disinherit a murderer. Do you understand me?"

Nichola's eyes were downcast; a single tear glistened on his cheek. His body had begun to shake. "Yes, Signor. I didn't mean—"

Savinus shook his head. "Ah, but you did, Nichola, you did. I saw the definite swing of that paddle; there was no hesitation in it. You may take a horse and go home. I do not wish to ever see your face again."

∞

Returning home, Savinus staggered inside, leaning against the wall. Agnese helped him into his chamber where he stripped off his wet clothes, pulled on his nightgown, and fell into bed. Offers of food and drink were refused. Worried, Agnese and Giulia lingered at the door, desperate to know what had happened. He did not wake and they sat down at the kitchen table with Piero. It was unusual for Agnese to eat with Giulia, but they felt their time together was coming to an end. Their conversation was minimal as they ate a light meal of polenta and fish. Piero was unaware of the drama surrounding them, shovelling in his food and making them laugh. Since escaping from the asylum, his appetite had been as incessant as his good humour.

Savinus was awakened at dawn by a cool breeze touching his cheeks. Agnese had been into his chamber and opened the window.

She stood just outside the door, impatient for him to wake.

"Good morning, sir. It's time to wake now. My old bones are feeling uneasy today."

Savinus pushed himself upright. Fatigue seeped through his body and he ached all over.

He gave her a wan smile. "Good morning, Agnese. I do believe this is our last morning together—your bones have not lied. Relax a little. Everything went to plan last night. Hello, my dearest."

Giulia raced in and threw her arms around him. "Papa, we missed you last night. Are you all right? You look very pale."

"I think I am paying for the nocturnal swim. Trying to climb back into the boat was another challenge. He's fine, waiting for you in the cave. A little cold perhaps, but alive."

"I want to go to Antonius now. I'm ready."

"I was hoping we could have our last breakfast in Pesaro together."

"Yes, you're right. That would be lovely. Agnese, you must join us, if it's all right with you, Papa?"

"Yes, it is. If you two could let me dress I will be out shortly. Agnese, I think strawberries, bread, and butter would be in order, thank you."

"Yes, sir. I'll go and prepare it."

They sat down for breakfast. Piero consumed five slices of thick bread, washing them down with milk. Agnese ate little, pausing every few minutes to wipe her eyes. Giulia patted her arm and found her own eyes welling up. Her father seemed withdrawn—his mind was planning the intricacies of their escape, checking for loopholes.

When it was time for Giulia to leave, both women sobbed with abandon. They hugged each other, Giulia feeling the older woman's bony frame through her housedress.

"You must come and join us, promise me you will."

"I'm not sure. It's something that must be discussed with my family. I will try to come. In any case, I'll be bringing your father's most precious belongings, his books and equipment. For the time being, they are safe in my family's house."

Giulia nodded. "I understand." She smoothed her boy's tunic down, startled for a moment to see her legs encased in breeches. The rough fabric itched her skin. A suede cap hid her long hair.

She turned to her father, who was standing to the side with a pensive droop to his shoulders. He tried to straighten up and regain his usual composure.

"Good luck, my dear. The vegetable seller who is taking you is a good man, very competent and smart. He knows some smaller roads where you are less likely to be stopped. Lorenzo di Montefiore will meet you at the town square in Genoa. You will stay with him until alternative lodgings can be found."

He pulled her to him. "Goodbye."

She detected anxiety in the firmness of the embrace. He had always projected confidence and it unnerved her. Reaching out, she touched the side of his face and their eyes met. In his blue gaze, all she could see was devotion.

Patting Piero on the shoulder, she left. The moment she was out the door, Savinus sank into a chair, cradling his head in his hands.

Giulia mounted Jocanda, pulling the reins to steer her up the path. It was only then she realized her father had not spoken of himself finding lodgings in Genoa.

∞

Inside the villa, Savinus declined the offer of a drink from Agnese, and set himself to the task of waiting. As he did so, he shuffled out to the courtyard and lowered himself onto a stool, preparing a fire and the salt, sulphur and mercury for the ritual. With a shaking hand, he measured out the required quantities and tipped them in three bowls, ready to be placed on the flames. Sensing time was running out, he tipped the contents onto the fire and chanted. His mind became clear and his trepidation floated away like the acrid smoke. He heard as if from a long distance, several loud raps at the door, followed by aggressive voices. Agnese could be heard, her voice rising in agitation. A heavy thud as the door was forced open.

"We know he's in here! Get out of the way!"

Savinus closed his eyes and felt the waves of transformation undulate through his body, his organs shrinking, and a sound like a fierce wind in his ears. He opened his eyes and was the size of the pots of red geraniums lining the courtyard. Rapid staccato footsteps could be heard from the workroom, headed in his direction. Beating his wings, he rose up, the courtyard becoming smaller below, the three men looking up in amazement. His shadow fell on their faces before he flew higher, then out of sight. It did not take long for him to find the road to Genoa, north of the town. The sun warmed his back as he glided, surveying the tiny houses giving way to golden wheat fields. The workers were concentrated on their scythes, but from his vantage point, appeared like coloured insects on the landscape.

The pain in his heart thrummed just as he was over the forest. He watched the deep green trees as they swayed and became blurred. His strength made a rapid retreat and it felt as if a vice were crushing his chest. In a vertiginous circle, he tried to regain his balance, before the earth swam around him, faster and faster, pulling him into an excruciating vortex. In terror he plummeted, and the forest took him into her heart.

CHAPTER 36

The cave was cloaked in silence. For a moment, Giulia worried he was not there. Then she heard the crunch of stones and Antonius emerged, grinning with relief. She ran to him and buried her face in his chest, breathing in his familiar scent. He pulled her closer and kissed the top of her head, then her lips.

They sat down at the mouth of the cave, wrapped around one another. The herons had returned. They called out and one plucked a fish from the water, sending droplets in all directions. The sun was hot. Giulia thought about lying under a cloth with all the vegetables and the long journey ahead. A sharp pain erupted in her chest and she clutched it, sitting up.

"What is it?"

"I'm not sure, my chest hurts."

Tears sprang into her eyes and deep anguish flooded through her. She could not speak, and shook with sobs.

"Giulia, please, tell me what's wrong? You're scaring me."

A vision came, forcing him to shut his eyes and watch. An eagle, with ink-black wings, fell in a spiral from the sky into a forest. He saw its yellow eyes, the life departing.

He held her and let the pain seize him, his face contorted and wet. It was infinite and they could have sat for a long time. Giulia sobbed until her voice was hoarse, then fell quiet, her chest convulsing.

Antonius glanced up and saw a stocky figure on the shore: the vegetable seller. The man lifted his arm and waved and Antonius helped Giulia stand, pointing at their rescuer.

They stepped into the boat and he rowed. For the last time, they saw the reeds, the rippled water, and the shimmering blue sky, but all the colours seemed faded and dull. Their limbs were heavy as they climbed onto the sand and greeted the man.

A thick black beard covered half his face, and he smiled at them, his teeth a stark white against the black. The skin around his brown eyes crinkled up.

"Good day. I am Bruno. My cart is over here. Please, come this way."

He gestured to the wooden cart, the vegetables stacked in neat rows. A space had been cleared in the middle and a sheet flung to the side.

"I'm sorry, but the seer told me you must be hidden. The sheet will conceal you and at least you will have plenty to eat."

Antonius was embarrassed. "But Bruno, that is your livelihood, surely you don't want us to eat it?"

He laughed. "Well, why don't you choose three vegetables each and then stop?"

"That sounds more than enough."

As Giulia had imagined, it was stifling under the sheet, with little air for them to breathe. In her misery, she was immune to further suffering and lay prone on her side. Antonius tried to comfort her, but soon realized she needed to retreat. He understood, having lost his own father. Every so often, he lifted up the sheet and allowed fresh air to flow over their bodies. The road was uneven in parts, and they crashed into one another as the cart lurched. After this happened a few times, she allowed him to hold her, keeping her face averted. Bruno knew many people on the road and called out effusive greetings as he passed.

They paused in several towns during the journey. Bruno found verdant trees away from the sight of the villagers and stopped the cart. He bought them panini and fruit juice, telling them about his travels and his young family. On the second night, he found an inn and asked them if they would like to stay there. Giulia shook her head.

"There might be people looking for me. I can't risk it. We can sleep under a tree."

He shrugged and wished them good night, taking a small bag with him inside.

"I'm going to have an ale and then turn in. Are you sure you will be comfortable enough?"

Antonius assured him they enjoyed sleeping outdoors.

They lay under an ancient oak, listening to the calls of an owl resting in its wide branches. Above them, the stars glinted, the constellations punctuating the blackness with their diamond swirls. The grass was soft and cool beneath them and they covered themselves with the sheet from the cart. Antonius drew her to him and exhaustion allowed them to sleep.

The road to Genoa was often isolated, with few villages. The landscape was varied. Raising the sheet and peering over the edge of the cart, they saw forest-covered mountains, fields of cornflowers, then arid plains of jagged taupe-coloured rocks and pale green patches of grass. As they progressed further north, the sea came into view, its silver-tipped waves blue and endless.

It was three days before they came to the outskirts of Genoa. Antonius lifted the sheet and saw a sky streaked with mauve and pink above the vast sea. At the horizon, the last of the orange sun lingered, bleeding light into the dark water, before slipping down. The sky transformed to more sombre hues of indigo and grey. Giulia had not spoken more than a few words since they had left. He grazed her cheek with the back of his hand, catching her eye, willing her to life.

"We are here, Giulia. Just a few minutes now."

The beginnings of a smile curved on her lips and she took his hand. Lifting the sheet, she peered at the sandstone ramparts of the town. They were lit with flaming torches sending sparks careening into the sky. The ramparts joined an immense arched gate flanked by two round towers—the Porto Soprana. As they passed through the archway, she threw the sheet aside and sat up, tearing off her cap and shaking out her hair. There were many people on the streets, lined with villas. Through the windows they could see families eating their supper.

Antonius called out. "Take us to the town square, please, Bruno."

"Yes, those were my instructions."

She sent him a thought. *We are home. This will be our home.*

Tears streaked her face but her eyes shone with life.

ACKNOWLEDGEMENTS

In writing and editing this novel, I have been fortunate to receive the guidance of other writers. *Stone Circle* was polished and has emerged as a result of this support.

My heartfelt thanks to Peter Campbell, Sebnem Sanders, Sheena Macleod, Jackie Bates, Kali Napier, Tabatha Stirling, Cindra Spencer and my agent Sarah McKenzie. Thanks also to my husband and my ever-supportive mother.

ABOUT THE AUTHOR

Artist turned writer Kate Murdoch is the author of Stone Circle (2017) and The Orange Grove (2019).

Her short-form fiction has been published in literary journals and anthologies in Australia, United Kingdom, United States and Canada.

Stone Circle was a First in Category winner in the Chaucer Awards 2018 for pre-1750's historical fiction. The Orange Grove was a finalist in the Chaucer Awards 2019 for pre-1750's historical fiction.

Kate was awarded a KSP Fellowship at the KSP Writers' Centre in 2019. In 2024, she travelled to France for a writing residency at the Chateau d'Orquevaux.

For more about Kate:
www.katemurdochauthor.com/
www.instagram.com/katemurdoch2/
www.facebook.com/katemurdochauthor
www.x.com/KateMurdoch3

ALSO BY KATE MURDOCH